Never Just a Memory

Never Just a Memory

Gloria Cook

CANELO

First published in the United Kingdom in 2005 by Severn House

This edition published in the United Kingdom in 2019 by

Canelo Digital Publishing Limited
57 Shepherds Lane
Beaconsfield, Bucks HP9 2DU
United Kingdom

A CIP catalogue record for this book is available from the British Library.

Print ISBN 978 1 78863 341 3
Ebook ISBN 978 1 78863 067 2

Look for more great books at www.canelo.co

Printed and bound in Great Britain by Clays Ltd, Elcograf S.p.A.

To Tracy and Simon, and 'the boys', Max and Midas

Chapter One

1943

Dusk was crowding in and the mist was turning into drizzly rain. The smells of damp earth and wild herbage were pungent and overpowering. The trees, bushes and the high hedgerows seemed to press in all around her. Jill Laity was used to the countryside but she felt she was in a strange, unfriendly world that might fall in on her at any moment and trap her. She told herself not to be silly. That it was simply the apprehension of venturing out into a new situation. The farm was going to be more than a new workplace and new home, it was the only place she could call home now. She mustn't brood and get anxious. She would be fine when she reached her destination. She hoped.

Peering through the gloom she rounded another bend. From the information received a short time ago in the village of Hennaford, she should soon reach a fork in the road where she should veer to the right, then climb up a short, steep hill, and Ford Farm would be there; impossible to miss. The road straightened out and just ahead was yet another curving crook. Hopefully the fork would come into view after that. The lane tapered even more and dripping foliage from the banks brushed her from each side. If she was fated to meet a cart or motor vehicle in this impossibly narrow space there'd be nothing for it but to clamber up a hedge for safety, and then what a state she'd be in. She must already look a mess.

A sudden strong whiff of farmyard manure gave her hope that she was at last closing in on her goal. The nervousness of finding herself among strangers churned away inside her. It seemed she had been trudging along for ages. Tension tightened its grip. She would find the farm. Surely she would. She couldn't have missed it. Could she? It was getting darker every second. Her torch, which she could only use pointed to the ground and covered with layers of tissue paper because the wartime restrictions forbade lights at night, was, unfortunately, packed in her bags.

Something snagged her coat. 'Oh no!' It was only a bramble but it took several moments to disentangle herself. She could only see a few inches ahead now. Praying she wouldn't fall into a ditch, and perhaps ruin everything by breaking a leg, she kept to what she hoped was the middle of the lane. She stepped into something deep and smelly and disgusting. It was probably only a cowpat but it might be part of some dead creature. She mustn't imagine silly things. Everything would look different tomorrow in the daylight and she would smile about this. Smile as she wrote to Ronnie about it.

She came to the fork in the road. There to the right, as stated, was the hill, stretching up like a big black shadow in front of her. Heaving a sigh of relief, she strode on. Then shrieked in fright and horror as she splashed into several inches of cold water. Now she knew, and had foolishly experienced, the source of Ford Farm's name. How could she have been so stupid to forget about the ford and walk straight into it? She'd been told she must venture across a ford and that there was a footbridge at the side of it. The ground had suddenly sloped and she hadn't cottoned on.

She backtracked clumsily. Putting her things down on the stone bridge, while balancing precariously, she shook the water out of her shoes. She should have worn her boots but she'd wanted to arrive looking smart. She crossed over the bridge with humiliating squelchy steps, then braced herself to begin the final part of her journey.

She was anxious now about the late hour. What sort of welcome would she receive at a time when every knock on a door was treated with dread of bad news and sometimes suspicion? She trudged on, the top of the hill seeming never to get any nearer. But finally, there it was, the rambling silhouette of a building, the farmhouse.

Her next step was cut short. She froze. A tall figure, dark and looming, was directly in her path.

Tom Harvey thought he was seeing a ghost. He was just slipping down to the village, a route so familiar that the darkness held no problem to him, when he'd looked up from the ground and in the dimming light he'd distinguished an outline. A hazy, still outline. A chill rode up his back. Biting his lip, he leaned forward, peering. The figure was small, not quite small enough to be a child. It had odd protrusions, and he wasn't sure if it was a man or a woman. Or something else.

Clearing his throat, Tom ventured, 'Hello, is someone there?'

His heart leapt when he received a reply. 'Yes. Are you from the farm? I'm the new Land Army girl.'

'Oh! Oh, good.' Feeling a fool, for he could now make out a girl burdened with a suitcase, two bags and a respirator box, Tom went to meet her. 'We weren't expecting you until tomorrow. How did you manage to get here at this time of night?'

It was a great relief to meet a friendly person from Ford Farm. 'I was fortunate enough to come across someone from the village at the railway station, a Mr Sidney Eathorne, the butcher, and he kindly offered me a lift and then gave me the directions here. My name's Jill Laity.' She did not clarify that the railway station was at Truro and that she had travelled up from Bosahan, the large house taken over on the Helford River as the Women's Land Army training centre. Security dictated that place names should not be mentioned aloud.

'You're very welcome, Miss Laity. Here, let me take your things.' Tom liked her soft, clear voice. The reason for his foray down to the village, an assignation with a local girl, could wait. 'It's cold for a June night. Come into the house. I'm afraid you've missed supper. Tilda the housekeeper's out with the Sewing Guild, but my mother will make you a warming mug of Oxo or something. You need to meet her anyway, she owns the farm.'

'Your mother? Then you must be Tom Harvey.' Jill gladly relinquished her baggage, which had become like lead weights dragging down on her arms.

'Keep close,' Tom said. 'Tuck your arm through mine so you don't come a cropper in the dark. I'll take you in through the front door.'

'Thank you.' This close she felt the good cloth of his clothes and smelled the brilliantine on his hair. Was he missing out on a drink in the pub which she had passed

4

at the entrance to the lane because of her? She had to pick up her pace to keep up with his long, easy strides. 'I know your mother owns the farm. The County Organizer of the Land Army informed me. I actually know a good deal about your family. I'm afraid Mr Eathorne proved to be quite a chatterbox. You're the second son of the squire, but there isn't a squire any more. Your father died twelve years ago and your mother has remarried. She's now Mrs Perry Bosweld. Your older brother Will is an aerial photographer in the RAF; your cousin Jonny, a flyer. Your sister Lottie is the village beauty at seventeen years old. Your grandfather – on your mother's side – is an ARP warden. He manages the farm.'

'All correct. But I manage the farm now,' Tom said quickly. It wasn't a matter of vanity to inform her of that – he liked to impress any new girl. He wished Will was on leave. It would be fun to indulge in some light-hearted rivalry to win over this pleasing young woman. He was looking forward to taking a good look at her once they were inside.

'Of course, Mr Harvey.' Jill was worried she had made a blunder. Tom Harvey might not want to be thought of as a labourer.

'Tom will do. We don't go in for titles round here.'

She was relieved to hear that, to have learned how easy-going the farm manager was. 'I'm Jill.'

'Good.' Good she was a friendly sort. 'Your room's in the older part of the house, but it's directly over the kitchen, so it'll be quite cosy.'

Jill was pleased there was a spare bedroom for her, it meant she didn't have to billet elsewhere. It would make the very early starts, something her training hadn't got her used to, and the long hours expected of her, a little easier.

'Did you do anything before, Jill?' From her well-toned voice he imagined her of the ilk who before the war had sat about prettily, learning dinner menus, waiting for a husband to come along who would provide her with a daily help and weekly gardener.

'I was a telephonist. I lived with my grandmother. She died recently and my uncle and his family took over the house. There wasn't really any room for me, so I decided to go off and train for something more useful for the war effort.'

'You must be finding farm work very different.'

'I'm doing my best to rise to the challenge.' Jill's reply was typical of her unassuming nature.

Tom chewed his lip, a habit of his when concerned. Lottie wasn't happy about not having an experienced land girl. Jill Laity was rather refined and insignificant of build. Lottie was strong in constitution and will. She was no respecter of any form of male domination or anyone's weaknesses, and she was often impossible. Some impatience and intolerance was probably ahead. Which was a pity, for Lottie would benefit from female company her own age, and Jill Laity seemed, if given the chance, that she might be a good influence on her. It still sometimes shocked Tom how Lottie would smoke, joke and even cuss like a man. It was a good thing it was Lottie's turn to stay outside for fire-watching. It would give Jill time to settle in.

They turned off from the lane and were crunching over the wide gravelled approach to the house. In the last filter of daylight, Jill glimpsed that the front door was set in an imposing Victorian wing, and that the rest of the farmhouse, standing at a right angle, was at least a century older, and, presumably, looked over the yards. Altogether, the building was huge and imposing. Sidney Eathorne had said it had seen 'some history'.

Tom opened the door and hurried Jill through it so as to allow out no more than a dash of light. While he ensured the blackout curtain was firmly back in place, Jill gazed down the long tiled passage, from which many rooms branched off. It was lit by a single lantern, no doubt to conserve electricity. The furniture, from a mahogany side table and a square gilt wood mirror to a walking-stick stand, was handsome but reassuringly unpretentious. There was a homely smell mixed with lavender polish.

'Come through to the kitchen,' he said, sweeping his eyes over her. He got a close enough look in the dimness to see she had marble-pale skin, pretty honey-blond hair, and an appealing, modest demeanour. When she gave a brief, shy smile, he was enchanted to discover a delicious dimple each side of her sweet mouth. He didn't care for the brash, forward type of woman; this one was perfect. 'I'll take your things along with us. Your room is reached quicker by the back stairs. My room's in the old wing too, by the way. I'll go in first so you don't get overwhelmed by the dogs.'

Tom went through the door at the other end of the passage. Jill followed him and felt the warmth in the kitchen reach out to her like a welcome. She was given only an instant to enjoy it. Tom suddenly dumped her things on the floor and shot off, crying, 'Mum!'

Jill ran up behind him. 'What's happened?' She found herself looking down on the inert form of a woman, lying next to a small armchair, near the range. A group of Jack Russells were fussing round her and trampling over some airforce-blue knitting.

'She's collapsed!' Tom flung over his shoulder. 'My stepfather should be in the den. Go back and shout for help.'

Chapter Two

Lottie Harvey flicked on the electric light and gazed down on the slumbering girl in the bed. She had the girl's alarm clock in her hand, which was set to ring at 5 am. Any moment now. Jill Laity would be woken with a start and would, no doubt, search frantically for the clock to switch it off. But Lottie had it. Out of reach.

She smiled and smiled. Should she?

No. It would be cruel. Pressing down the alarm stopper, she put the clock back in its place on the little bedside cabinet. Then reaching out she shook Jill's shoulder. 'Wake up, sleepyhead! There's no place for lie-abeds here.'

'What?' Jill shot up straight, her eyes wide and shocked, her hands clutching the covers up to her neck. 'Oh, no! Have I overslept?' She looked from the stranger who was towering over her to her alarm clock, then thumped a hand over her hammering heart. 'No, I haven't. What...?'

'Sorry. Can't resist a joke,' Lottie said, grinning. 'It drives Tom mad. It's childish of me, I know, but his wiggings only make me do it all the more. I'm Lottie, if you haven't already guessed. Didn't get the chance to say hello to you last night because you went to bed immediately after the little family crisis. I never go up before midnight, I thrive on only three or four hours' sleep.

9

Thanks, by the way, for rushing to my mum's aid. She told me how you fetched my stepdad and how you helped get her up to bed. Didn't need the doctor. Perry – Pappa, I call him – was once an army surgeon. Come along then. I'm afraid you're going to have to brave your first early start here. We're in the middle of the corn harvest. The weather let us down yesterday but it's going to be bright and sunny today. Are you shy? Want me to turn my back or leave the room?'

'No, no, please stay.' Jill threw back the covers and stepped out on to the square rug that covered most of the polished planked floor. She was just about recovering from her fright. She felt vulnerable in her thin winceyette nightdress, which had received some 'make do and mend' attention, and would have preferred her privacy, but more than anything she wanted to make friends with Lottie Harvey. The village butcher had mentioned that Lottie was high-spirited, a rebel, and that although her mother and stepfather indulged her, other parents wouldn't tolerate such blatant disrespect. Tom had also said ominously last night, 'You mustn't take any notice of Lottie. You'll get used to her.' While sorry about her new employer's ill health, Jill was glad to have made a good impression right from the start. Jill went to her uniform, which she had unpacked and hung up outside the single walnut wardrobe. She acknowledged she didn't look as good in it as Lottie did in her brown coverall. Lottie had the height and gently curving figure that would look wonderful in rags. Her coppery-brown hair, of the same shiny tint as her mother's and Tom's, was tied back young-American style with a flag-red ribbon, and fell in the sort of extravagant waves Jill wished for herself.

'How is Mrs Bosweld this morning? She came round quickly and told Mr Bosweld she'd merely fainted, but I could see he was worried. Tom was anxious.' It had been evident how much affection and concern there was in this house. Something outside of Jill's experience, for her grandmother had been conservative and undemonstrative and had rarely offered a word of encouragement.

'She's up and about, although she'll be taking things a little easier than usual. Pappa's insisting.' Lottie was studying the few things Jill had placed on the deep window shelf. She looked Jill straight in the eye. 'It's turned out there's nothing wrong with her as such. After eleven years of marriage to Pappa, she's expecting a baby.'

'A baby? Mrs Bosweld's…?' Jill blushed a vivid red. She was not used to having such a thing mentioned in a patent manner. Obviously, few things embarrassed Lottie Harvey.

Lottie giggled, then sighed, becoming bored. Jill Laity seemed pleasant but she was dull, and probably strait-laced. Tom had reported in the sort of annoying male talk that spoke of intimate desire, 'Give her a go, Lottie. Please. She's got the sweetest nature and is a divine little thing.'

Impatiently, Lottie had demanded, 'Since when did I pick on anyone? If she puts in a hard day's work and never slacks, then I won't be asking for anything more.' Secretly, Lottie had hoped to make a friend, a confidante to chew over things like clothes and boyfriends. She'd never had one of the latter. The previous land girl had been a decade older and absolutely no fun.

Lottie shrugged off her disappointment. 'Call my mum Mrs Em. Everyone does. Do you like your room?'

'Oh, yes. It's pretty and so comfortable.' Jill's reply held enthusiasm. In contrast to her dreary, puritan room at her old home, everything here was furnished in a distinctly feminine style. The curtains were chintz, there were lace-trimmed cushions on the upholstered chair and the walls were crowded with pictures of roses. When Tom had carried her things inside last night it had been necessary for him to duck his head under the overhead oak beams.

Lottie picked up the one photograph Jill had brought with her. 'Who's this, may I ask? Your brother?'

Jill went pink. 'That's my sweetheart, Ronnie. The only family I've ever known is my grandmother and Uncle Stanley. She died in February. I've never been close to my uncle. Even though he lived just across town, I only saw him and his wife and two young children once or twice a year.'

'Ronnie's in army uniform, I see. An officer.' Lottie put the photograph down carefully, changing her opinion of Jill. *She actually had a boyfriend.* There were a hundred questions Lottie wanted to ask but she settled for something appropriate. 'He has a nice smile. You're not about to rush off and get married, I hope. Your predecessor suddenly did.'

'We haven't thought that far ahead,' Jill said, washing her face in the cold water left from last night on the washstand. She buried her face in the towel. Her feelings for Ronnie were private.

'Is he overseas?'

'No. He's currently at the light infantry depot at Bodmin. Not too far away but, of course, I get very little chance to see him.' Loneliness ate a path into Jill. She ached for the only security she had left. Of being with the caring, intelligent boy she had grown up as neighbour to, of planning a future together. Whenever difficulties fell on her she replaced it with the last image she had of Ronnie, as he'd left her at the end of his last leave. His brave smile hadn't hid the little amount of fear in his soft blue eyes. He felt he wasn't a natural leader of men, and sooner or later he'd have to serve on a battlefield. She prayed ceaselessly for him to prevail.

Lottie observed her mingled hopes. 'You must worry about him. It's a shame about your grandmother. Mine died last year. I loved her dearly. Now, Jill, get a move on! Tom's bringing in the herd. I'm off to get the milking shed ready. Mum has said, as this is your first day, to let you off any work until after breakfast. She's a softie. But I'm not.' She wagged a finger, partly in playfulness, partly in warning. 'One last word, Jill. I know you're spoken for, but watch out for Tom. He's good-natured but he's a heartbreaker. Ask any girl in the village.'

Jill nodded to show she had taken everything in. She couldn't imagine there was anything ruthless about Tom. He had an arresting smile, just like his sister did, but there was a boyishness about him, and, so Jill thought, a gentleness too. As she made haste to get ready to go downstairs, she was amazed at how uplifted she felt. Lottie Harvey bubbled with a raw energy, and although she obviously wasn't a sufferer of fools, she seemed thoughtful and fun-loving. After pulling her khaki overall on over her Aertex shirt and knee socks, she gazed into the small mirror on the wall and fastened her tie with its Women's Land Army badge. Soon, she might get the chance to stride off down to the village wearing her knee breeches, green V-necked pullover, and her round-brimmed, somewhat unflattering hat. She couldn't hold back a burst of joy. She felt the way Ronnie made her feel, that she was somebody, that she had a purpose, was even a little important.

She switched off the light and threw back the heavy curtains to meet the burgeoning daylight, and as she flung open the window, every last scrap of boldness left her. A burst of confused noises, that in her anticipation had escaped her before, joined forces with the busy scene below to scare and taunt her. While calling and cajoling, Tom and two other men, presumably his grandfather and the cowman, and a border collie, were guiding a long line of brown and brown-and-white cattle into the outer yard from the lane. Sheds and outhouses and barns and farm machinery straggled seemingly into the distance and animals and poultry sprawled everywhere. Fields and meadows stretched away in all directions.

How different, quieter and safer, most noticeably, her life was going to be here than in the dignified house in Melvill Road, at Falmouth. Day and night, the harbour underwent regular raids from German Stukka bombers, and residential parts also took hits. The docks and boat-yards were a frenzy of activity, repairing and constructing and loading ships. The United States Navy was there in force and had erected a huge Nissen hut and brought in the largest crane ever seen. There, and all along the river banks of the tidal estuary, they were building strange-looking boats, obviously landing craft, with ridged ramps that would enable troops to walk off straight on to the shore – enemy-occupied shores. The endless racket and constant bustle had been wearisome and unnerving, not least because it all pointed to a secret that was too big a secret to be kept, that these were preparations to open up a

Second Front, to liberate Europe, an undertaking so vast it was beyond the comprehension of most. It made one feel insecure and apprehensive yet confident and proud all at the same time. The contrast here of ancient hills and trees and farmland, the tip of the tower of the parish church just in view, rather than soothing Jill, made her feel an outsider.

Lottie was striding away from the back door between her mother and stepfather, their arms all linked together. Jill had found both the Boswelds open and friendly last night, but Emilia Bosweld, who was a striking-looking woman, had an air of strength and resolution, and Perry Bosweld had a hint of authority. It had been impossible not to take in his dark, amazingly good looks. He walked slowly with a roll to the right, having lost half his right leg in the last war. Jill had been surprised at the contrast in her new employer's ordinary accent and her husband's pleasant cut-glass one – Mrs Bosweld – Mrs Em – had apparently, as Jill's grandmother would have put it, married twice above her station. The strong affection between the Boswelds, their deep connection, was distinct. The family happiness, the prospect of a new baby to be born into it, cut into Jill and made her feel even further out of place.

Moments of unreality swept over her. Early loss of her parents had robbed her of confidence and she had often fought to feel she existed, that she was alive and real and mattered. Then she lifted her head high. She mattered to Ronnie and the war effort. 'I'll make good with my life or I'll die trying,' she whispered the vow.

The scrubbed pine table in the kitchen was long and wide, and laid for several people. A plate of thinly cut bread, spread with just a scrape of butter, sat importantly in the middle, making Jill's mouth water with longing. Should she sit down at the table? Call hello, see if anyone was about? She smoothed at her rolled-under, shoulder-length hair, which she had tied back with a scarf, then she made sure she had a hanky in her overall pocket. These moments of being new somewhere were always excruciatingly awful.

A collection of cats lolled and slept on the hearth rug. Jill had always wanted a pet but never been allowed one. She bent to the nearest cat, which was washing its paws. It was set a little apart, as if chief of the clan. It was thin, its rough black coat showing patches of rusty plum. Jill reached for it and the cat lashed out, clawing her wrist. 'Ow!' She shot back. Drops of blood cascaded over the back of her stinging hand.

'No, no! You mustn't touch he!' a horrified female voice cried from behind her.

'I'm sorry.' The sudden attack and her foolishness left Jill trembling. She clamped her hanky over the wound, fearing she'd drip blood on the rug.

'Aw, he's hurt you.' The woman had come out of the walk-in larder and was carrying a large crock, labelled 'salt'. 'He's not supposed to be in here. Motley creature. He's a yard cat but he keeps sneaking in. It's Mr Tom's fault, he's too soft with him. Lazarus! Out with 'ee. Go on! Get!' She put the crock down and opened the door to the back kitchen and then the stable door beyond it to the yard, then after coming back she flapped the brilliant-white apron around her stout body at the cat. It ignored her until she fetched a broom, then it hissed at her as she chased it outside. Back inside again, she said, 'He's called Lazarus because he keeps escaping the fate he deserves, though I s'pose we shouldn't wish no harm on one of God's creatures.'

Dabbing at the scratch, Jill repeated, 'I'm sorry. Are you Tilda? I'm Jill.'

'Tilda Lawry.' The housekeeper straightened the turban that covered most of her scraped-back, greying ginger hair. 'Sit yourself down then, maid. Just as well I've fetched the salt. You'd better clean that hand. My, you're a little thing. The last land girl we had was built like an ox. I come here to work in the Great War. Never thought we'd have another on the same catastrophic scale. Sometimes I can hardly believe it's happening again. Mrs Em lost her brother Billy at Passchendaele, now she's worrying over her eldest boy Will, who's named after him. And there's Mr Tristan Harvey's son, Jonny, to worry about too. You come from Falmouth I hear, Jill? They're always in for it there, poor souls. Hope you didn't suffer anything bad there, eh?'

'So far the family house has been spared. Some of the surrounding villages have fared even worse than the town because of the mishits. No details were reported in the newspapers, of course, but word gets round.'

''Tis wise to keep our lips buttoned,' Tilda said approvingly. While putting a glass bowl of hot, salted water on the table, she gazed at Jill's hands, which were a little roughened, small and well formed. 'You speak well. Not brought up to work on the land, I s'pose?'

Jill wanted to say she had a medical certificate to prove she was capable of hard physical work. She sat on the form and sank her hand into the salt water and forced herself not to flinch at the intensified stinging. 'When I get my ration book adjusted, should I give it to you or Mrs Em?'

Tilda placed a cup of weak, stewed tea – rationing meant tea leaves were used several times – beside the bowl, then she leaned forward with her hands on her knees and stared at Jill. 'I do the shopping. If you don't mind me asking, are you sure you're old enough to leave home? You look very young.'

'But I'm twenty!' Jill protested. She hated the habitual comments she received about her age.

'Mmm. You're as pale as a lily and as thin as a yard of pump water. Mind you, a month or two out working in all weathers should pink you up, and rationing or no, I'll find something to put a bit of weight on you.'

There was a loud rap on the back kitchen door. Frowning, Tilda's head shot round in that direction. 'What on earth? People don't usually hammer like someone gone mazed.'

A man came in. He was dark and very good looking. For an instant Jill thought it was Perry Bosweld, but this man had an arrogant demeanour. The sight in his left eye was marred and a small scar ran above it. From his clothes he appeared to be a farmer.

'Well! Mr Ben! Fancy seeing you here. It's been ages.' Tilda folded her plump hands primly, then added in a tart tone, 'You don't usually darken Mrs Em's door.'

Jill stopped bathing her hand and stood up. Although this man wasn't welcome here he somehow commanded respect.

He glanced at her, an eyebrow raised, then rounded on Tilda. 'I'd no wish to come but there's bad news. Jonny's plane has crash-landed.'

Chapter Three

'What? Oh, no! I'll run and fetch Mrs Em!' Tilda hurried off.

The man stepped smoothly out of her way. Jill guessed he was in his early forties, about the same age as Mrs Em. He had a powerful build and a tremendous sense of presence. 'Your name? I take it you've just arrived?' She took exception to his bluntness and the way he was looking her over. She stared at him. 'I'm Jill Laity. I'm sorry to hear you've brought bad news.'

'Thank you.' He smiled. It was an indolent smile, a handsome smile. The stiffness about his mouth made Jill think he didn't smile often. Why was he willing to be friendly with her? Perhaps he shared Tom's penchant for women. 'I'm sorry. I must have sounded rude. Jill? A pretty, uncomplicated name. I'm Ben Harvey.' He approached her with quick, athletic strides. 'Uncle of Tom and Lottie. And to Jonny, whom I've just mentioned. I own Tremore Farm on the other side of the village, and a lot of other property and businesses locally and in Truro. I don't have the benefit of family working for me but I do have three Land Army girls. You're very welcome, Jill, to call on your colleagues.' Now he showed no humour at all. 'You won't find any agreeable companionship in the females here. They're tenacious, and my niece is a bolshie little fiend. You'll need to be wary of her.'

Obviously there was a rift between the two branches of the family that lived in Hennaford. This man's boastfulness, the inflexibility she sensed in him, made Jill reason much of it had to be his fault. 'Really? I've found Lottie to be very pleasant.'

He shook his head as if amused. 'You'll learn.'

A crowd came in all at once. The Boswelds, who were holding hands, and Tom, Lottie and Tilda. Ben Harvey's stance became confrontational. Jill didn't like him staying so close to her, giving the impression they had become familiar. She shuffled several steps away, but watched, fascinated somehow, as he, declining to speak to the members of his family, flicked open a slim gold case and nonchalantly, in blatant disdain, tapped the tip of a cigarette on the case.

'Well? What's happened?' Emilia Bosweld tossed her hands towards him. Displeasure with her former brother-in-law sang out of every strong angle of her face. Jill saw that she wasn't the least bit intimidated. Although dressed in an old shirt, trousers and boots, she was wholly feminine. Combs swept back her wealth of hair in flattering swathes. She was statuesque, stately, something of a goddess. Here was a woman who would never be ignored. 'Is Jonny…?'

'No. He was lucky though. He has a broken collarbone, cracked ribs and a small head wound.' Every word Ben Harvey uttered was given with a begrudging grimace. 'His plane took a hit over enemy territory – Berlin, no doubt – but, thank God, as an experienced pilot, he managed to shunt it back on three engines and underbelly damage all the way to the airfield, then get his crew out before the flames reached them. It happened two nights ago. Tris has just heard. The telephone lines are a bit dodgy and he asked me to pass on the news.' He advanced towards the gathering, forming impatient sweeps with his large hands – in effect ordering them out of his way. 'I've done my duty, I'm off.'

With a supercilious grin, he threw over his shoulder, 'It was a pleasure to meet you, Jill.'

All except Emilia gave him leeway. Her intense dark eyes were stern. 'I'm relieved the news wasn't the worst. Does this mean Jonny's likely to be on his way home soon to recuperate?'

'No idea.' Ben placed the cigarette between his lips and brought a lighter up to it. 'You know what you can do if you need more info. Move.'

'Thanks for coming,' Emilia said, with faint sincerity. 'Light that up outside.'

He pushed past her and left.

Emilia gazed at her husband. 'Thank God!'

Perry Bosweld encircled her in an unselfconsciously warm embrace. 'I'm sure that wherever Will is, he's safe too, darling.'

'I hope so.'

There was a moment's silence, a pause from everyone in the room as each thought about their loved ones involved in the war and far from home. A linking of anxiety, hopes, wishes and prayers.

Jill caught Lottie staring at her scratched hand. Was Lottie thinking her weak and soft for managing to hurt herself before she'd even stepped outside into the farmyard? Jill wanted to show she was ready and willing. 'Is there anything I can do, Mrs Em?'

'Well, if you want to go straight to it, Jill—' Emilia smiled at her – 'come and join us in the milking shed.'

'I'll wait for you to put your boots on,' Tom said, when his mother and stepfather were on their way back across the yard.

'No, you won't.' Lottie pushed him out through the stable doorway and hissed in his ear. 'Don't you dare bother Jill. You know what I mean. Besides, she's got a boyfriend.'

'Well, bully for him,' Tom grinned, ambling off with his hands in his pockets, whistling 'You Are My Sunshine'.

'I want you to know something, Jill,' Lottie said vehemently, making Jill pause with just one gumboot on. 'Heed these words carefully. My Uncle Ben is a loathsome man! You've seen for yourself how he shuns my mother. If he can cause trouble for my stepfather he doesn't hesitate to do so. He's jealous of their happiness. His American wife left him years ago when she was pregnant with their second child. It took months but he tracked her down in the States, then he returned almost at once and has never spoken of her or their two children since. He's even made it known that he's cut the children out of his will. You mustn't mix with him. If you do, the family, me in particular, will see it as disloyalty. And while Tom may be a heartbreaker, my Uncle Ben is a merciless seducer.'

Jill had listened amazed at such frank information.

'Do you understand?'

'Yes, Lottie. I do.'

As they started across the yard, Lottie suddenly pushed her arm through Jill's. 'Good. Then I'm sure we'll get along fine.'

—

Someone else turned up in Hennaford, but unlike Jill, she was neither expected nor welcomed.

Ben Harvey had barely got back inside Tremore House when his ageing, stick-thin housekeeper hurried to the library with news that he had a visitor.

From his desk, Ben scowled at her puffed face as he impatiently pushed a sheaf of papers together. The trip to Ford Farm, clashing with Emilia, as he had done so often over the years, had put him in the darkest mood. He pulled off his round-rimmed spectacles and rubbed at his partially blinded eye. Tension made it ache and sting. 'Is it anyone important, Agnes? I'm about to slip off to the farm. I've a very busy day ahead.' He was extremely patriotic and saw it as his duty to king and country to put in several hours of hard physical work on the land almost every day.

'You must come at once, Mr Ben!' Agnes blustered, wringing her bony hands and making the veins on them stand out ugly and blue. 'It's Miss Faye! She's here. She's actually here.'

'Who? Don't be silly!' Ben cried in anger at the mention of his daughter.

'It's her, I swear. I'd know her anywhere. She's changed quite a bit but 'tis certainly the same little maid that used to live here. She's come with bags and everything and is standing out there in the hall. Asking to see you, Mr Ben.'

Ben sank down slowly onto his plush buttoned leather chair. He dragged a hand down over his face. 'I… I. What does she want? What on earth's she doing here?' Everything inside him seized up. He swore under his breath. 'Um… show her into the drawing room. Tell her I'll be along in a minute. I need to think.'

Faye Harvey followed the housekeeper into the appointed room. She looked all around. Little had changed since she'd last been here, twelve years ago. Mirrors and reflective ornaments and highly polished furniture, crafted in the last two decades, gave the illusion of there being more light and space to the long room. There was still the same enormous brick-red Tabriz rug on which she had spread out her toys. There was little she remembered about her father, it had seemed that he could never be much bothered with her, but he hadn't minded where she'd played. On the lofty mantelpiece was a copy of a photograph that her mother kept displayed in her own drawing room, of a sad-looking, black-haired man. It was of her late Uncle Alec, who had been Hennaford's squire. Her brother, born a few months after her mother had taken her away from here, was his namesake and looked very much like him. And like their father too; the older Harvey men shared the same dark, rugged, grey-eyed looks. Hopefully, she'd get to meet her Uncle Tristan, whom she remembered to be very good-natured. Her Aunt Emilia too. If her father turned her out, her next stop would be Ford Farm, where she was sure she'd receive a welcome.

She heard a deep step out in the hall. She sucked in her breath. A plethora of emotions surged through her. Curiosity. Indignation. Anger. Hurt and rejection were the strongest. Although none of these were her real reason for being here, she had a desperate need for an explanation as to why she and her brother had been totally forgotten by the owner of this grand house. She wanted to smack this man's face, but also to hear him say he was sorry and to beg her for forgiveness. She ached to have him hold out his arms to her and offer all the paternal love she had missed out on.

On the other side of the door, Ben was hardly breathing. It was wrong of him, but although his daughter was the one person in the world he should be closest to, she was the last one he wanted to see. He had loved her once, but not greatly. He had wanted a son, to inherit his achievements and fortune. If he'd got that, then perhaps he'd have felt more for the fluffy, tidy little thing who'd lacked charm and spirit. Why had she come? What did she want from him? It could only be to bring bad news – which he wouldn't be interested in – or to take issue with him. Damn the girl! Damn himself. Why couldn't he have loved her? Why had he been fated to love only one person? Emilia. Damn her most of all! He touched his injured eye. He had blamed her all those years ago in their youth for blinding him. His bitterness had destroyed the love she'd had for him. He'd been unable to stand the fact that shortly afterwards she had fallen in love and married Alec. And after his death, Perry Bosweld. He had taken refuge in hating her. He couldn't stop and it was gradually destroying him. Dear God, don't let Faye see that in him!

Swallowing the painful lump in his throat, he went into the drawing room. And stood stock still. This young woman with the figure of a fashion model, wearing a tailored jersey dress and open-toe slingbacks, her ebony hair finished in kiss-curls in front of her ears, was Faye? His daughter? Agnes might have recognized her but he as sure as hell didn't. Brooke, his ex-wife, was attractive but neat and homely. This stranger was the picture of sophistication.

Narrowing his good eye, he said guardedly, 'I'm Ben Harvey.'

Faye felt she had been sliced through, as if her heart had been grated. Her father hadn't changed a bit. He was a fine sight. Many men of his age thickened round the middle and their hair thinned, but he was still in his prime, handsome and magnificent. She could have borne this meeting better if he had deteriorated in stature. Worst of all, he was as cool towards her as on the last occasion he'd seen her. 'Hello, sir.' Her accent was educated with a soft hint of American.

'Are you really…?'

She tilted her chin, a confident pose yet more than that, and Ben saw a touch of his own arrogance in her. He shrugged, unusually lost. He had been prepared to ward off any sentimental feelings but it wasn't necessary. Faye was a stranger to him. It made him realize that all he had in the world was his elder brother, Tristan. Never before had he felt so lonely. And afraid. Fear was new to him. Insecurity had suddenly been bred in him. 'Well. Faye. This is…'

'An unwelcome surprise?'

'I… don't know what to say.' It was rare for Ben to have to clutch at composure. 'Um, sit down. I'll ring for Agnes to bring some tea.'

Keeping her eyes on him, Faye lowered herself into a leather armchair near the tall windows. 'It was good to see Agnes again. She remembered my favourite childhood drink, raspberry and elderberry cordial.'

Ben did not miss the accusation in her words. He made to sit but was too restless, and he paced the length of the room, staying at a distance. Then he frowned. 'How did you get here? What in God's name made you undertake the treacherous journey across the Atlantic? What was your mother thinking of, allowing you to compromise your safety? She's well, is she? Brooke?'

'Mom's fine. She married again, ten years ago. I've got two half-siblings.'

'Mom?' Ben pulled a face.

'A long time ago I slipped out of calling her Mummy.' Faye glanced down, then fastened her eyes back on him with a sort of pleading. 'I'm sorry to have just arrived unannounced. I should have written first. Neither Mom or I have done anything foolhardy. I was actually here in the country before the war broke out, at boarding school in south London, training for the ballet. The school was evacuated to Scotland. It wasn't considered safe for me to get a passage home.'

His stare was full of incredulity. She had been close in location to him for years. If she had written to him he wouldn't have replied. She must have known that. Yet here she was. In person. It showed she had courage.

Faye was having trouble keeping control. He was furious with her. Hating her being here. Oh, what had compelled her to behave so irrationally? Yet she'd had to come. And why shouldn't she? This man owed her a hell of a lot. Deep down, she would like to build up a relationship with him, but if that wasn't possible, then she'd use the heartless brute.

Ben couldn't put his thoughts together, so again he shrugged. He scratched his tumbling black hair. Then reached for his cigarettes. 'I haven't a clue what to say. I take it you've left the boarding school, that you're now a professional dancer?'

'I'm afraid not. I grew too tall, and to be honest I wasn't destined to scale the heights for a company like the Royal Ballet. I've been employed as a secretary for a Highland estate for the last couple of years, but… a short while ago the laird considered there wasn't enough work there to justify my wages.' She fumbled with her skirt, waited for him to respond.

'So what do you intend to do now? Enlist in one of the services?' It was unthinkable to Ben that an able-bodied nineteen-year-old would not be willing to serve the country.

Faye blushed. 'I'd like to do something eventually but first I need a place to settle.'

'So you thought you'd look me up? Why now? Do you need money?'

Faye flew to her feet. 'I didn't come here for a handout! I came here because you're my father. It took a lot of nerve to come here after so many years. I was hoping you'd at least be curious to see me again.'

Ben looked down at the smoking effects in his hands. Then at her. How could he meet her eyes and feel nothing? 'Yes, I should be, shouldn't I? Look, you've caught me totally unawares. You're welcome to stay.' He nearly added, 'I suppose,' but managed to grind out, 'Of course. Use your old room, if you like. I'm afraid there's nothing of yours left there. Look, Faye, I know I'm being rotten, but I can't come to terms with you being here. I

28

was about to leave to work on my farm. We'll talk later, if that's what you want. If you're still here.' He hoped with all his strength she wouldn't be.

She stared at him. How could he be so cold? Over the years her mother had warned her that she would never be accepted by him. 'Aren't you going to ask about Alec?'

The arctic storm that invaded Ben's guts nearly made him sick. He must have looked ferocious because Faye gasped as if she had received a physical blow. While cursing her for mentioning the boy's name, he checked himself. Pride, and pride alone, prevented him for blurting out what was on his lips. 'Well, how is he?'

'Mom sent me some photos last month.' She twisted her mouth to the side. 'I'll show them to you later.'

At the door, because he needed to know, Ben asked, 'How long are you thinking of staying?' He softened it. 'I mean, how long before you seek a recruitment office?'

She couldn't join up. She had a responsibility. She replied with equally cold meaning, 'I might not be bothering you for long, sir.'

With a brisk nod, he was gone.

Faye had told herself if she got an icy reception she wouldn't weep. But she did. Pools of hot, stinging tears. Ben Harvey was her father. And Alec's. Yet he acted as if he loathed them both. Why was her father so disconnected from her? The reasons her mother had given for leaving and divorcing him were that he was a contentious snob, that he had always been jealous of his eldest brother, coveting the position of squire for himself. And that he had overlooked her as his wife and had yearned for another woman. Whoever that woman had been, her father had not used his freedom to marry her. But those reasons all together were not good enough excuses for him being such an unloving father. And right now she could do with a caring and concerned parent.

'You're a complicated person, Ben Harvey,' she said, drying her eyes. 'That's something we have in common. It's why, like you, I've made a mess of my life. I don't care what's behind all your bitterness. I won't let you force me to leave here.'

Chapter Four

Was there any skin left on her hands without a blister? Jill felt along each finger and thumb, then scrutinized both sore, stinging palms. Her knuckles were raw and bruised. The scratch on her wrist seemed insignificant now. It seemed hours, a lifetime ago, since the cat had attacked her. Thistles had become her new enemy as she'd slogged away in the cornfield, endlessly turning stooks – made up of eight heavy sheaves – inside out to dry in preparation for rick-making. She'd kept her sleeves buttoned down but stalks had scratched paths up to her elbows and chaff had rubbed inside her collar and even her underwear. Her ankles too were tender and her nose and throat felt choked with dust. The work had been hard during her few weeks of training, but not undertaken at anything like Lottie's furious pace.

She and Lottie and the rest of the workforce, including Mrs Em and Edwin Rowse – Lottie's grandfather – and a few villagers, were now moving on to the next field, where Tom was busy with the horses and cutter and binder. Fresh sheaves were thrown out of the machine and new stooks had to be formed. Although her back and limbs were aching, Jill managed to keep up with Lottie, labouring on without pause or complaint. While the others chatted and sometimes laughed and joked, she concentrated, storing up each experience inside her head to word in the letter she would write to Ronnie tonight, particularly the wildlife she saw. Harvest mice scuttling away from the machinery, a kestrel hovering overhead for the easy, exposed prey, and as they were near the stream that emerged from the woods, there had been a grass snake skulking through the long grass.

'I've never met anyone as quiet as you.' Lottie passed her a mug of tea during the afternoon break. 'Rub some soil well into your hands, it will harden them up. Getting worn out?'

'Just a little,' she replied, ignoring her woes. The first sip of tea was hard to swallow but tasted like something sent from heaven.

Lottie expertly squashed a stinging winged insect on the back of her hand with a slap from the other. 'When we finish up here we'll bring in the herd for milking. Then your first day will be over. What do you think of it then? Of us?'

Jill resisted the desire to close her eyes and doze. 'It hasn't been too bad. And you've all been very patient with me. Your granddad's a sweetie. I'm really looking forward to the bath Mrs Em's promised I can take, and then my bed.'

'Granddad would be amused at that description of him.' Lottie looked fondly at Edwin Rowse. Short and work- weathered, with full side whiskers, he had been content to hand over his managerial responsibilities to Tom a couple of years ago. Firstly Ford Farm's cowman, he'd lived in a tied cottage in the village and had moved into the farmhouse, with his late wife, when Emilia, formerly the dairymaid, had married the squire. Lottie was proud of the two differing branches of her ancestry. With so many forebears in the churchyard, a short distance along the lanes, and the fact that she, like her two brothers, would inherit a third of the farm, she had a strong sense of belonging, of continuity. Something, she sensed, that Jill did not.

In the early evening, in the milking shed, copying the encouraging noises Lottie had made to the herd along the lane from pasture, Jill sought to head the cows into the stalls.

Midge Roach, the wrinkled, brown-skinned cowman, was nearby, chaining up a cow. 'You don't need to do that, maid. They'll go straight in on their own.'

Jill didn't hear him above the mooing and lowing. She turned and was frightened to be suddenly faced with a big, heavy, brown creature that looked as if it was about to trample her underfoot. She just managed to escape her feet being trodden on, then lost her balance and collided with someone. 'Oh! Sorry.'

'Don't worry, you're doing fine,' Tom said. 'Come with me and help me measure out the feed.'

'All right, but first I'll just get this beast in.' She edged round the cow and pushed on its rump in the hope of guiding it into the next empty stall. But it stubbornly refused, heading for the stall beside it. 'No, no! In there, silly!'

A hand dragged her away. It was Lottie. 'That's Briar. She won't go into any stall but her own. None of them will. See above? Their names are painted in. Didn't they teach you that at training? Now move back so Buttercup can go through. Well, don't just stand about gawping, little mouse.' It was just one of the nicknames Lottie had taken to calling her. 'Buttercup's not the most patient creature. You'll come a cropper in a minute and you're slowing us up. Pappa's insisting Mum takes a rest, so you're taking her place.'

'Sorry.' Jill was so weary she could hardly catch her breath.

'You've been saying sorry all day and there's no need. Come on. We'll wash the udders. Tom and Midge will put on the machines. Granddad will write in the yields and hump the churns.'

Jill had been surprised that morning to see the herd wasn't hand-milked, but Mrs Em had explained that all the larger farms had machinery. She had watched while the many shiny metal parts had been put together and attached to the teats. It had seemed a complicated procedure and she was nervous she'd make a hash of it when she was called on to do it. Long before the process of dismantling and sterilizing the machinery was over, of hand-stripping each cow's udder to ensure the last drop of milk was gained, and the herd was unchained and led out again by Midge and Edwin, Jill was almost sleeping on her feet.

'Right. Now to wash down.' She heard Tom's voice as if from a distance. She felt his hand on the small of her back. 'You all right, Jill?'

'What? Oh, just a bit tired, that's all.'

'This won't take long. I'll fetch you a brush. Just follow what I do. Lottie will use the hose.'

Follow him? With every muscle in her body screaming at breaking point, it was impossible to keep up with his expert pace, of reaching up and reaching down, of scouring every corner, of brushing the waste into the channel at the back of the stalls, where it would be loaded into a wheelbarrow to be taken away to the dung heap. And all the while hopping out of the way as Lottie sprayed. Jill was overcome by a wave of dizziness. Next instant she screamed as she was hit by a jet of cold water.

Shortly afterwards, sodden and weak, she was being supported on either side through the yards by the laughing brother and sister. 'I'm so sorry, Jill,' Lottie said, chuckling. 'But you looked so funny. It was hysterical.'

'You're game, I'll give you that, Jill,' Tom said, sliding his arm firmly round her waist. 'You put in every effort today.'

'Do you think Mrs Em is pleased with me?' Jill was willing her eyes to stay open, holding back a groan as her body, relaxing at last, throbbed all over in complaint.

'We all are,' Lottie said. 'I must admit I had my doubts. You seemed so delicate. But you were soon pulling the stooks together as if you'd been doing it all your life.'

Jill wished Ronnie was here to listen to this. She'd love to see him right now. He'd be so proud. They'd enjoy discussing every detail of her first day here. Ronnie was a mathematics scholar. He had a fine methodical mind. He'd make mental lists of every good point and every point that could be improved on, and with a little prayer, soothe her over anything that couldn't be changed but simply endured. That way he'd give her strength. And in his own doting way he'd smile at her, occasionally reaching for her hand. He'd say she looked pretty in her work clothes, even though she didn't. At the end, as with all of their meetings – secret meetings, for Ronnie insisted their love stay a secret until he'd graduated from university – he would kiss her. Kiss her softly. Ronnie was gentle and not at all forward. She wished now she'd worn her engagement ring on arrival here, but she was too used to keeping everything about Ronnie to herself.

She copied Lottie and Tom and pulled off her boots outside the back kitchen door. Her limbs trembling uncomfortably, she leaned against the wall and joined them for a cigarette. 'My grandmother was so old-fashioned she'd have had a fit if she could have seen me now.' She'd nearly had a fit herself when Lottie had offered her a smoke during the morning crib break.

'Take it, Miss Prim.' Lottie had pushed a Woodbine between her fingers. 'Everybody smokes these days. My mum can't see us. Anyway, why worry about anything when the future's so uncertain?'

'We are winning the war.' Jill thought it unpatri-otic to believe otherwise. After four years of hostilities, many countries under German and Italian control had been retaken and Allied troops now occupied the Axis stronghold in the Mediterranean. She had stared at the cigarette with equal amounts of excitement and distaste. And on each of the first three puffs she'd dared take she'd coughed like a bronchitic.

'Glad you're an optimist. We're not doing too badly,' Tom had said. He'd gazed across the shorn field then up at the pale-blue, lightly clouded sky. He'd gone so quiet, Jill had wondered what he was thinking.

This time, the nicotine steadied her. Screwing her eyes up against the smoke, she brought the cigarette up for the next inhalation and noticed the ingrained dirt in her hands, the ragged nails. She reached up and felt at her hair, her face. Felt dirt on both. 'Oh, what must I look like?'

'A grubby urchin,' Lottie stated.

'I don't look that bad, do I?'

She felt Tom's eyes on her. They had often strayed to her throughout the day. She didn't mind. His looks had not been invasive. Every time, however, Lottie had showed that she minded. Jill was amused but she found it reassuring to have someone looking out for her honour.

Tom said, 'If you look exactly as you do now, I'd be proud to escort you to the dance next month.'

'Dance?' Jill stifled a yawn. 'I've never been to a dance before.'

'It's nowhere special,' Lottie said, ushering her inside to clean up. 'Just in the village, the Methodist social rooms. But the proceeds will go to the Linen League, for the infirmary. A friend of ours, Louisa, has helped with the fund ever since the infirmary was bombed last year. Mum and Pappa are arranging the dance. Uncle Tris will come. You'll like him, Jill. He's a darling. Sometimes he stays with us. He lives at Watergate Bay, near Newquay, and he's been so lonely since our cousin Adele joined the WRENS, and his stepdaughter Vera Rose moved up to London to work for a government ministry. Tragically last year our Aunt Winnie was killed when she was hit by a car after dark.'

'Jonny should be well enough to travel and attend the dance by then,' Tom said, waiting his turn for the soap. 'He and I together will liven things up.'

'You must spread it around that he's coming anyway,' Lottie said. 'That way we'll get girls from the other villages and Truro. There's always a shortage of male partners. Jonny's the most gorgeous man you'll ever set eyes on,' she explained for Jill's benefit, then she cast a meaningful look at her brother. 'Although he's another who has the morals of a tom cat. We might be unlucky to attract some boring American servicemen at the dance. They seem to hear about all the social events. They're so boastful. They think they're God's gift.'

'Lottie, you're so uncharitable,' Tom chided. He still smarted over her observable amusement back in the spring, when their American allies had led the Wings for Victory march, part of the fundraising for a new Spitfire, past the war memorial in Truro and had been virtually ignored by the public. They must have been annoyed and embarrassed when the British servicemen following on after them had been loudly and passionately cheered. Tom hated what he saw as unfair behaviour. Give everyone a chance, was his philosophy.

'Do they usually come?' Jill asked. Her grandmother's worsening senility had caused her to liken GIs to German troops. Evangeline Laity had been so afraid of the expected enemy invasion of 1940 she had threatened to kill both herself and Jill if it took place, to spare them rape and capture. While not despising the Americans, of which there were increasing amou'nts packing in and around Falmouth, it had not bred a security in Jill about them either.

'So you've never been to a dance before, Jill? Does that mean you can't dance at all?' Tom moved in to take the bar of soap from her.

'Well, I've done some country dancing at school.' Gingerly, she dried her sore hands on the towel.

He studied her closely. 'Well, you have got a lot to learn. Haven't you?'

Emilia had agreed to rest but not to stop work. She was busy in the den with the farm accounts, inserting the amounts received from hotels, restaurants, cafes and canteens for dairy produce, eggs and vegetables. The telephone rang. After she put the receiver down she went to the open window and called to Perry. He was hoeing long rows of runner beans. Once roses had been grown here. Now, except for a small plot they kept as a memorial garden to dead loved ones, every scrap of earth had been given over to edible produce.

'Darling?' He came to lean over the windowsill. 'What is it? You're looking very serious. Was that more news about Jonny?'

'Jonny? Oh, yes, that was Tris who rang and Jonny should be home in a few days. He's a bit battered but on the mend. They will be coming to stay, which will be lovely. But it's Tris's other news that's astonished me. I'm surprised it hasn't swept round the village by now. Ben had phoned Tris, and you'll never guess what's happened! It's Faye, Ben's daughter. She suddenly turned up on his doorstep this morning. She's been over from America for years. I wonder why she's come to him after all this time. There has to be a reason. Apparently, Ben's so shocked he hasn't a clue what to do about it. He should make things up to her, that's what!'

Perry reached in through the window and laid a restraining hand on Emilia's shoulder. 'You're not thinking of racing over to Tremore, are you, Em?' She was a firm believer in family love and loyalty, and as a champion of rights she could be impulsive and stubborn.

'I'd love to be a fly on the wall there for a day or two, but Ben and Faye need time alone and lots of it. I hope she calls on us. I'd love to hear all about young Alec.'

'I'm sure you'll see her about the village. She'll be able to pass on our good news to Brooke. Perhaps Brooke will get in touch at last. It wasn't as if we fell out with her or anything when she left Ben.'

'Who could blame her for that? Ben must have really hurt Brooke for her to cut herself off so completely. I often wonder what happened when he went to America. Why he decided to reject his own children. Ben's despicable. It's hard to believe that he used to be happy-go-lucky like Tom. Just one small accident and all this...'

'But if it weren't for that he'd have fought in the Great War and wouldn't have become bitter for missing out on service, and if he'd survived, you and he would have married and there'd be no Will, Tom or Lottie. And you wouldn't have married me after Alec died and there'd be no child of ours on the way.' He laid a hand tenderly on her tummy, still flat but not for long, all being well. 'Em, darling, are you hoping for a girl?'

'Because we've both lost a daughter, you mean? I don't mind.' She raised her arms round his neck and hugged him tight. 'Are you hoping for a son to carry on the Bosweld name?'

He kissed her, and as always couldn't hold back the passion he felt for her. 'I don't mind at all.'

'I just hope everything will turn out all right. I shall be an older mother, after all. To be bringing a baby into such an uncertain world is not the best thing to do, but to have your child, Perry, I can't think of anything I want more. I just pray this war will end soon and Will and Jonny will come back safely and we can all be together again.'

Chapter Five

'Excuse me? Don't I know you from somewhere?'

'I beg your pardon?' Faye looked up from the criss-crossed taped shop window of a shoe shop in Princes Street, in Truro, at the young woman who had spoken to her. She was about seven years older than herself, and looked vaguely familiar. Slender and fair, she had a small, ragged pink birthmark on her right cheek. Her short-sleeved dress, like Faye's, was utility inspired, and also worn with flair. With clothes so plain it was the fashion to have hats that were obvious, but while Faye's had a high crown tilted towards the forehead, the other's was round, of straw and undecorated. 'Oh, yes. Is it Louisa? Louisa Hetherton-Andrews? I'm Faye Harvey.'

'Faye Harvey! Of course, I can see the resemblance to your father. I'm now Mrs Carlyon, but sadly a widow. My husband David was killed during the withdrawal from Dunkirk. Well, what a surprise to see Uncle Ben's daughter. Of course your father's not my real uncle but it's what I've always called him. He must be delighted to see you.' Her last comment was unlikely to be true; it was the usual sort of thing to say. 'Well, how long have you been in Cornwall?'

'Just a few days. My father isn't at all pleased to see me.' Faye watched the delight die in Louisa's soft blue eyes. She deflected attention away from herself. 'I'm sorry about your husband. How is your Aunt Polly? Does she still live up at Kenwyn?'

'Sadly, Aunt Polly died years ago. I live in the house with Ada – do you remember the maid? I think of her as a friend now. She works full time in a… workshop, not far from here actually.' Faye took it to mean one of the workshops of HTP Motors, which had been given over to vital war work. The noise of the welding could be heard from a couple of streets away. 'David and I were hoping for children but it wasn't to be. Faye, please feel free to call on me at any time.' Louisa spoke with her head in a forwards direction, showing she was fully interested in her conversant. 'I'm kept busy with voluntary work, but I pop along to Tremore when I can. And Ford Farm too to see Aunt Em. How long are you planning to stay at Tremore?'

'I shall be sticking around.' Faye had still not been given an opportunity by her father to talk to him at length. He never responded to mention of young Alec and she had not bothered to show him the photographs of him, or those of herself taken throughout her childhood. He didn't care about her past or future. The longest sentences she had got out of him this morning were, 'Do you know the time of the bus back? Don't miss it. There won't be another and you'll have to walk.' Sometimes she didn't think she could stand much more of his indifference, but she couldn't give up. She still had time to get on better terms with him before making some vital arrangements.

Louisa saw how downcast she was. 'Faye,' she said carefully, 'I can imagine how strained things must be between you and Uncle Ben. If you ever want someone to talk to… Well, what I'm trying to say is that I know how difficult it must be for you. Aunt Polly wasn't my real aunt and I've no idea who my parents were. I know about that awful feeling of being lost and uncertain. Of not quite belonging.'

'Thank you, Louisa.' The kindness touched Faye and she choked back a rush of tears. It would be nice to make a firm friend of this gentle-natured woman, but she recalled the closeness that existed between Louisa and her father. He, and her late Uncle Alec, and Aunt Emilia, had been very protective towards Louisa, who had been shy and lacking in confidence. It had given her an appealing vulnerability. She was now unassumingly poised, but still retained a fragility that made Faye sure people would always rally to her cause. Hurt and angry, Faye wondered what it was about herself that had made her father so easily reject her. Unable to hide her suffering, she barked, 'So you've always kept in touch with the family?'

'Yes, I have.' Louisa understood the other young woman's resentment. There was something she hoped would give them empathy. 'But I'm afraid that for some inexplicable reason your Uncle Tristan can't seem to bear the very sight of me. He makes it plain he doesn't like me being friendly with Jonny. It's very unsettling.' Now she tried a way to cheer Faye. 'Uncle Ben's informed me that Jonny will shortly be staying at Ford Farm. I can't wait to see him again. We get on particularly well. He can be a riot, you know. You'll enjoy catching up with him, Faye.' Louisa glanced at her silver bracelet watch. 'Well, I'd better make a move. Got a Red Cross meeting to attend – we'll be packing up parcels for our POWs. I'll let you get on with your shopping. Are you going inside? Sampson's sell very good quality footwear.'

'I'm thinking of buying a pair of gumboots so I can help out on the farm. If I'm allowed.' Faye repressed a heavy sigh. Her father preferred that she kept to helping Agnes in the house.

'Have you been over to Ford Farm?'

'Not yet.' The animosity her father bore towards those who lived at Ford Farm made her wary of antagonizing him. But no matter how much he hated it, she was determined to live under his roof. And to be joined there by another.

Chapter Six

'You are comfortable?' Tristan Harvey glanced at the front-seat passenger in his twenty-year-old Citroën. 'Want me to slow down?'

'There's no need to fuss. I'm fine,' his son replied. In RAF officer's uniform, his left arm in a sling to keep his upper body stable, and a dashing-looking dressing above one bold black eyebrow, thirty-year-old Jonny Harvey was in good spirits. Although sitting and confined, the energy that readily flowed through him was evident, like something instantly available for ignition. He'd been given many glowing labels about his good looks, usually by women: a dreamboat; a warrior; a demi-god. He was well structured, unlike his father, who had always been rangy, but was now worryingly thin. 'And if you drive any slower, Dad, we won't arrive until the middle of next week. I want us to get to Aunt Em's so she can start feeding you up.'

'Now it's my turn to tell you not to fuss,' Tristan said. He found it easy to smile, filled with relief as he was that Jonny had survived the plane crash. He didn't feel at all guilty for wishing it had left him slightly maimed, so he'd have to sit out the rest of the war behind a desk. This war, and the last one, had cost Tristan immensely and he couldn't bear another loss.

Jonny pressed his free hand on the warm leather seat. He was serious now. He had come through many perilous bombing raids. Planes of his had developed fuel problems or taken flak before, but because of the powerful cannon fire from a crafty German night-fighter a few nights ago, it had taken every scrap of sheer nerve, bloody-mindedness and impassioned prayer to bring the Lancaster back on the dreadful, achingly long ten-hour trip and land it without most of its undercarriage. Those last dreadful minutes of violent impact, then skidding down the runway, of feeling the aircraft juddering and breaking up, of hearing its dying screams, along with the terrified cries and shrieks of his crew, and his own, would stay with him for ever. He'd thought he was going to die. How he and the five other men had managed to scramble out, all battered but alive, was a mystery, a miracle. Faulkner, the flight engineer, was deeply religious and had quietly said they had been spared for a purpose. To die another day, Jonny had thought, after he had solemnly agreed. Now he took an affectionate but sorrowful pleasure in valuing everything familiar to him. Touching things as if he'd never felt them before.

'Where did you get the petrol coupons to have the jalopy running today?'

'The colonel who's sleeping in my bedroom fixed me up,' Tristan said blandly. His Victorian clifftop house at Watergate Bay had been requisitioned as a billet for officers and he was living in the original servants' quarters. He'd wanted to stay close to his late wife but the loneliness had become too much to bear. Too much had changed. The once peaceful sands fifty feet below the house had been laid with mines, and now they had been cleared and young American servicemen were training to land in

46

strange-looking craft. He was planning on alternating a long stay between Ford Farm and Tremore. He had closed his antiques and curio shop in Newquay shortly after the outbreak of hostilities – there was going to be little demand for the wares – and he could easily carry out his other work, for ex-servicemen charities, at either place. An extra pair of hands at either farm would be welcome. He took a bend in Henna Lane at prudent speed; Jonny would have taken the Citroën round so fast there would have been a noisy swiping off of the heads of the creamy-white cow parsley in the hedge. 'Jonny, I'm thinking of moving out of Roskerne for good. There's nothing for me there now. Your stepmother never made a will and although the house is legally mine, I feel it's only right it goes to Vera Rose. She'll need it when she settles down after this current mess is over. She doesn't intend to stay on for ever in London.'

Jonny thought about his stepsister, who, because his father's late wife had been a Harvey cousin, was also his second cousin. 'Vee will appreciate the gesture. But where will you live? What about Adele when she comes back from Portsmouth?'

'I'll find us somewhere to live. I accept that she'll probably want her own home in due course. Hennaford will do for me for the time being. Well, son, it'll be interesting to catch up with Faye. I suppose she'll return to America eventually and then we might never see her again. I wish everything would stop changing. I feel life is slipping away from me.'

'Don't get depressed, Dad. You're still a young man. There's time enough for you to start all over again. It's very odd, about Faye.' Jonny puffed on a cigarette, ponderous, frowning. 'I hope she gets some sort of justice for herself and young Alec. It's time Uncle Ben received what's due him.'

'What do you mean?' Tristan frowned. He'd driven to the end of the lane and stopped at the crossroads. At one time only a pause and a brief look to the left and right would have been necessary, but with the county's main road cutting through the village there were often military lorries, jeeps, and even the odd-looking American bulldozers passing through. He waited for an American naval staff car to pass. The sailors saluted Jonny and waved to them both, and they reciprocated. 'On their way to somewhere on the Fal or Helford, no doubt.'

'Yanks everywhere,' Jonny said dryly. 'About Uncle Ben? Well, it's no way to treat your children, is it?' He turned his head sideways and set his strong, dark grey eyes on his father. 'Or any young person.'

Tristan tightened his narrow mouth, making his neat moustache jump up as if to attention. Jonny was referring to his stiff manner towards the Carlyon woman. Louisa. It was something Jonny hated, but Jonny didn't know the truth about her, how her very existence caused terrible hurt to him even now. Tristan would never come to terms with the death of his unfaithful first wife during the birth of her lover's child. The child who had been adopted and raised in Truro against his wishes. Louisa Carlyon. Jonny had been told his half-sister had died the same day as his mother. It tortured Tristan how Jonny and Louisa were so struck on each other. For years it had been the devil's own job keeping them apart, more so since she'd been widowed. Apart from the obvious worry of them getting together, there was also what Jonny's reaction would be if he learned the truth now. He was bound to be upset and furious and that might make him careless when he was on ops again. And the very thought of Jonny hating him for the deception chilled Tristan to his bones.

'Don't go across the road and take the route by the back lane, Dad,' Jonny said. 'Drive through the village, then back again. I'd like to wave to a few familiar faces.' Raised in Hennaford during his early years, he felt it was his home rather than Roskerne and he savoured taking in much-loved people and places. Just past the pub, across from the little village square, housewives in turbans and pinnies were queuing outside the butcher's. 'Dear old Sidney must be enjoying the whole damned show. He's a worse gossip than the women. I spoke to Tom on the blower last night. He says the new Land Army girl's a little smasher. Got a sweetheart, apparently, but we've put up ten bob on being the first to at least get a kiss out of her.'

Tristan shook his head, but couldn't help grinning. 'You're a couple of bounders. One day you'll meet your match. Fall in love, I mean. Then you'll regret all this messing about.'

'Marriage and I are not destined to ever meet. Afraid you'll have to look to Adele for grandchildren.' As they reached the last tiny cottage of the straggling village, its many-paned windows dutifully criss-crossed with tape so as not to shatter dangerously in the event of a bombing raid, Jonny threw his dog-end in the ditch and thrust out his chest. 'There's only one thing to do with life, live it to the full. Well, I've got the uniform to impress this girl with, but Tom's had the advantage of time to soften her up. Jill, that's her name. Whoever wins, she's a Harvey notch-up anyway.'

Jill was sweeping the pigsties, her dungarees wet and splattered in meal. Cleaning in here wasn't too unpleasant as the pigs did not soil their bedding but used the long passage at the rear. She was enjoying her excursion among the friendly, softly squealing pink piglets and their docile mothers. Each pen was divided and there was a centre gangway, which had made filling the feed troughs an easy task.

She'd got the pile of muck up to the door at the end when she felt eyes upon her. Lottie, no doubt, who often kindly checked up on everything she did.

She did meet the gaze of a pair of dark Harvey eyes but these belonged to a rugged man in RAF uniform, with a kitbag hanging off his shoulder. His hair was coal-black, but otherwise he was much like Tom. With an air of self-assurance he was taking in everything about her. 'Hello,' he drawled.

'Um, hello. You must be Squadron Leader Jonny Harvey. I'm Jill Laity.' To be polite, she rested her broom aside and stepped out to him.

'It's a very real pleasure to meet you, Jill Laity. But you're wrong about who I am. I'm Group Captain Will Harvey. Got a spot of unexpected leave.'

For an instant Jill felt silly. Of course he wasn't Jonny Harvey, he had no wounds from a plane crash. Her excitement grew. 'Does Mrs Em know you're coming? She didn't mention it at breakfast.'

'No one knows I'm here. Except you, Jill.' He had a striking sort of smile.

'Well, everyone's going to be happy.' Jill clapped her hands together. 'Your cousin Jonny is due to arrive this very morning. I don't know if you've been told that he had a prang with his plane but got away with fairly light injuries, thank the Lord.'

'Thank the Lord indeed. I heard about that. It'll be good to see the old boy.' Will moved close to her, bent his head and spoke into her ear: 'As long as he remembers that I saw you first. Had your crib yet, Jill? Come inside for a cuppa. Mmm, the next few days are going to be a lot of fun.'

As he set off for the house in quick, agile steps, Jill blurted out, 'There's more news. I mean, you might not have heard…'

He returned to her so fast that Jill thought she should make a hasty retreat into the pigsties. 'What news?'

'That another cousin of yours is in Hennaford. I haven't met her yet. Her name is Faye.'

'Faye? Faye! From Tremore? Or rather, from America. Blood and bones! And here I was thinking I'd returned to the usual sleepy old place. Before I really do go, is there anything else I should know? Jill?'

Jill wished she hadn't spoken. He was not as much like Tom as she'd first thought. There was something a little disagreeable about Will Harvey. Perhaps he had more in common with his Uncle Ben, whom, in the light of what she'd learned about him as a parent, she felt she could never like. 'Actually, there is, but it's Mrs Em's place to tell you that, if she hasn't already.'

–

'A sprog?!' Will exclaimed in disbelief in the farmhouse kitchen. 'Mum, you're actually expecting a sprog?'

'Yes, Will, I'm having a baby,' Emilia replied cheerfully, although her delight at his unexpected appearance was dampened a little. Will bore some resentment over the fact that his father had left the farm to her, denying him sole inheritance, and she had been weighing up when to relay her news to him.

'Well, congrats, Aunty Em!' Jonny, who had entered the house with Tristan almost at the same second as Will, encircled her in an affectionate embrace. He playfully punched Perry on the arm. 'You too, old chap. Took your time, but got there in the end, eh? Dad, why didn't you tell me?'

'It slipped my mind,' Tristan said. It hadn't. The grief of losing his beloved second wife was still too keen to enable him to revel in the happiness of others, and he was anxious about Emilia carrying a baby at this stage in her life. 'Hope you're keeping well, Em.'

'Jonny, it's so good to have you with us.' Emilia hugged him. She had acted as his foster mother during the last war and had strong maternal feelings for him.

Tilda was kept busy with the teapot as all present sat round the table and listened to a glossed-over account of Jonny's crash-landing.

There was a tap on the door. Jill peeped round it. 'Is it all right…?'

'Of course.' Emilia beckoned to her. 'Tilda's got a potato cake for you.' The farm grew a lot of potatoes, and with so many shortages, the housekeeper was kept at full stretch fashioning new recipes for the humble vegetable.

As Jill crept in on stockinged feet, Jonny leaned back in his chair and winked at Will. 'I say…'

Emilia introduced Jill to the newcomers.

'Jill and I have met already.' Will eyed his cousin in distinct one-upmanship. 'Come and sit by me, Jill. I've saved you a space on the form.'

'Thank you, Group Captain,' she said coolly, and a typical no-nonsense Lottie-type glare slipped into her eyes.

'That's told you,' Jonny crowed in a whisper across the table to Will.

'A guinea says you're wrong,' he returned in kind.

–

Tom knew his older brother and cousin were inside but he didn't join them. He carried a bundle of newly hewn wooden posts and a mallet to the pigsties. Lit a cigarette. Then, as if suddenly losing all his energy, he fell down on to his haunches. Sighed. Cursed.

His features drawn tight, he stared up at the sky. It was deceptively free and peaceful, a warm sun romancing the pale- blue dome. Often, with the airfields of St Eval, Portreath, Trevellas, Predannack and the American-occupied St Mawgan all fairly nearby, it was speckled with Spitfires, Hurricanes, Beaufighters and Blenheims, and occasionally a scare was created by the emergence of enemy bombers. He lowered his eyes to the ground and smoked in continuous dejected drags until the stub was burning his fingers. 'It's not fair,' he muttered under his breath, keeping his head bent. It wasn't himself he was referring to.

A pair of gumboots arrived in sight.

'Tom, are you all right?'

He rose and tossed the stub away. He loosened his shoulders and swept a hand through his thick hair. 'Just taking a breather, Jill.'

'Mrs Em and Tilda are wondering why you haven't come inside for your tea break. I've just met—'

'Will, Jonny and my Uncle Tris,' he broke her off. 'I know they're arrived. I'll see them later. What are you doing here?'

Tetchiness wasn't something she expected to find in Tom. 'Um, Mrs Em's sent me to help you.'

Seeing her confusion, he shook his head over his grouchy behaviour. Although he was the manager of the farm, it didn't bother him that his mother was mostly in charge. 'Sorry. Didn't mean to sound like a crosspatch. I've got...' He thought to tell her what was troubling him, but he didn't know her well enough to trust her as a confidante, and she got on so well with Lottie she'd probably tell her, so he said, 'I've got a headache. Right! The fencing needs renewing. We'd better get to it. You can steady the posts while I hit them home.'

It was good working with Jill. She just got on with things and she didn't chatter or give silly giggles or try to be clever. She was a nice, quiet presence. While he dug out and lifted away the old posts, she used a claw hammer to pull out the staples used to keep the wires taut, setting aside those that could be reused, and then rolling up the wires. She stacked the old posts by the woodshed. He hammered in the new pre-treated posts while she held them steady, and a trust was built up, that he wouldn't allow the heavy blows to slip and injure her.

'Well, we made quick work of that,' he said, banging in the final staple. He felt his friendly grin returning. 'We make a good team, Jill.'

'Yes, we do.' She smiled back. It was natural to smile at Tom. He joked about his fondness for girls but she felt he was also a steady sort. 'Has your headache gone? I've got some aspirin in my room.'

He pressed a hand on her shoulder. 'That's very sweet. Actually, I'm fine.' He proffered his cigarette packet.

'Thanks, but I can't keep smoking yours or Lottie's.'

'Take one. There's a chap I meet in the pub who fixes me up with anything I need on the cheap.'

Their heads close together, they lit up from the same match.

'Well, little brother. Looks like you're keeping busy.'

The pair turned round and saw Will, his brow raised in amusement. He was holding a mug of steaming tea and a plate with half a pasty on it.

'You're very naughty,' Will said in mock chiding. 'Mum's making a fuss about your whereabouts. I practically had to stop her from coming to look for you. After all, if Jill hadn't found you here she would've come back and said so. I hope you haven't taken unfair advantage, old chap, and bagged every dance with her on Saturday evening.'

'I've promised the first and the last dance to Tom.' Jill had no idea why she'd blurted out the lie. She and Tom had not discussed the dance since he'd first brought it up. She hoped it didn't make her sound racy. But she had no wish to be dallied with by the two Harvey men in uniform, even though she had to agree with Lottie's declaration that Jonny Harvey was the most handsome man she was ever likely to see. Ronnie was all she wanted. He was perfect for her.

'It's really good to see you, Will,' Tom said, his tone mild. 'By the way, Jill's spoken for. Her bloke's a lieutenant in the footsloggers.'

'Well, God bless him then. Lucky chap. Jill, I'm to tell you that when you've finished here, you're to join Lottie lifting spuds. You'll find her roughly where you were yesterday.'

'Thanks for your help, Jill,' Tom said, as she left him and his brother.

'A very interesting little piece.' Will stared after her before handing Tom the refreshment. 'Let's sit and chat. You can tell me what's the matter.'

'There's nothing the matter,' Tom said, taking a very welcome gulp of tea. Unfortunately, Will, always the bossy big brother, would insist on the chat, so Tom started off for where family powwows were often held, midway on the granite steps that ran up an outside wall of the goat house.

'Don't give me that. You've never shunned Jonny or me before.' Will sounded concerned rather than cross. 'What's up with you? Surely you're not lovesick? Is it her? The land girl? You've fallen for Jill and can't take the fact she won't give up her bloke for you?'

'Jill's a lovely girl but my feelings for her are the same as yours. Well, not quite. I like her, wouldn't want to seduce her and hurt her. She's thoroughly decent, very nice. Best of all, she's good for Lottie. Lottie's fond of her. She's teaching her to dance and sharing girly stuff with her. She's taken Jill under her wing, so take warning.' Tom chewed a mouthful of pasty. Made to take another bite, but Will nudged the food away from his mouth.

'I'm not giving up. I want to know what's wrong with you, Tom. I know you're miserable. Oh, don't tell me you've got someone into trouble? Well, I suppose it might not be too bad. Depending on what she's like, of course. Do I know her? Is she from the village?'

'It's nothing like that.' Tom put his mug down on the step and threw the remains of the pasty down to the pack of Jack Russells, who were gazing up at him hopefully from the foot of the steps. There was a vociferous mad rush to gain the crumbs, with the geese, hens, ducks and turkeys joining in.

'I'm bored, Will. Fed up with the same routine every day. I want to enlist.'

'What? You can't! Just forget all about it, Tom. You can't possibly leave now Mum's in the family way – of all the silly things she and Perry could do. My neck's on the line nearly all the time, and so is Jonny's. You have to carry on here, Tom, for Mum's sake. Forget this silly longing.'

'But it's not right that I live out this war in comparative ease and safety while men are fighting and dying every minute of every day. I want to do my bit.'

'You are! You're slogging your guts out from dawn until hours after darkness to help keep the nation alive. Britain's so cut off that thousands would have starved to death without hard and willing workers like you. The country needs you here. So does Mum, and the farm.'

'But there's Lottie.'

'She's just a child.'

'She's more mature than you give her credit for.'

57

'Look, Tom, the Ministry wouldn't let you join up anyway. The only men here are Perry, who's disabled, and Granddad and Midge, and they're old. Face it. You're going to have to see the war out here. If it's a different life you're after, if you want to see the world, you'll have to wait until we've succeeded in sorting out Hitler and his cohorts.'

'But I want to fight! I feel so underused here every day. I know how Uncle Ben felt all those years ago.'

'Whatever you're feeling, Tom, it's nothing at all like what goes on inside his wretched mind. You want to serve your country and fellow men. So did Uncle Ben, but he also longed for honour and glory for himself. He didn't have to become bitter about partially losing his sight. He made that decision and it's cost others dear.' Will patted his shoulder. 'Come on, cheer up. You must believe you're doing essential work in this war, otherwise you'll drag yourself down and Mum with you. You've got too much backbone for that. You're too good, Tom. And that's the truth, even if you don't want to accept it. Leave being a bit of a swine to Jonny and me. It's natural to us.' Will was laughing, but although there was some jollity in it there didn't seem to be enough. Tom studied him. 'You and Jonny talk as if you're convinced you're going to die. Are you scared?'

'All the time, but it's something you learn to keep under control. It's a brilliant feeling though when I succeed in getting back some crucial intelligence, say of the whereabouts of a German munitions factory or a fleet of U-boats. I feel proud that I've taken on Dad's passion for photography. If I do manage to get through all this it's what I want to do, set up as a professional, to scour the world for new and astonishing sights. I don't particularly want my third of the farm. There wouldn't be enough land for us all to share after Mum's gone anyway. It won't be that easy in the future for you and Lottie when you have your own families, all living here together. You don't really want to turn your back on the farm, do you?'

'No. It means everything to me,' Tom replied truthfully.

'Then have I made you feel more settled?'

'Yes. I suppose so.'

'Tom—' Will became intense – 'I need to know that I can rely on you to look after Mum and Lottie, if… you know what I'm saying?'

Tom lifted his head and stared into Will's eyes. The usual potency in them had gone, replaced by a sad resignation. 'You'll come through, Will. You must believe that. You've made me feel humble. Of course I'll see they're all right. You can trust me. I'll make you proud.'

'Me too.'

They shared a hushed moment.

Then Will pulled back his lips into the widest smile. 'Our raffish cousin has taken up my wager of a guinea to be the first to gain our wicked way with sweet young Jill. Are we going to allow him to win?'

Tom didn't think about his answer. 'No. And I'll tell you why. I'm adding Jill to the list of those I'm determined to protect.'

Chapter Seven

Ben was in the restaurant of the Red Lion Hotel, in the wide sett-paved street of Truro. He had no appetite but was making a half-hearted attempt to eat the vegetable soup in front of him. To his mind, wasting food was a crime. Before the war he had been extravagant, eager to show off his wealth, but although he charged extortionate prices for the wines he still had in stock in his warehouse, the business most threatened by the war, he wouldn't dream of buying anything on the black market that was vital to the country winning the war, like petrol for his filling station on the outskirts of Hennaford. He'd rather the military vehicles and factories had it. He saw it as his place to set a good example. He never made an unnecessary journey in his motor car but usually walked, cycled or rode.

He was thinking about Faye. He was still avoiding her company but she was never out of his head. She was trying to make herself at home. When he'd glossed over her suggestion that she spend time working on the land, she'd immediately taken over the kitchen garden and set up thrice-weekly women's knit-ins at the house. She clicked away all evening, turning out mufflers, gloves and socks for the troops. Although she didn't go far, and as of yet had not rambled over to Ford Farm, she was becoming liked and respected in Hennaford. Tristan and Jonny had come for dinner and were besotted with her. Every time he arrived home, he hoped to find she'd packed up and gone, left to join the person she stole away to make regular telephone calls to. From the snatches of conversation he'd unwillingly overheard, the person wasn't a boyfriend; perhaps it was her best friend. Often she looked as if she wanted to tell him something – he sensed it wasn't about her childhood, and he always forestalled what he thought might be a revelation he wouldn't care to hear.

Yet part of him was curious about her. He was afraid to ask her questions, afraid he'd respond favourably and form a desire to get close to her. She'd again demand to know why he had totally abandoned her to a new life and why he still chose to shun her brother. The simple reason for rejecting her was that he hadn't loved her enough. If Faye learned this she'd rightly hate him for ever, and although she resented him now, he didn't want that. He didn't want her to entertain hatred, as he did. Hatred was slowly destroying him. It would be better for Faye to leave and forget all about him. He ought to put her back in his will though. She deserved at least to inherit his assets.

He dropped his soup spoon and twisted his fingers into his brow until it hurt. Oh, why did she have to look him up? It had never occurred to him that she would. A worse thought was her brother showing up some day. People would understand why he'd disowned the boy if they knew the truth, which he'd discovered when Brooke had hurled it at him on their one and only meeting in America. That she'd had a one-off fling with his older brother. Alec had been dying of a brain tumour then. He'd been behaving very oddly and Ben didn't blame him for the indiscretion. But it had made him hate Brooke and her subsequent offspring – adding to the hatred he felt for Emilia. He'd like to tell Faye who her brother's real father was and make her see that her mother wasn't perfect. Most of all he'd love to fling the whole story in Emilia's face – the smug bitch, she believed Alec had loved her exclusively – but his pride wouldn't allow him to be thought of as a cuckold. He'd rather be assumed callous.

He snarled at his cold meal. He had no appetite but he'd swallow it down. Then he'd seek an interlude with female company. Despite his ruthless approach to women, there were many willing to entertain him at his whim, some fooling themselves that he'd grow to care for them. Abruptly, he had no appetite for pretence and not even for sex. His daughter might be back in his life but his world was growing ever smaller.

When he raised his head he noticed a man at the next table. The stranger, full-faced, bespectacled, portly, wearing a tweed sports coat, a well-knotted tie and immaculately polished shoes, his grey hair parted precisely, had been glancing at him for some time, endeavouring to make eye contact. Ben shot him an aggressive look. He picked up his spoon, determined to finish the soup, but he would tell the maître d' that he'd changed his mind about the subsequent courses. It was Saturday night. He'd cycle home and get ready for the dance. He'd already contributed generously to the hospital linen fund, but he thought it important to show his face on every such occasion. He wasn't looking forward to this evening's event. Although it was always good to see Tristan and Jonny, the rest of his insufferable relatives would also be there, and despite his efforts to put her off, Faye was determined to go and make herself known properly at last in the village.

'It's time I saw my cousins, Aunt Em and Perry Bosweld again,' she'd said, tossing her head as if it was her right. 'We don't need to arrive together, sir.'

He hated her calling him 'sir' but he couldn't bring himself to ask her to call him Father. She might not want to, and who could blame her?

He was swallowing his last mouthful when the man from the next table approached him with confident steps. 'Mr Benjamin Harvey? I wonder if I might have a word.'

'Look, old man, bugger off!' Ben hissed, clenching a fist. 'You're barking up the wrong tree. I'm strictly for the ladies.'

Unruffled, the man peered down over a superior nose. He produced a scrap of paper and held it for a moment under Ben's eyes. Ben didn't need his glasses to read the initials of a certain organization, in Baker Street, London, written on it. 'My name's Goodrington. Maxwell Goodrington.' He destroyed the paper by ripping it into shreds. 'I believe you could be of good use to us, Mr Harvey. Now may I sit down?'

A heady joy broke into Ben's expression. A healthy, excited colour lit up his cheeks. His posture changed from sluggish to parade squareness. 'Yes, indeed, Mr Goodrington. What are you drinking?'

–

Lottie put on her best dress and angled herself in front of her full-length mirror. Copied from a *Vogue* pattern, it was of violet-blue silky cloth, rested just below her knee and clung beguilingly to her figure. She'd had the dress for some time but had not fully valued its qualities until now. She admired her reflection, saw what others had been saying about her for years, that she looked lovely. Although never lacking in confidence, it gave her a new self-assurance. Jill's friendship had made her appreciate her femininity, made her seriously explore the prospect of falling in love, something she now thought she'd rather like.

She began to whistle, checked herself – it wasn't lady-like – and picked up her curling tongs and went to Jill's bedroom. 'We'll have to go down to the kitchen to heat these in the range. The men have been banned from the room until we're ready. Jill, why have you put that on? You look as if you're going to church.'

Jill pulled ruefully at her frumpish long skirt and white cotton blouse, both about ten years old and styled to suit a much older woman. 'These were my grandmother's. I used to give her nearly all my clothing coupons, I felt I owed it to her. I'm afraid I haven't got any high heels either. Look, I think I'll stay here and have a quiet evening instead. I'll write a postcard to Ronnie. I don't mind,' she lied, as Lottie's face fell.

'You will not stay here. I've got something you can wear. A pale yellow frock with piping and a dear little belt. It'll suit your colouring perfectly. And you can borrow my sandals. You need a social life, Jill. I'm sure your Ronnie would agree. You do really want to go tonight?'

'Oh, yes,' Jill replied emphatically.

'Right then. Let's get ready to dazzle. Mum lets me wear lipstick. You can put some on too. I don't suppose you've got any jewellery?'

'Actually, I have.' Jill held out her left hand.

'Wow!' Lottie stared at the diamond cluster on Jill's ring finger. 'It's beautiful. Ronnie must really adore you to fork out for something like that. You lucky thing.'

'You want to get married, Lottie? I'd imagined you were much too independent to consider it for several years.'

'Well, I don't want to settle down next week or next year, but I hope one day to find someone I'll love as much as Mum loves Pappa. Mind you, if my over-amorous brothers and cousin are anything to go by, I'm not likely to meet someone like Pappa round here.'

'You never know. There's a lot of good and honest men in the world. Ronnie's not at all like…' Jill looked down coyly.

Lottie joined her in blushing softly. 'You mean he's happy to wait before… bedroom activities. I'll say it again, Jill, you are lucky.'

Lucky if he survives the fighting and comes back to me, Jill thought, filling up with a terrible ache to see Ronnie's gentle face again, to hold him in her arms. She pleaded with the Almighty to spare him. Communications were sometimes difficult but she hadn't received a reply to any of her letters informing Ronnie of her new address.

-

Will and Jonny were in the pub, the Ploughshare. Tom was at the other end of the bar room, sitting at a table with five American servicemen. He'd deserted his brother and cousin almost from the moment they'd entered the place.

'What is my brother up to? Why has he got in with that lot?' Will asked the landlady, handing over his and Jonny's empty half-pint glasses for refills. He tossed the change in the war fund savings box. The beer was watered down for the duration but palatable. He looked with annoyance round the dark, smoky confines. There were Yanks crowding his local. In general, they had the cheek to complain about the beer, and, damn their eyes, they made advances to the women. The RAF, 'the cream of the British defence', were able to 'walk tall' and cut a dash, but otherwise the crisp, high-quality uniforms and higher pay of the Americans put the ordinary squaddie at a disadvantage.

'Mmm…' Ruby Brokenshaw, who was just past retiring age but still sparky and nimble, pursed her bright-red lips. She motioned to the cousins to bring their heads closer to her. 'Dodgy dealing. I'd have thought Tom of all people would know better. One of them GIs he's with can get his hands on just about anything you please. That's him there, with the curly hair, swarthy complexion, and voice like a twanging guitar. He's got a funny name. Most of 'em have. He's called Herv Brunstein.'

'You're joking!' Jonny whistled through his perfectly straight white teeth. 'Tom? A bit of a spiv? He'll be wearing a wide-striped suit next. No, no, I take that back. Can't see it myself. Tom's always been the sensible one. Good-natured and all that. He's just being friendly to that ruddy lot.'

'Oh, your Tom's full of surprises. You'd think he's as soft as steam pudding but I've known him to belt a bloke for just being bad-mannered in front of a woman. Your mother don't know half of what he gets up to. There's many a woman who can thank him for the stockings on her legs. Young Lottie's never short of niceties, you know. Still, I like the Americans, specially that lot there. They're jolly and generous. They're stationed at Devoran. Some of their division will be helping to provide the music for the dance. Shall go 'cross there myself later on.'

'Oh, yes, they're generous, particularly with their—' Will stopped, remembering he was talking to a woman. Ruby prided herself on being a bit of a lady. 'Come on, drink up, Jonny. The girls should be there by now. I don't intend to fight my way through a posse of blasted Yanks to get to the delectable Jill.'

–

Faye hesitated outside the Methodist social rooms, which were attached to the chapel, across the road from the pub. She had walked along the series of lanes with Tremore's three land girls, but had insisted they go in ahead of her. Why bother with this dance at all? she asked herself. She'd only be a subject of curiosity. And suffer more humiliation when her father snubbed her in public. Strangely, when he'd got back from Truro he'd surprised her and Agnes by singing loudly while he'd washed and changed, but whatever the reason for his uncharacteristic good humour was, it wouldn't be reflected on her and she hadn't waited for him to escort her here. She felt all alone in this village, but reminded herself that she wasn't totally alone in the world and soon she would go to fetch the most important person in her life. Then she doubted the wisdom of doing so.

She gazed soulfully at the double chapel-style doors in front of her. Now she was here, she might as well go in and say hi to the rest of her family. It would be interesting to see how her cousins had turned out. She put her hand on the heavy iron latch.

There was a shout from the distance. 'Faye, hang on! Wait for me.'

She was amazed to see her father running towards her. Amazed to see him actually grinning at her. She was speechless as he crooked her arm through his and took her inside.

–

'Everything seems to be going well,' Emilia said happily to Perry. They were helping to serve the lemonade, cups of tea and other refreshments from behind a long, white-clothed trestle table. It amused the villagers how Perry's unconventional approach meant he wasn't afraid to be seen to be doing 'women's work'.

It was nine o'clock and the creaking planked floor was packed with adults of all ages. The band, made up of locals and American servicemen, had played together success-fully before and were producing a medley of popular big band tunes. Some people were in black or wearing black armbands, having lost husbands, sons or brothers in the fighting, or, in one or two cases, civilian relatives in the bombing. Others were in dull utility fashions. Only the young brought colour with them, but overall there was a sense of gaiety and purpose. 'Oh, Perry, look! It must be Faye. Doesn't she look a picture? And good heavens! She's with Ben.'

Before Perry could caution her to mind what she said in front of Ben, Emilia was heading for the newcomers.

'Jill, care to dance with a chap with his arm in a sling?' Jonny was asking slickly. He had just beaten Will to her by shoving him aside with a sly elbow in the ribs.

Jill was in conversation with a plainly dressed, sweet-faced woman in her mid-forties. 'I'm quite happy talking to Mrs Killigrew,' she said firmly, knowing his intention, like his irreverent cousin's, was only to manoeuvre her outside to the back of the building.

A master of tactics, Jonny aimed a smile heaped with charm at the other woman, who was the local land army representative. She was married to the local builder, who was currently serving in the merchant navy. 'How's Jim, Mrs Killigrew? I suppose you know, Jill, that Jim used to work for my Uncle Alec? He and I are close friends.'

'Yes, I do know,' Jill replied, polite but dismissive. 'I've been telling Mrs Killigrew about my fiancé.'

Knowing when he was on a lost cause, Jonny listened to Elena Killigrew's reply that the last news she had heard from her husband was that he was about to go to sea again. They all knew this meant he would be part of a convoy in the dangerous South Atlantic, bringing back vital supplies. God willing, a U-boat or enemy aircraft didn't sink his ship: the merchant navy had suffered great losses. With-drawing sportingly, he prodded Will in the direction of their uncle Ben's land girls. 'None as appealing as Jill, but we do have the choice of three. Ten bob on the brunette?'

Will studied the girl in question. She didn't seem the shy sort, there wasn't going to be much of a contest. His eyes returned to Jill. He never gave up easily hunting down a quarry.

'Forget about them.' Tom put himself in their path. He had been watching the two airmen, making sure they didn't get the chance to proposition Jill, and suddenly he did not like their, or his own, caddish behaviour. He had been getting mixed looks of hope and reproach from a couple of girls he'd let down and he saw himself as juvenile and selfish. He wouldn't like it if some bloke came on in the same way to Lottie. 'Uncle Ben's just turned up and he's brought Faye. Let's go and say hello to her.'

Tristan had also seen Ben and Faye enter and he beat Emilia and the younger men to them. He hoped the good sign of them arriving together would last. 'Well, I say, Ben. Faye's a stunner. You must be proud.'

'Of course, Tris.'

Her father released her so she could accept a kiss from her uncle. He didn't let her go at once and she wondered again what was behind his tremendous change in attitude. Had he softened at last? If only they'd talked before coming in. She could really enjoy the evening if she knew there wasn't likely to be a repeat of his rejection, or conflict in the future. 'It's a pity Adele isn't here. It seems a lifetime ago when she and I and cousin Lottie all played together.'

Lottie was on her way back to Jill and Elena Killigrew with drinks. Spying Faye through the throng, she excitedly changed course but was wrong-footed. 'Hello, sweetcake.'

'Don't call me that!' she snapped at the owner of the nasal American voice who'd planted himself in front of her. Like his compatriots grouped around him, he was in uniform of low rank. To Lottie's mind, every one of them had a wider than necessary grin.

'Hey, baby, we're on the same side, ya know. You're supposed to be nice to me.' The American pointed to himself then spread his hands. 'To all of us. Let me carry those for you. The name's Herv. And this is Todd, and Jeff and Mort and Brad. Pleased to meet ya, I'm sure. How about a dance?'

'How about you drop dead? And all your friends too?'

She barged past the GIs, leaving them laughing good-humouredly after her. Then the three drinks in her hands were slipping, about to hit the floor. She'd make an awful mess and a fool of herself. 'Oh no!'

'Here, let me help you.'

'Oh, thank you.'

A pair of warm, strong hands enveloped hers and the tumblers. Satisfied all was under control, she looked up and found herself gazing up into the gentlest, brownest pair of eyes she had ever seen. Into the quiet face of another American. A corporal, with insignia indicating he was a medic. 'I hope the men weren't bothering you, miss. They don't mean to be rude.'

'No... no, they weren't.' Lottie realized how disrespectful she had been, and she should never have told men that might soon be called on to go into battle to drop dead. She hoped this non-commissioned officer hadn't overheard.

'Lottie, I'm here. I'll take the drinks.' It was Jill.

The corporal took his hands away from Lottie's.

'Thank you, Jill,' she said, using the politest voice of her life. 'Thank you, Corporal.'

'You're welcome, miss.' His voice was as strong as his hands yet as soft as his eyes, and those eyes were flickering over her, as if with interest. Lottie was apt to stare shamelessly back at others but she was temperate while she took in everything about him. He exuded a sense of command yet there was also something free and easy about him. His features were well balanced, as if fashioned by a perfectionist. His sandy hair was tidy, not slick, and a few strands fell carelessly across his hardy forehead.

She stared on, inquisitive about him, and he gazed back, unhurried. For once she was not restless, eager to get on to the next thing. Then he blinked, his lashes fell, and she got the sinking feeling she was losing his attention. She was desperate to make a good impression on him, and not just to make amends for her belligerence towards his comrades. She offered him her hand. 'Miss Harvey. Lottie Harvey. From Ford Farm. In the village.'

He shook her hand, more lightly than she would have liked. 'Nate Harmon. I'm pleased to make your acquaintance.'

When he let his hand fall from hers, her skin was left feeling it had suddenly leapt alive. It tingled, and she placed her other hand round it to share this strange, desirable sensation. 'This is my friend Jill Laity. She's a land girl. On the farm. She's engaged.' Why had she thrown in that last remark? He'd think she was making some sort of statement aimed at showing that she, herself, was unencumbered. She was embarrassed but it didn't really matter. She wanted to keep him talking. He was so unlike the rest of his boisterous, chatty contingent.

She let out a small shriek when an arm was thrown round her waist and she was furious to be unceremoniously hauled away. By Will. 'Come and meet Faye. It's brilliant catching up on old times.' She looked back urgently, intending to apologize to Corporal Nate Harmon, but he was nowhere in sight.

Tristan still couldn't fathom why Ben was suddenly being so attentive to Faye and nor could she by the puzzled looks she was aiming at him. Then he had something more pressing to consider. Louisa Carlyon had arrived and she was weaving her way towards Jonny. He left the family to head the woman off.

'Mrs Carlyon! Good evening to you. Would you care to dance?' Tristan had never imposed himself on a woman before but he put a firm grasp round Louisa's wrist and pulled her into the middle of the dance floor. She struggled against him. The music, 'Moonlight Serenade', stopped and there was a brief round of clapping, then a different, louder, raucous tune, played only by the American musicians, broke out.

'Now what, Mr Harvey?' Louisa cried above the din. 'I shouldn't think for a moment that you know how to jitterbug.'

'What? No! No, we can't possibly dance to this.' Tristan could hardly believe he was doing it again as he wrapped a hand around her arm. At all costs he must keep her away from Jonny. All through his injury leave the name most frequently on Jonny's lips was Louisa Carlyon's. Jonny was in the grip of a condition Tristan had seen in the last war, of men getting emotional, seeing the things most precious to them in a shining light, straining to reach out and retain them, for they believed they were unlikely to survive their next battle. He had felt like this himself about his first wife, Ursula, whom he had adored, while in the barbaric trenches on the Western Front, where he had been nearly blown up and killed; he still bore the physical and mental scars. If his son thought he was in love with this woman, if they got to be alone together, it might lead to terrible consequences. 'Let me get you a drink instead.'

Louisa allowed herself to be propelled to the end of the queue for refreshments. Tristan Harvey's behaviour was inexplicable. Who the hell did he think he was? But at least she had the chance at last to talk to him. He usually evaded her presence, unless Jonny was around, when he'd watch them both from eagle eyes. 'It seems you'll go to any lengths to keep me away from Jonny.'

'Not at all.' He blushed, deeply embarrassed. He'd put himself in a fix. And his ploy wouldn't work anyway. If Jonny wanted to talk to Louisa, to dance with her, or do anything else with her, he'd go ahead and do it, such was his son's determined nature. 'Um… um, sorry about the queue. Seems that's all we do nowadays.'

'You mean women do. I don't recall seeing many men in the food queues.' She sensed he wanted to escape now but she wasn't having that. She took a grip on his jacket sleeve. 'Mr Harvey, what's all this about?'

'J-just thought it was time I was sociable to you. Look, you don't have to stay with me. There's plenty of young people here. I'm sure you'd rather be with them.'

'Actually I'd rather talk to you. I want to know why you hate me so much.'

She looked hurt and sad. Vulnerable and humiliated. And it was all his doing. He had first looked at her briefly on the day of her birth and had taken against her, seeing her only as the offspring of a hated enemy, the handsome, no-good lounge lizard who had seduced his wife. But now, although Louisa shared the contemptible Bruce Ashley's fair colouring, she had a strong hint of Ursula about her, and Tristan was shaken to the core of his being to realize that even now, after twenty-five years, and his subsequent happy marriage, he still felt his first passionate love for Ursula. 'But I don't hate you, Louisa! Not that.' Certainly not now.

'How can you say that? You've always been beastly towards me. You don't think I'm good enough to spend time in Jonny's company, that much is certain. Why? I have to know.'

'Hey, Louisa, why aren't you dancing?' Tom had witnessed the awkward conversation and had come to Louisa's rescue. He shot his uncle a look of reproach. It was beyond imagination why anyone didn't like Louisa. She was wholly good and thoughtful, absolutely delightful. 'Excuse me, Uncle Tris. I'm going to steal her away.'

Throughout the rest of the evening Louisa glanced at Tristan Harvey. Sometimes he looked away, sometimes he dropped his head, always he fought off eye contact. Except once. When he looked at her strangely, almost longingly. What had that meant? She'd seek the first opportunity to find out.

While Faye enjoyed getting reacquainted with family members she remained stunned by her father's mystifying reversal of attitude towards her. While he seemed to be happy, as if celebrating something personal only to him, he acted as if he was actually proud of her. At one point, he said, 'I think you'll agree, everyone, that Faye has turned out very well indeed.'

She and Lottie had immediately fallen back into their girlhood friendship. Lottie admired her organdie frock and matching bolero jacket. 'You look like a screen idol. You must have men queuing up to ask you out.'

'Not really,' Faye replied, quickly placing the focus on Lottie. 'Have you got anyone?'

'No.' Lottie couldn't resist scouring the hall for the American corporal. Sadly, it seemed he had left. She told herself she didn't care. Got a niggle in her tummy because she knew it wasn't true.

'Well, Faye,' Emilia said. 'There was no need to keep yourself a stranger from the rest of us. I was on the verge of coming over to see you at Tremore.'

'Sorry about that, Aunt Em.' Faye remembered how much more cheerful and relaxed life was at Ford Farm. 'I'll be over soon, I promise.' She watched her father for his reaction to this now he wasn't being his usual grumpy, rigid self. Apart from either ignoring or casting smug looks at Aunt Em, he was animated. Passing round cigars and laughing at anything anyone said even if only slightly funny. What had happened since he'd left the house this morning? It was all very peculiar, and disquieting.

Lottie said, 'You must tell us all about Aunt Brooke and young Alec. Has Mum told you her news? She's got to be very careful. She and Perry are going to have a baby.'

The good humour, put on Ben's face because he had been so unexpectedly and wonderfully given a real sense of purpose at last, an opportunity to fulfil his lifelong ambition, was swiped off as violently as if he had been dealt a physical blow. Emilia was pregnant! God damn her. Damn her life! It was his babies she should have had. By now he would have had the son he'd wanted so much. She'd had two sons with Alec and now she might be bearing one for Bosweld.

Only Jill, who was coming towards the Harvey huddle, saw his shock and fury. And, so she thought, his pain. He'd obviously been shaken by the news of Mrs Em's expected happy event. Jill was no expert on matters of the heart but she reasoned there could only be one reason for Ben

Harvey's reaction. Lottie had filled her in on her mother and uncle's past. He was still in love with Mrs Em.

Ben saw Jill looking at him. With sympathy and kindness. He went to her, and somehow managed to keep his voice light. 'Good evening, Jill. I hope you're enjoying yourself amongst our little community. Would you care to dance with me?'

'Thank you, Mr Harvey. Thankfully, it's a foxtrot now. I don't think I'm up to the more modern, fast styles. And yes, I like Hennaford and its inhabitants very much.' She felt it wasn't sensitive to mention her work on Ford Farm.

'My name's Ben.' He held her firmly but not tightly and danced in smooth steps. Jill was aware of him shaking. 'Your daughter is beautiful.' Jill had swept her sight over Faye Harvey's clothes and classiness in envy, but only for a moment. Ronnie loved her for exactly how she was, pleasantly ordinary and content with the simple things in life. Sophistication, high fashion and well-applied make-up wasn't for her.

'Yes, she is. She never used to be. She was a plain little girl.' Ben needed comfort and this young woman's tender, slight body soothed him a little. Thank God he'd not long ago met Maxwell Goodrington or he'd go mad. He was longing for the next communication, which he had been told could come at any time of night or day, when he must be ready to travel wherever he was told to go immediately. Goodrington had said, 'I was down in this neck of the woods on other business and I happened to hear someone mention your trips to, as I shall say carefully, certain foreign parts for the wine trade. I take it you're fluent in the language? Good. I shall speak to my superiors. Someone might be in touch with you soon.'

Please God, Ben prayed more earnestly than he ever had in his life. *Let it happen and let it be very soon.*

He said, 'Have you spoken to the girls working for me yet, Jill?'

'Yes. We've all had a pleasant conversation with Mrs Killigrew.'

'When you can manage a spare minute you must come over to Tremore and spend time with them.' He slid in a little closer to her and gazed into her eyes. 'Come to the house. You must have dinner with me.'

'Thank you for the invitation, Ben, but I must not. I'm engaged.'

Ben slackened his hold on her, silent for a while. 'So you should be. A nice girl like you should be in love with some decent sort and get married and have a happy life. Is your fiancé in the services?'

'Ronnie's in the Duke of Cornwall Light Infantry. He was studying to be a scientist before.'

Her devotion for her man radiated out of her and Ben was pleased to see that at least one woman could stay faithful to her true love. Emilia had soon turned to Alec after his own quarrel with her, and she was almost certainly entertaining Bosweld before Alec's death. The bloody, bloody bitch. He loved her and he hated her. He hoped something terrible would happen to her, but nothing to do with her baby. The last time he'd ill-wished Emilia her baby girl of just three and a half weeks old had died. He only wished Emilia harm. With a vengeance.

'Are you all right, Ben?' He became aware of Jill's anxious voice. 'You look quite drained.'

'Oh, yes, I—I think I need some fresh air. I hope Ronnie returns safely to you.' The dance came to an end

and he relinquished her. 'I'll say goodnight, Jill. I've ha
enough of this place.'

Jill wasn't left alone for long. She was spun round on
her feet. 'What the hell were you doing dancing with
him?' Lottie bawled at her. 'And where's he slunk off to?'

Firmly releasing herself from Lottie's grip, Jill said, 'I
shall dance with whomever I please. You don't own me,
Lottie. Your uncle didn't seem well. I think that's why he
left.'

Faye had followed Lottie. 'He's behaved very strangely
this evening. Well, he's back on form, paying me no
consideration.'

'Hey, little lady, was that an American accent I just
heard?' Herv and his mates were crowding round the girls,
eager to speak to Faye and claim dances from them all.

'I was brought up in Washington,' Faye explained, her
eyes on the door her father had not long banged through.
She'd have something to say to him when she got back
to his house. She would not be picked up and dropped
at his whim. Yet there had been a dejected droop to his
shoulders at the end and she couldn't help feeling worried
about him.

Lottie had gone silent over Jill's unexpected retaliation.
She had warned her to keep away from her rotten uncle.
Well, if the land girl wanted to be stroppy and show favour
where she shouldn't then she could damned well look
elsewhere for a friend. Oh! And as for these damned Yanks
now bantering down her ears! Why did they have to take
over everything? Tossing her head, she made to steam
away. And found Corporal Nate Harmon in her path.

He stepped sideways. 'Let me give you space, Miss
Harvey. I can see my friends are annoying you.'

A scolding path of red burned all the way up Lottie's neck and face. For the second time in the same evening she was being forced to acknowledge just how bad-mannered and childish she was. She'd had no right to be dictatorial with Jill. 'No, I...'

Nate Harmon walked away from her.

Chapter Eight

Two nights later, there was a knock on Jill's bedroom door.

'Come in,' she called, frowning after a moment when no one appeared. If it was Lottie, Mrs Em or Tilda seeking to disturb her nightly jottings to Ronnie they would have entered. It had better not be Will come to pester her. He and Jonny had backed off, but until Jonny had left this morning, with his father, to stay at Tremore, sign language of the innuendo kind, plainly about her, had passed between them.

Yet she shouldn't be wholly suspicious about Will. This morning he had joined her in the dairy, usually the women's domain. He had kept his hands, as if innocently, behind his back. 'Don't worry. Tom, your new guardian's not far away. Anyway, I've just popped in to ask you to come outside. I've pulled everyone together, including Faye, who's here. I want to take a photo of everyone. It will be nice to look at when I get back to camp.'

'You want me in it?' She'd been delighted to be included.

'Of course. You're part of the gang now. Jonny's very disappointed Louisa Carlyon is not here.'

Thinking the Harvey airmen weren't so bad, Jill hauled herself off the bed and opened the door. And changed her mind about Will again. He was leaning forward, smiling disarmingly but in a way that was too familiar. 'What do you want?'

'Don't be like that, Jill. Perhaps I should have chosen a more appropriate place to come to you. You know I'm catching the early train back tomorrow. I want to say a private farewell to you.' He glanced over her shoulder into the room. 'Busy with the writing paper and pen again, I see. Your Ronnie's a lucky blighter. I know a few chaps, well, a good many of them are dead now, who've received "Dear Johns". A loyal woman waiting for them at home goes a long way in the comfort stakes.'

Staying wary of him, she was nonetheless glad for this chance to bid him a proper goodbye. It might be the last time he saw his home. 'I hope you have a good journey, Will. I'll pray for you. Good luck.'

'Thanks. Fancy a stroll round the garden?'

So he couldn't resist making another move on her. 'Hardly.' She tossed her head. 'Listen. I am not going to have sex with you.'

She was expecting ridicule, perhaps scorn – Will could be sharp when crossed – but he threw back his head and howled with laughter. 'Blood and bones. Can't blame a chap for making one last try. You have been spending time with Lottie, haven't you?' He dropped his voice melodramatically. 'Don't think you'll get away with it often, putting Lottie in her place like you did at the dance. She's been rather quiet since then. It means she's brooding. Likely to turn into a she-cat at any moment. She can be fiendish when she gets going. Then no one can control her. Even I hate being at the receiving end of her most vicious temper.'

'I don't believe anything of the sort.' Jill was annoyed. Lottie was a young adult, of an age much given to rapid changes of mood. 'Lottie can be strong-willed and that's all.'

Will's attractive dark face broke into a giveaway smile. 'Perhaps you're right. You must know her better than I do now. I've been away from the farm for the last four years. I worry about Lottie. Seriously though, Jill. I would like to talk to you away from the house. Come outside for a cigarette?' At her look of doubt, he raised crossed fingers. 'Promise it's not an excuse to make a pass. On Harvey honour.'

Jill had gained enough insight about the younger Harvey men to know that when they swore an oath then heaven or hell wouldn't make them renege on it.

A weak moon provided some light. More ominous lights were provided by the faint criss-crossing of faraway searchlights moving through the cloud-pathed sky. A pipistrelle bat, out searching for moths, a more innocent hunter than an enemy bomber, was picked up in the searchlights. To avoid the glow of their cigarettes pin-pricking the darkness they lit up inside the dugout shelter at the bottom of the back garden. 'Will, what did you mean about Lottie? Why are you worried about her?'

'Not just her.' Will rubbed at the tension in his neck. 'All of them. My whole family. Even Perry. And dear old Tilda. And I wish to God that my mother wasn't pregnant.' Jill listened patiently as he rambled on. 'I'm glad I've at least had the chance to see Faye again. Pity Uncle Ben isn't treating her properly. He went through some peculiar moods at the dance and he's remained uncommunicative towards her since. She's his daughter, for goodness sake!

My father wasn't particularly close to Lottie, but he was ill, couldn't stand a noisy little brat like she was back then buzzing around him. I don't know what's the matter with Uncle Ben. Or Uncle Tris. He behaves so badly towards poor Louisa. Well, you can see what a lovely sort she is. I'd propose to her if I wasn't called on for active service. She'd make a splendid wife, always so interested in what others do. A chap could count on her to always be loyal and supportive.'

Will had revealed a side that Jill would never have dreamt he owned. Apart from the understandable concerns of Mrs Em bearing a baby at forty-two years old, Jill thought it a shame he was otherwise troubled.

'Silly isn't it?' he went on. 'When I'm on a mission, or thinking about how dangerous my next one's likely to be, I think about them worrying about me, and it makes me worry like hell about them. I mean, what if something was to happen to one of them? Uncle Tris's wife was killed because of this damned war. She stepped out into the road without realizing there was a motor car there with its lights dimmed out. Kaput! She was killed instantly. Gone in a second. Lottie and Mum and Tom and the others work half the time in the dark. One of them might become victim of a terrible accident. Sorry, I'm getting morbid. I'm glad you don't have to worry about your Ronnie being involved in the fighting at the moment.'

'Yes,' Jill said gloomily. 'But I wish he would write.'

Will placed a comforting hand on her shoulder. He longed to put his arm round her. Both his arms to offer her comfort, and he needed comfort too. Another's gentle touch. But his earlier advances forbade it. 'Sorry.'

'It's OK.'

'It's a pity you've never known a close family life as I have. I'd never appreciated it until the war started. Through most of my childhood I'd expected to inherit the farm and all my father's property, but just before he died he changed his will, leaving everything to Mum. I felt a fool. I resented it. Was quite often difficult with her after that, as if blaming her. I love her very much. I hope to have her see me settle down, but well… the odds are against me surviving this war. Tom and Lottie can give her grandchildren. She'll love that. She deserves it.'

In the dim light, Jill could swear tears were glistening in his eyes. 'Have you told your mother you love her?'

'Not in years. Can't now. Not really, can I?'

'Why not?'

'Mum would think I was fearing the worst. That I knew my number was about to come up. That I was saying goodbye to her for good. Couldn't do that to her.'

'Oh, yes. I understand.'

'Tom was right about you, Jill. You are a good sort. It's a comfort to know you're here at the farm, that everyone likes and trusts you. Jill, if I write a letter to Mum, just in case… I mean, if I am killed, would you give it to her for me?'

'Yes, Will, of course.'

'Thanks. I hope that you'll know lasting happiness with Ronnie.'

'Thank you.'

There wasn't any need for more words, so they stayed silent until they went back inside.

Chapter Nine

Emilia strode into the cobbled yard of Tremore Farm, having been told at the big house it was where she would find Ben. One of the land girls, driving a tractor out to the fields, shouted to her that he was attending a birth in the calving shed.

She found him with the sleeves of his striped shirt rolled up nearly to his shoulders, crouching, while vigorously rubbing a handful of straw over a newly born addition to his herd of pedigree shorthorns. He was gaunt, a shadow of what he had once been, what he should be. His hair was tumbling across his brow in the way it had done in his youth, but he looked old and beaten. She went up close to him, making plenty of noise so he knew he was no longer alone.

Caring for the new life in his hands, while casting anxious glances at the heifer, who was struggling to remain standing on the slippery floor, he couldn't see whose company he had gained. 'Who is it?'

'Emilia. You're going to need a hand with the cow. I'll fetch fresh straw.'

Ben whirled his head round so she was in full vision. 'What the hell are you doing here? What gives you the right to think you can trespass on my land?'

Emilia made an impatient expression, as if she was gazing down on a difficult child, a nuisance. 'Must you always be beastly? I've come to talk to you.'

'You never talk to me unless you can possibly help it, any more than I do to you. Come to poke your nose into something that's none of your business, is what you mean. I know that stubborn look in your eyes. Well, you can bugger off! Turn straight round and take yourself back to the other side of the village. I won't tolerate your uppity ways. You always were a bossy cow.'

'I've never been uppity in my life and well you know it. I won't go until I've said what I've come to say. You know that too. So you might as well listen. I'll fetch the straw.'

'No you won't!' Despite his anger he couldn't help being interested in why she had come to him, something that hadn't happened for years. And again, despite his hostile feelings for her, Emilia was always worth looking at. She was earthily beautiful, unconsciously sensual; she had something of a warrior queen about her. She would always hold a powerful draw to him. He was taken back down the years to when she had made a similar appearance, then, like now, in early pregnancy; her first pregnancy back then, having just married Alec. She'd come to take him to task over his treatment of an old friend of hers, a girl he'd been engaged to, and she'd been stricken with pains and had feared she'd miscarry. He had been kind to her that day, had taken her home and made sure Alec and the doctor had been sent for. What would he do today if she was taken ill? Did he hate her so much that he'd rather leave her to suffer? He didn't want to find out.

'Shout for someone to help in here. Then I'll allow you five minutes and not a second more!'

Ben's longest-serving employee, a mannish woman called Eliza Shore, answered Emilia's shouts. Ben wouldn't hear of Emilia helping them with the struggle to right the cow on to its four legs. Emilia waited for them outside, taking in Ben's property. When he had bought Tremore, cheating Alec out of its purchase, it had consisted of a few run-down buildings, small acreage and the former Tremore steward's dwelling, now the big house, which he'd had greatly extended and modernized. The farmstead was also extended and well equipped and he owned almost every field, meadow, hedgerow and tree stretching into each horizon. Here and there his land converged with hers. The walls here in the yard were chalked with 'V for Victory' signs. Emilia was sure Ben would have done it himself.

'Haven't seen 'ee here for ages, Mrs Em,' Eliza Shore deliberated, foregoing a trip to the yard pump and wiping her huge soiled hands down her baggy corduroy trousers, then through her hair, which was dry and grey and had a hacked-off appearance. Although past retiring age she was healthy and strong. She towered over Emilia. She blew her thread-veined nose on a dirty hanky. 'Haven't come with bad news, I hope.'

'It's not bad news, Eliza.'

'So Will's all right then? Fine young man he is. And Jonny. You can be proud of your Tom too. Now he do give the maids some runaround but he's good and kind to the core.' Eliza shot her boss, who was emerging from the calving shed, tight-faced and clench-fisted, a meaningful look. 'You've got a lovely daughter too, Mrs Em. Your children are a credit to you. And you are a blessing to them.'

'Thank you, Eliza.'

'On your way, Eliza. I don't pay you to stand about spouting useless nonsense,' Ben snarled at her. He had washed his hands and arms in the bucket of soapy water in the calving shed and was rolling his sleeves down to his elbows.

Eliza was unruffled. She had worked for the farm's previous owner and had given 'no nevermind' to everyone in a superior position all her life. She saw the man she still thought of as 'Young Mr Ben' as misguided and sadly lonely. She searched behind her ear and was rewarded with a cigarette stub. Slowly and calmly she stuck it between her rough lips. 'I'm going inside t'get my crib. Been hard at it since an ungodly hour and I'm bleddy parched. G'day to 'ee, Mrs Em. My prayers go with the young men.' Eliza plodded away.

'I'm glad to see there's someone else who isn't intimidated by your snappy tongue,' Emilia said.

'Five minutes,' Ben warned, breathing heavily.

'It's about Faye. She came to see me yesterday.'

'Straight to the point as usual, eh, Emilia? I thought it couldn't be about anyone else but her.' He tossed his head. 'What did she want with you?'

'She asked for advice, about how she could talk to you and get you to listen to her.'

'What about?' he huffed.

'I don't know. She didn't go on to confide in me but she obviously needs to confide in you,' Emilia snapped impatiently. 'She seems quite troubled. You need to give her some of your precious time, Ben.'

'Faye isn't any of your affair.'

'She is. She's family. She's—'

'She's not a member of *your* family!' he hurled at her, storming off, then shouting back, 'You were just a dairy-maid when my brother married you and now you're a bloody Bosweld!'

His venom left Emilia blinking. He was shaking in rage but she went after him. 'You thought me good enough to marry you back-along. And it makes no difference who I'm married to now. It was painfully clear how unhappy Faye was yesterday.' He kept striding on, leaving her behind, so she ran to catch him up and reached out and grabbed his arm.

Ben halted, spun round and faced her, his face a theatre of fury.

She snatched away her hand, not so sure of herself now but still determined to tackle him. 'Faye is your daughter and young Alec is your son. I don't know what went on between you and Brooke all those years ago but Faye is here now, by choice, staying under your roof, and it's time you stopped treating her like a stranger. Like she's someone detestable to you. Do you want to risk losing her for good? What on earth is the matter with you, Ben? Is your heart so dark and cold that you don't care about her at all? If you don't start showing her some interest soon, she might pack her bags and never come back. Do you really want to die a lonely old man?'

'Why should you care about how I die? If I dropped dead this instant you'd celebrate. You want to know what it's all about, do you, Emilia? Are you really sure about that?'

His colour was so high, his expression so fierce, she recoiled. He'd repeated many times over the years that he hated her but she hadn't realized he'd felt so strongly. 'What's this got to do with me? What has your shunning of Faye and disowning of Alec to do with me?'

For a very long time Ben had wanted to see Emilia without her usual fighting spirit. With pleasure he watched as her stately bearing melted a little. He wanted to hurt her badly and he wanted to do it so much, he thought he'd rather die on the spot than be denied the triumph. Why had he kept his secret for so long? Why had he let his pride rule him, when, instead, he could have seen the confidence, the annoying edge of superiority, wiped off the face of this woman years ago? He had once loved her more than anyone else, but witnessing her love for Perry Bosweld, just a few weeks after his brother's death, losing the second chance he'd hoped to have with her, had shattered his ability to ever love again.

He clawed through the air and seized the hand that had had the affront to grab him. Sliding his grip down to her wrist, he held on tight. 'You asked for the truth and now you're going to get it! Every last tiny bit of it and I hope every word chokes you. I hope it shakes your cosy little world so badly that you'll never know a minute's peace, that it makes you as miserable as I am. Well, here it comes, Emilia. Faye's brother is not my son. He's really Alec Harvey the second. Alec's bastard! And before you accuse me of being a liar, let me tell you that Brooke told me this herself. She'd had a fling with Alec. It was just the once, but the child couldn't be mine because, remember, she was refusing to give me another child, fearing another miscarriage. Yet she lay down on the river bank for Alec, conceived and happily carried his damnable brat! And do you know what's really funny, Emilia? All the while you were carrying on your sordid secret affair with your precious Perry Bosweld, Alec had screwed my wife. That's why Alec left you the farm. Not out of some great love for you, but because he was feeling guilty!'

Horror and shock rooted Emilia to the spot. She hadn't taken a breath for several seconds and was forced to gulp in air. Ben let her go. He went in and out of her vision. She staggered past him to the pump, lowered herself down on to the side of the granite horse trough below it. She felt dizzy and nauseous and kept her eyes shut. Her heart was pounding in her ears. She was aware of Ben coming up to her, staying at a dispassionate distance. He said nothing.

Moments ticked by like hours. Finally she gazed up at him. He was staring at her, his stony grey eyes moving as he watched for her expression. She wouldn't give him the satisfaction of allowing him to see how much hurt she was suffering. That even yet she hadn't absorbed the full force of what he'd launched at her. 'I take it Faye doesn't know any of this?'

He shook his head.

'Why haven't you told her?

'I don't want to talk to her. I never want to listen to her. I'd rather she left despising me.'

'Why? I can understand why you've no interest in her brother, but she's your flesh and blood! Are you so sure you don't want some sort of relationship with her? You escorted her so brightly into the dance. It doesn't make sense.'

'Still asking questions. Still poking your nose into where it isn't welcome. Let me just say that nothing's made sense in my life for a good many years, Emilia.' His taunting expression turned into one of sneering. 'Aren't you going to tell me how you feel about Alec? What he did to you?'

Calling on the inner strength that had rarely let her down, mustering her dignity, Emilia rose, resting a steadying hand on the pump. 'Do you really think I'd share my personal feelings with you? And what have you actually said, Ben? You've told me some truths, truths that I'd rather not have heard, and that's all. And all that you've done for yourself is to gloat. There's nothing to congratulate yourself over. I *pity* you, Ben Harvey. Back in your youth it seemed you were as fine as the young men Eliza not long ago remarked about. Now you're bitter and all eaten away. And all because you're jealous. You once thought you were in love with me but you couldn't possibly have been. You weren't capable of loving anyone even back then. You envy anyone who has more of anything than yourself, for having anything that you think you want. You are the most selfish person I know and for that I *pity* you.'

She stepped away from the pump and was relieved her legs were able to hold her up. His face was blank. As if there was no life behind it. She said, walking away, 'Whatever happens, I'll never set foot on your land again. And I don't expect you to ever come near mine.'

Ben remained rooted to the ground for five minutes. The same length of time he'd got to glory in triumph over Emilia. Now it was all gone and he was desolate. He saw his life for what it was. A failure. Barren. Futile. In reality he had nothing. He was nothing. Struck by a terrible numbness, on legs like cardboard he stumbled out into the lane, leaned against the hedge, and with hands that trembled like an old man's he scrabbled for a cigarette. He didn't light up because he couldn't breathe. There was a terrible tightness in his chest, his guts had turned to water and he broke out in a sweat. The hedge across the road, the dusty ground, swam in and out of sight. He thought he was going to die. Hoped he was. Anything was better than this revolting emptiness.

Gradually he felt a little strength returning to his beleaguered limbs and his sight cleared. He managed to light up but he couldn't stop shaking. He was cold, as if he'd been left outside naked in a storm. He was certainly exposed. Exposed for what he was. Emilia had seen to that.

He walked off like a drunkard. In the opposite direction to home. He trudged on and on. Keeping in the lanes. Slowly, he was able to pick up pace. Until he was jogging. Then running. Running as if for his life. He could run for ever but it was impossible to get away from the one person he wanted most of all to leave behind. Himself.

–

Faye was whispering down the telephone. 'So I can come up tomorrow and make the arrangements to take him off your hands? Oh, thank God! I've missed him so much. I can't thank you enough, Mrs McPherson. I shall get on the next available train. When Simon wakes up from his nap give him a kiss from me. Tell him Mummy loves him.'

She packed an overnight bag. Supper time arrived. She went downstairs to the dining room, endeavouring to keep her excitement in check. There was a space at the head of the table. 'Has my father not come in, Uncle Tris?'

'No sign of him yet,' Tristan tried to put some brightness in his reply. In contrast to Ford Farm there was a strained atmosphere here. Jonny was all for returning across the village. 'Agnes says we're having yesterday's leftovers. She's made it into a fish envelope. Can't really keep it warm.'

'That's strange,' Faye frowned. 'I haven't got to know him very well but one thing he is keen on is punctuality.'

The meal was eaten. Darkness fell and Jonny poured tiny whisky nightcaps. 'He must be tucked up somewhere with a woman and forgot to mention he wasn't coming home.'

'But he's in his working clothes,' Faye said, wishing she could peep out of the blackout blinds and see if he was on his way.

'I don't think it's likely Ben's come to any harm,' Tristan said.

No, he's just being awkward, Faye thought grimly.

She stayed awake all night hoping to hear him come in. Each excruciating hour stretched on – one hour less to try to commit him to an all-important talk. Just before dawn she wondered about waking Tristan and confiding in him. She didn't think he'd be too shocked by her confession that she had a child, but he behaved unreasonably towards Louisa, so she cancelled him out. There was no point in telling Jonny. What could he do? It was looking as if she'd have to go away and keep her secret a little longer. She hated secrets. She had been at the receiving end of a very humiliating one.

Next morning, she carried her overnight bag down-stairs.

'You're leaving?' It was the dry, breathless voice of her father. He'd just come through the front door. He looked as if he'd stayed out all night and slept in the woods.

'I was hoping to see you before I go. I haven't got time to talk now, I'm expecting a cab. I'm, ah, planning on coming back fairly soon and bringing someone with me.'

'Are you?' he asked, as if his mind was in a fog.

'Do you mind?' She tried to read what was going on through the muddle of him. She'd spoken in challenge, but she was coming back anyway. He might not want to forge a father and daughter relationship but he owed her, owed her a lot. Simon too, for he was his own flesh and blood.

'No. Do what you like, Faye.' He held up his hands, saw the layers of dirt on them. Became aware of the shabby, sweaty state of his clothes. He had his work boots on, they were caked in mud. He'd never entered the house before in his boots. 'Do forgive me. I must freshen up.'

Faye didn't know what to make of him. 'Has something happened?'

'What?' he said stupidly. 'Um, nothing… not really.'

She wished she could think of a way to bring him out of this extraordinary haze. He had been horrid to her but she didn't like seeing him like this. Like someone broken and utterly lost. 'Are you all right, Dad?'

'I just need a bath and a rest. Excuse me, Faye.'

He lurched off, heading for the stairs. Tristan was coming down for breakfast. 'What the heck?'

The telephone rang. Faye froze, afraid she was about to hear complications to her plans. Tristan answered it.

'Can you try later? I'm afraid my brother's temporarily indisposed.' He argued for another couple of sentences. 'Ben, it's for you. The chap's most insistent, he refuses to talk to anyone but you. He says it's very important.'

Ben had no strength left in him. He juddered to the bottom stair and fell down on it. Tristan put the receiver into his hand. 'Yes, I'm he, Benjamin Harvey. Yes. Yes. I understand. Of course. Thank you for ringing.'

'Who was it?' Tristan asked, trading an anxious glance with Faye.

'Can't say.' Ben gazed up at his daughter and his brother and there was now a glimmer of life in his drawn face. 'You're going to have to manage without me being around for a long time. I have to go away.'

Chapter Ten

Lottie was in Truro. Free time was scarce, but her mother insisted every family member took an afternoon off at least once a fortnight. Usually, she went riding, or if it was very wet weather she'd curl up in her room with a book. Occasionally, she went into town and trawled through the clothes shops, as she was today with the bonus of some precious clothes coupons.

She wished Jill could be with her, to try on things together, to have fun. Jill had given her the few coupons she had. 'Would you mind seeing what you could do with these? I don't care what you choose. It can be a blouse, nightie or undies. You have such good taste. I've never really had the confidence to buy things for myself.' Jill's clothes were either her grandmother's hand-me-downs or juvenile. She'd get something pretty for Jill, even glamorous, to dazzle Ronnie when he – Lottie crossed her fingers – when he eventually got leave.

As she crossed over the threshold of a quality fashion shop in King Street, Lottie broke into a smile. Right in front of her on a mannequin was just the thing for Jill. A frock with intricate detail on the bodice and a cowl neck in a fabulous shade of pink. Dark rose pink, the assistant who hastened to serve Lottie proudly announced. And to go with it Lottie chose a little piece of frivolity, a red, velvet-look hat with a net front. Jill deserved something chic and daring. Lottie would add her coupons and the rest of the required price, three pounds, nine shillings and tuppence, to Jill's meagre lot and take home a prize to delight her friend.

She hurried out of the shop, eager to get back. She'd slip straight up to Jill's room and put the frock on a hanger and leave it suspended outside the wardrobe, and she'd place the hat on the chair and place the chair beside the frock. She'd accompany Jill upstairs immediately after supper, and make her close her eyes before entering her bedroom.

Picturing Jill's expected gasps of wonder, Lottie nearly collided with someone outside on the pavement. 'Oh! Sorry!'

'My pleasure, miss,' a friendly American voice replied. The GI was with a group of others. All expressed animated interest in her, all wore highly polished shoes, all were chewing gum.

Lottie scanned their faces and was disappointed not to find Herv, or Jeff, or Todd, or Mort, or Brad among them. Or Corporal Nate Harmon. She was keen to show them, and the quiet-eyed sergeant in particular, that she wasn't ill-mannered, or childish, or an English snob, as she must have seemed to them in Hennaford's social rooms. She had never cared before what people thought of her but she wanted to make amends for her behaviour. Again, particularly to the corporal. 'Excuse me, please,' she mumbled, dodging round the GIs.

She went on her way, climbing up the hill of Pydar Street, pinking up as she was followed by a shower of wolf whistles. 'Come back, honey,' one of the GIs called after her.

Once she would have uttered under her breath, 'Buzz off!' But Nate would be offended. Damn! Why did she keep thinking about a man whom she had only met once, for a few minutes? Why was it important what he thought of her? He probably had a wife or a girlfriend back home anyway. Why on earth did she care about his marital status? How was it someone could affect her in such a way? She had asked Jill if she had fallen in love with Ronnie at first sight.

'No,' had been Jill's amused reply. 'We lived next door to each other, remember? Love was something that grew gradually between us. I suppose we took it for granted that we would marry one day. The war hurried things along, our feelings for each other, I mean. When the war's over, Ronnie will return to university and finish his degree.'

'And when you get married I will be your bridesmaid, won't I?'

'Of course. I'd like that.'

'Good. Pappa can give you away. He'd be honoured to. When the war's over, you must continue living here with us, do you hear?'

She'd enjoyed the thrill shining out of Jill's face. 'I'd love to stay on, if Mrs Em will have me.'

'None of us would have it any other way. Tom thinks of you as another sister, you know.'

Jill had become emotional on hearing that. They had exchanged a hug. 'Why did you ask me about being in love, Lottie?'

'Oh, I don't know really. Just curious.' She couldn't admit she had been thinking about Nate Harmon. She'd feel a fool, especially as on every mention of Americans before she had haughtily disparaged them.

She had walked the six miles into town, the distance being little more than a stroll to her. Rather than ride on the noisy, stuffy, boneshaker bus on the way back, and wanting to think over the strange new insight of thinking continually about a stranger, a stranger who had been abrupt with her, she continued on her way home. Nate Harmon had put her in her place. Something she wouldn't have tolerated before. She had been noticeably quieter ever since. Tom had asked her if she was sickening for something. Her mother and Tilda were concerned about why she wasn't eating properly.

She had to cross over the road and she stepped up to the edge of the pavement. An American jeep pulled up and the driver, close to her due to the left-hand drive, motioned to her to pass by. It was Corporal Nate Harmon. Without thinking twice she smiled at him. He lifted his hand in a little wave. She knew she was blushing fiercely but it didn't matter. All that was important was that he saw her this time as friendly and polite. She crossed over to the opposite pavement. She turned round immediately and nodded to him and called, 'Thank you.'

He returned the nod, put the jeep in gear and drove on, turning left, heading towards Castle Hill.

For the first time in her life Lottie knew the meaning of frustration. And dejection. And misery. She had wanted so much for him to stay and talk or something. Pulling in her mouth and keeping her head down, she trudged on and upwards. Arguing with herself. *So he really did think I was unforgiveably rude. Well, I deserved to be ignored. If he's married or spoken for he wouldn't be interested in me anyway.*

It's a good thing he drove on. I'm glad he's not too free and easy. There are too many people seeking cheap thrills nowadays.

She trudged on, turning off before reaching the Kenwyn area, passing a solid group of Victorian houses, taking the route home through the quiet lanes. This way took her past the entrance to the back steps leading up to St Keyne's churchyard and then on through the tiny hamlet of Idless, a heavily wooded area with a complement of a mill and a few whitewashed dwellings.

She travelled on and on, her shopping only a light burden, the business now of walking under a blue sky and warming sun both calming and uplifting. Half a mile away from home she came to the lonesome parish church of Hennaford, the minerals in the ancient stones of the tower glinting sagely in the strong light. The main body of the church and the graves were screened by yews and oaks, and high hedgerows massed with burdock, wild garlic and foxgloves, and walls creeping with stonecrop and feverfew. She thought to stand awhile at the Harvey grave plot, its newest incumbents her baby sister and father. Death had snatched them both away at very young ages. Death was disintegrating innumerable families on a daily basis. What was the point of being where the sister she had never known was lain, or her father who'd died when she was only five years old. It was better to be with the living. To forget that there was a narrow line between happiness and security and loss and tragedy.

She was on Harvey land, but wanting to stay alone for as long as she could, she climbed over the next field gate and headed for a secluded spot. A hillock in the middle of a long field where bullocks were pastured, and within the hillock, capped with small leafy trees and banked with golden gorse, was a natural depression. She sank down in this little valley, sharing it with fritillary butterflies flitting on the bracken fronds. Putting her parcels carefully aside on the fragrant grass, she rested her face on her knees. Who needed romance? A boyfriend? Especially a foreign national who didn't approve of her, when she had – war permitting – part of all this to inherit and a close family and good friends? She stayed perfectly still in peace and lazy contentment.

'Hi.'

She thought she had imagined the word, so quietly spoken. It was just the breeze lightly stirring the low, encircling branches, or whispering through the long grasses. An echo of a childhood dream. She hugged her knees and closed her eyes to meditate, breathing in the clean air and soothing warm scents of nature's finest. Here she felt safe, at one with the land she loved.

'Miss Harvey. Lottie…'

'What?' She lifted her head. 'Corporal Harmon! Nate! How…? I mean, how did you know I was here?' She could almost believe she was seeing a vision of him, tall and dominant, yet unassuming, unconscientiously trailing his cap from his fingertips.

'I've driven through Hennaford a few times. When I came off duty a short while ago I thought I'd take another look at it. I knew roughly where to find the farm. I came across Jill, the land girl, in the lane. She told me she saw you from a vantage point, strolling this way. Hope you don't mind me showing up like this. Can I join you?'

Mind his unexpected appearance? It thrilled her. He had driven this way to see her. After their earlier fraught history, her mixed feelings about him, she was surprised at how at ease she was with him. 'Yes. Of course.'

He sat down at her side, facing her. 'This is a nice, peaceful little place.'

'It is today.' She smiled. 'As a child I used to play very noisy games with my older brothers and cousins. I could never keep a frock clean.'

He returned the smile. 'I can imagine that. It's good to be somewhere peaceful, away from the constant hustle of camp. I miss the peace of my home. We have something in common. I'm a farmer's son. Well, a rancher's.'

'Really? Where? Texas?'

'That's right. Can you tell from the drawl?'

'Not really,' she admitted. 'My brother Tom could, I'm sure. He goes to the pictures when he gets the chance. He likes Western films. I don't think you've got much of a drawl actually. My uncle married an American, but they're divorced. She originated from Wyoming, but when she returned to America she settled in Washington. Wyoming is all prairie and cattle country, isn't it? Their daughter Faye was at the dance. Perhaps you spoke to her. She's up in Scotland at the moment. I'm hoping she'll return soon. I like to have as many members of the family as possible round me. You must be missing your family. Is your ranch very big?'

'I noticed the commotion your cousin caused when she arrived in your little village hall. And the ranch, well, Hennaford could be swallowed up in one tiny corner of it, but I don't mean that in a boastful way. A lot of you English seem to think that some of my countrymen and I have big mouths.'

'Oh…' Lottie thought he was making a dig at her, until she saw the humorous glint in his eyes. How gentle his eyes were. She had read romantic stories about velvety eyes and scoffed over it, but it was just how Nate's were. She had read about girls wanting to gaze into a man's eyes all day long and thought it daft, but it was exactly what she wanted to do now. Gaze and gaze into Nate's gorgeous eyes, eyes that were settled firmly on her.

He took in the trees, the dots of red, yellow, white, pink and blue of the wild flowers, the banks of fern, the sky overhead, where cottony clouds floated by as if careful not to blot out the friendly sun, giving no clue that up there in the heavens, day and night, tragedy was played out on a daily basis. 'I really like it here. It feels like you could just fall asleep and find yourself in another world, one where there's only peace and harmony.' His voice, so soft and rich, dropped to a huskier tone.

'This is my mother's land.'

'So I understand. I had a pleasant conversation with your mom at the dance. She seems a fine woman.' He raised an eyebrow. It was steeped in meaning. 'I'd like to meet her again.'

'I'm sure she wouldn't mind if you came back with me for tea. Mum loves a houseful. I'm lucky to have a big, close family. Have you got brothers and sisters, Nate?'

'No. My daddy died six months ago. I've got no folks at all now, Lottie.'

'Oh, that's sad.' She paused, then asked with lowered eyes, 'So you're not married? Or attached?'

'The girl I had in mind not long ago married the local pastor. Do you have anyone? Anyone special, I mean.'

'No.'

'Can't say I'm sorry to hear that, Lottie.'

She was rapt to hear him say that, but was now a little shy. She searched her brain for something to say. 'So you like England? Cornwall?'

'I sure do. I like your sleepy old churches, your bluebell woods. Everywhere is so green. It's different to how I imagined it on the troop ship coming over.' He didn't mention how primitive he and his countrymen found the country, especially the outdoor privies. It touched many a man's heart at how much the shortages made people, particularly the children, go without. 'And you're different to what I first thought of you, Lottie.'

'You didn't like me?'

He gave her a sideways glance. 'I thought you were cute. Very cute. I was about to ask you to dance, then I overheard you giving poor Herv plenty of lip. Uh oh, I thought. This little honey's got a sting in her tail.'

'But you do like me now?'

'I do. I like you very much, Lottie. If that's not too forward.'

'No. My question was rather forward.'

'Rather… I like the way you people say things like "rather". I'd like to hear you say a lot more things, Lottie. I have to get back fairly soon. Shall we go now so I can meet your folks again? I've parked the jeep by the field gate.'

Lottie realized the afternoon was drifting away. It was time she went home. It was going to be brilliant to be driving back with Nate. To show him off as her newest friend…

Chapter Eleven

Louisa picked sprays of apple blossom from her back garden and strolled along to the churchyard to place them on her adoptive uncle's grave. Julian Andrews, brother to her Aunt Polly, had died young, ten years ago, of a heart condition. She remembered little about him, so frail and quiet he had been, but she knew him as a kind, gentle person, and that he'd liked the glorious sweet fragrance of apple blossom.

The church of St Keyne appeared to be sleeping peacefully. As always when she came here, she paused near the porch and drank in the view of the three-spired cathedral down in the town, and the tidal river away in the background; its thickly wooded banks wound on, soon to converge with the River Fal. She tried to forget those not-too-distant waters and the surrounding areas, frantic with the preparations for the Second Front in Europe, the long-planned major assault on the German occupying enemy, assumed to be at the nearest port of Calais.

She carried on along the well-trodden path, much of the sky blotted out with ancient towering trees. To reach the grave she must begin the descent of the steep slopes that fell down towards the Idless valley. Nestled down among the headstones, as if he was a monument himself, was a man. Louisa would have to pass by him. She slowed her steps, wanting not to disturb him, but within moments she came to a halt. There would be nothing unusual in a mourner paying homage to a grave if it was not for whose body lay beneath this particular small expanse of sod. The almost blank headstone had been placed there reluctantly by the next of kin. The words it bore were few. Ursula Harvey. Died 1918. It was the grave of Tristan Harvey's first wife and no one except Jonny, her son, was known to visit it, for she had died in disgrace. Aunt Polly had mentioned that some people had voiced their objection to her being buried here.

Louisa crept up behind a high marble angel. There was something about the forlorn appearance of the man that bade he be left in privacy, but she couldn't help being curious. She had never seen him before. He was about sixty years old, white-haired, slightly bent over and leaning on a horn-handled walking stick. His clothes were a little shabby. He was holding a panama hat pressed to his chest as if he was having trouble breathing. Louisa could see he was weak. Every so often he gave a gasping cough.

She stole a little closer to him, then closer still. She heard him talking. In a rusty voice, he was talking to the deceased. Louisa caught a few words. 'Ursula... regret... the only... had to come...' Louisa sensed the overwhelming sadness in the man and felt sorry for him, wanting to offer him a few consoling words, but that would be inappropriate. She must go before she unforgiveably disturbed him.

To her dismay, the man looked up and saw her. It was obvious she was watching him. She couldn't make a hasty retreat: she would seem like a callous nosy parker riding off on a moral high horse. Flushing in shame, she went forward. 'I'm so sorry. Forgive me. I was bringing the blossom for my late uncle, and I, um…'

'Was curious about me?' he finished for her. He straightened up as much as he was able. A gentleman acknowledging the presence of a lady. Louisa revised her impression of his age. He was several years younger; illness and lack of nutrition had taken their toll of what must have once been finely honed fair looks. His blue eyes were pale and watery, yet compelling and expressive. He crumpled back over, coughing and breathing huskily. He banged a fist to his thin chest. He was shaking, growing ever more pale. 'My apologies, Miss, Mrs…?'

'Mrs Carlyon. Please don't think me impertinent. May I fetch you a drink of water? There's always some left in the church. Perhaps you'd like to sit a moment on one of the pews.'

With an effort that cost him another fit of coughing, he turned back to the grave. 'I can't leave her yet. It's been years and years, you see. And I may not be able to come again.'

He could only be one person. 'You were Mrs Harvey's… gentleman friend?'

'Her lover, yes. Bruce Ashley. I won't deny it. I was a cad, a good-for-nothing. I denied Ursula and she paid for it with her life. I abandoned her while she was giving birth to my child. It's down there with her. No mention of it on the headstone. It's as if it never existed. Excuse me speaking so frankly, but there's nothing to be gained now by false sensitivity, and you seem a sympathetic young lady. I don't even know if my child was born dead or died shortly afterwards. Or if it was a boy or a girl. Or how long Ursula lasted. As you can see, my own health is, to say the least, not so good. I have to know. Do you understand, Mrs Carlyon?'

'I do, Mr Ashley. Please allow me to make another suggestion. There's a high grass verge just over there. I happen to know something about Mrs Harvey and your child. If you would like to sit there, where you will be able to see her resting place, I'd be happy to inform you of what you want to know.'

'Why should you do that for me?' He displayed incredulity. 'Apart from my dubious reputation, I'm a stranger to you.'

'There's a war on, Mr Harvey. There's suffering enough. You've come to make your peace. There's not a better thing anyone can do.'

'I will be in your debt. But please, do lay your flowers and join me in a little while.' He dropped his head and Louisa fancied he had executed an old-fashioned bow. He shuffled off in the direction of the verge. She knew he was trying to retain his dignity, but she couldn't help glancing back to make sure he was making a safe passage. He was moving awkwardly, bit by bit. She took her time arranging the apple blossom on her uncle's grave and filling the flower pot with water, unaware that the dead young man had been present in the house when Bruce Ashley's child had been born, and that she was, in fact, the supposed dead baby.

When she joined Bruce Ashley he was sitting with both hands on his stick and his head bowed as if in prayer. 'Mr Ashley.'

'Oh, Mrs Carlyon. You came. I wondered if you'd think better of it. It's all rather unsavoury for a fine person such as yourself.'

Louisa sat down beside him. 'Mr Ashley, are you ready to hear the information?'

Never had she seen such an expression of longing, which he aimed at the grave. 'Yes. Please do go on. Tell me what I've wanted to know these past twenty-five years.'

'Your child was a girl. She was stillborn. Mrs Harvey haemorrhaged. There was nothing that could be done to save her. I know these facts because I am friends with the Harvey family of Hennaford.'

'A girl. I had a daughter.' He stared into space, as if making up images. 'I'm sure I would have loved her if she'd lived and I'd stayed around. But I wouldn't have made much of a father. Too irresponsible, too selfish. Perhaps it's better that she… Tell me, was it in Ford House, down the hill from the farm, where I last saw Ursula, that she died?'

'Yes, it was.'

'So Tristan Harvey never had her moved when she went into labour. The Harveys must hate me, especially the boy, Jonny. I deprived him of his mother and his half-sister. So you're friends with the family, Mrs Carlyon? I'm curious to know how Jonny turned out, if you'd be so good…'

Louisa always smiled when she talked about Jonny. 'He's intelligent, fun and free-spirited. He was already making a career in the RAF before the war started.' She related the rest about her friend.

'Well, I'm very pleased to hear it. I hope he continues to make it through.' Bruce Ashley lifted his jacket cuff as if to consult a wristwatch.

Louisa saw that the cuff was frayed and there was nothing to tell the time by. Once, his clothes, of the highest quality, had been smart. He must have fallen on hard times. By the fresh smell of him, the neatness of his hair, his close shave in an age when shortages required men to sharpen razor blades on glass, he was a man who cared about his appearance. She wondered how he had got here. There was no vehicle parked outside the churchyard. There was another approach, by many steps that led down to the road that wound to Idless. He appeared too frail to have mounted them. 'Do you have to go, Mr Ashley?'

'Shortly. I don't want to. I want to stay close to her. But...' he gave a thin, apologetic smile and indicated his woefully thin chest, 'I'm not quite up to it. Had a touch of pleurisy and pneumonia recently.'

'I'll leave you in peace. Goodbye, Mr Ashley.'

'Goodbye, Mrs Carlyon. Thank you for being so kind. I really don't deserve it.'

Louisa left but lingered on the path where she had a clear view of him. She owed him no more considera-tion but she couldn't bring herself to carry on her way and forget all about him. Where was he staying? Was he expecting a taxicab to come for him? She had to make sure he went safely on his way.

Moments later, awkwardly using his walking stick and the verge as levers, Bruce Ashley got to his feet. He coughed and fumbled for a handkerchief and wiped his mouth, returning the handkerchief back to his breast pocket with a shaky hand. His balance was precarious. Louisa caught her breath, afraid he'd fall over. He took a step, wobbled, threw out a desperate steadying hand and tumbled to the ground. He broke into a fit of coughing, a horrible hacking sound.

Louisa cried out and rushed to him. He was floundering, trying to get up. 'Mr Ashley! Please stay still. Let me help you.' She crouched down beside him. His coughing persisted and now he was gasping and choking, and sweating in streams. He kept his head lowered to his chest but what she could see of his face was a ghastly red and purple. He could hardly breathe. She patted his back, then pounded, careful not to hurt him, wrapping her arms around him in a manner to give him the best support and take his weight. 'Try to take a deep breath through your nose.'

The coughing, the pounding, her encouragements seemed to go on and on. Finally, he managed to snatch a longish breath, then after a few more fearsome seconds another one. Gradually, painfully slowly, his coughing eased. Louisa rubbed his back with the heel of her hand. 'That's right. Just keep breathing. Concentrate only on your breathing.' She reached round and pulled out his handkerchief, put it into his hand then lifted it up to his face.

His fingers trembling inside her firm grip, he dried his streaming eyes and mopped his chin and brow. 'Th… thanks,' he rasped feebly.

'There's no need to say thank you. Just stay calm. I'll get help.' She looked all around, hoping to see someone, but they were alone with the dead. 'Don't worry. I won't leave you.'

They stayed as they were for some time. Louisa was thankful that he was able to be calm. They were facing Ursula Harvey's grave, nine graves away, and with his head resting against her shoulder, he gazed at the bleak headstone. Louisa angled her head to peer around monuments and yew trees, and through the wild flowers and grasses, but no one came. It was still and silent. Even the rooks up in the dark trees neither stirred nor cawked.

His breathing was noisy but reasonably stable. She said, 'Mr Ashley, do you think you'll be able to stand now? I'll help you.'

'I think so. If I can get on to one knee…'

With a struggle that made him sweat again and cough and sniff and gulp, with Louisa plying every ounce of her physical strength, while remaining gentle and thoughtful, Bruce Ashley was righted. The stick in his hand shook. Louisa placed his free arm round her shoulders and put her arm firmly round his waist. 'We'll take one step at a time. When you need to rest you can lean on the tombs and the banks and then sit on one of the granite rests under the old schoolroom. I live not far along the road. I'll get you there and make you some tea. You can freshen up. Then, when you're ready, I'll phone for a cab to take you to your hotel.'

He said nothing, but with his eyes moist he gave a weak smile that spoke of gratitude.

They crept along and halted often. When finally they got to the lychgate, he pointed back with his stick to the holy well. 'I dropped my things beside it… if you'd be so kind.' She assumed he'd put something there to save the effort of carrying it. She found a small, scruffy suitcase. He must have come straight here from the railway station.

Clearly embarrassed, he was trying to hold himself upright. 'Perhaps you can recommend somewhere of reasonable price where I might find a room, Mrs Carlyon.'

'Let me get you settled into a comfortable chair, Mr Ashley, and then I'll make some enquiries for you.'

'I owe you a great debt of gratitude.' He flashed a smile. It was only there for an instant and she saw something of his former charm, the beguiling charm that had led Ursula Harvey to her tragic fate, and no doubt other unfortunate women, *rich* women, to heartbreak. Louisa felt a qualm of disquiet, but as Bruce Ashley's frailty threatened to overwhelm him again she saw only a broken man. He was very ill, he had come to visit the grave of the only woman he had ever loved. There could only be one reason for it. She felt distressed and it showed in her face.

He sighed, as if with the greatest regret. 'I'm practised at reading the thoughts of ladies, Mrs Carlyon. You're absolutely right. I am dying. I had to come to Ursula, to say how sorry I was. To tell her that I'd never forgotten her and how much I've always loved her. I've led a wasted life. All I want now is to join her. I'm sorry. I have no right to unburden myself on you. If you want to change your mind about your offer of hospitality, I'll understand.'

'The offer was genuine, Mr Ashley. Thank you for being so frank.'

She carried the suitcase. He had gained enough strength to enable him the dignity of walking to the house with her giving him no more than a supporting arm.

Chapter Twelve

Emilia was in the nursery, enjoying the delight of pulling off the dust covers of the cradle, the cot, the nursing chair, the rocking horse. It would be marvellous to soon be able to use these things again. Perry, the dear, wonderful man, didn't mind at all that these items had seen generations of Harveys. 'There's a war on, darling. New things aren't important, only our love for our baby is.' It was easy to love a man who was never jealous, never critical.

She was hit by a tight foreboding, followed immediately by a strange, terrible bareness which engulfed her whole being. Will! She was compelled to rush along to the end of the corridor to Will's room. Her nerves on edge, she groped for the door handle and went into the room where her firstborn child had slept a few weeks ago. Was it only weeks since she had last seen Will, had him at home? Looking after him. Doing all the motherly things, seeing to his laundry, brushing down the tunic that sat so proudly on his broad shoulders, making sure his favourite plum pudding was served at Sunday lunch. Playing chess with him; Will was unbeatable. Listening with satisfaction and pride at his enthusiasm to start up a photographic career. She was delighted he had inherited his father's love for the camera. She had a new album of photographs of the family which he had taken and developed in the darkroom built by his father.

'You'd be so proud of him, Alec,' she whispered through the quietness. Her words emerged as a strangled choke.

The curtains were kept drawn so the room was never forgotten in the nightly blackout. She could just make out the things in the room. The shelves and shelves of books; Will devoured information on all topics. The balsa wood and matchstick models of planes, ships, tractors and a gypsy caravan he'd made in boyhood. The precious rugby ball he'd been allowed to keep after leading his college team to its umpteenth victory. There, on his pillow, was the golden-brown teddy bear, somewhat reduced in fur and fatness, which he swore he kept not for sentimental reasons but to please her, his mother.

From somewhere up high came the distant grumbling of a solitary plane. It could be Will up there in the cold sky. Hopefully, he was safely at base. He had mentioned that he wasn't very far away and she had taken this to mean he was stationed in the county. She prayed he was safe. But she had this dread that he was not. She knew somehow, in the tiniest deepest place within her, as his mother, she *knew* he was not.

Unable to control her shivers, on feet she could barely bring to move, she went to the window. She had stood here before, during the last war, which had been fought at colossal cost and suffering to prevent another war on this horrendous scale ever happening again. The room had belonged to Henry Harvey then, the second son of the household. She had been a seventeen-year-old dairy-maid, running the house entirely on her own, seeing to all the yard work, and responsible for the care of Alec Harvey's senile grandmother, the first Lottie Harvey. At Alec's request she had moved into the house after the old lady had wandered off outside and fallen in the dark. The incident had led to Ben's blindness; in her panic, Lottie Harvey had thrust a handful of stones into his face. Ben had been her sweetheart. How different things were now.

Now, here she was again, praying and pleading, not as before for the safe return of Henry Harvey and her brother Billy – neither had survived the fighting on the Western Front – but for her son. Back then, Alec had joined her. Today, it was Perry.

Perry was a persistent guardian over Emilia. She had slept poorly since Will had gained his wings. She had hardly slept at all since the bitter confrontation with Ben. 'It's not so much because Alec went with Brooke, that her son is Alec's that's shaken me so,' she'd said, immediately on her return. 'After all, I fell in love with you and I was unfaithful to Alec. It's Ben's hatred that chills me. He's turned into a monster.'

Next day, he'd pointed out, 'Try to put it out of your mind, darling. He can't hurt you at the moment while he's away.'

'I'm concerned about Faye. He's hurt her so much, he could really bring her down.'

'She's gone away too. She might decide to stay on with her friend in the Highlands. It will be sad not to see her again but at least she wouldn't come under Ben's influence, have the youth frozen out of her. Ben might not come back. I hope to God he doesn't! I hope he stays wherever he's so mysteriously gone to. Life would be good with Tris running Tremore permanently. It's certainly been good for Tris.'

He and Emilia had another worry. Lottie's friendship with Nate Harmon. Although she saw little of him, and he didn't seem a forward young man, there was obviously something deep between them. Emilia, wise in her ways, had decided not to issue Lottie with any advice, saying that anything Lottie considered as a warning might drive her into Harmon's arms, and adding hopefully, 'It might not come to anything anyway.'

Perry found it hard not to pester Emilia with his troubles over the friendship. He might not be Lottie's father but he loved her as though he was, his love made strong and abiding when, during the same year, Lottie had lost her father and his own daughter had been drowned in the sea at Watergate Bay. His first fear was that Lottie, usually so down to earth, would be dazzled by the smart medical NCO. Although Harmon came across as a pleasant chap, although he had prospects in the vast acreage he now owned, had everything, it seemed, a caring stepfather could desire for his stepdaughter, Perry couldn't bear the thought that if Lottie became a GI bride he could lose her to Harmon's homeland. Also, in the not too distant future, when Harmon was inevitably pitched into battle on European soil, his possible death could mean heartbreak for Lottie.

At Will's bedroom window, Perry said, 'Darling...' Only that. He didn't offer useless platitudes. He couldn't promise her that Will would be all right.

It was a comfort to Emilia to have him with her. He wrapped his arms around her and she leaned against his strength and protection. The baby she was to bear moved inside her. It was a reassurance that it was alive and growing. But the fear, the wretched emptiness she felt for its eldest brother grew and grew into an ever greater void.

–

Jill hesitated outside the main bedroom of the farmhouse. She had only seen over the whole of the Victorian wing once before, when Lottie had shown her around, the surroundings luxurious to her. It was a hard thing to come here at this moment but it was the right thing to do. Will would have wanted her to. She had a duty to perform, a promise to keep to him. It was awful to have to disturb Mrs Em, who at her own request was spending some time alone, but poor, dear Mrs Em would undoubtedly feel a little better when she saw what she was bringing to her. Jill breathed in a long steadying breath and knocked on the door.

After a moment, Emilia called out, 'Come in.'

Her heart racing, Jill entered and closed the door with extra care. She shuffled awkwardly. 'Please forgive the intrusion, Mrs Em.'

Emilia looked up out of tear-stained eyes from where she was sitting at the window, a crumpled soaked hanky in her hand. She had a golden–brown teddy bear on her lap. 'You're not intruding, Jill. I was expecting the telegram. I knew, you see. I'm his mother. I knew the exact moment... when Will left this earth. He's with his father and little sister now. I shall find comfort in that.' She allowed herself to find comfort in Jill. She was glad it wasn't Perry who had come. She wanted some moments to think back over the time when her family was young, before Perry had come into her life. She owed Will, and

Alec, that. And she was glad it wasn't a member of the family. Lottie and Tom and her father too needed a little time alone to adjust to their loss. And Tilda, dear Tilda, needed to keep busy. This gentle newcomer, who had such a soothing effect on everyone, would make ideal company for a few minutes.

Jill perched on the foot of the bed. From her skirt pocket, she eased out the letter Will had placed in her keeping. 'Mrs Em, I've come because I've got something for you. I was hoping I'd never have to pass it on. This is from Will. He wrote it during his last leave. He asked me to give it to you in the event… in the event he...'

'He was killed,' Em finished for her. Fresh tears cascaded silently down her face. 'Th-thanks, Jill. I'm sure I'll treasure every word.'

With hot tears stinging her eyes, Jill placed Will's last gift to his mother into her hungry hands. Overcoming her shyness and awkwardness, she hugged Emilia and kissed her cheek. 'I'm so very sorry. I grew to like Will very much. I'll never forget him. I'll leave you alone to read his letter.'

When she reached the door, Emilia said, 'Thank you. You're such a kind person. You haven't heard from your Ronnie yet, have you?'

'No. There's been nothing.'

'I'm sorry. Sometimes it's hard, isn't it? The waiting, trying to be brave. Jill, you're always very welcome to come to me, if you want someone older than Lottie or Tom to talk to. You can come to me at any time.'

'Thanks, Mrs Em. That means a lot to me.' Jill hastened away. The instant she was out of hearing, she burst into tears. She cried fiercely for Will. For the grief of his family, now her friends. As she ran to her own quarters her heart was breaking over Ronnie's inexplicable silence. *Please God, please let Ronnie be all right.* She flung herself on to her bed and buried her head under the pillow. Lonely and afraid, she faced fully for the first time that for some reason she might have lost the man she loved.

Chapter Thirteen

With noisy effort, Bruce Ashley struggled to sit up straight on the couch while Louisa plumped up the pillows behind him. He was staying in one of her back bedrooms, which he'd only left, since the day of their first meeting, for the bathroom and a twice-weekly struggle to the churchyard.

'I don't deserve this,' he said in his rasp of a voice, panting as he collapsed back against the substantial padding. 'I can't come to terms with all your continuing kindness to me. I'm a stranger.'

'We've gone over this many times, Mr Ashley. I'm happy to have you and so is Ada.' Louisa had talked over the fate of her guest to Ada that first evening, after her shift at the workshops where parts for Spitfires were made, while they'd prepared dinner together. Bruce Ashley's sorrowful and regretful pilgrimage had stirred Ada's heart too. 'Well, 'tisn't as if he's up to hurting none of us,' Ada, a lanky, brightly natured thirty-five-year-old, had deliberated, cutting up rabbit meat – the rabbit sent over from Tremore Farm – for a stew that would last them two days at least. 'You can't just send him away, Miss Louisa. Wouldn't be right. Wouldn't be Christian. He's got a terrible wheeze on him. Noisy as a traction engine.'

Louisa had been biting her lip. 'Are you sure, Ada? Absolutely sure? We could take him in for a few days until he's a little stronger.'

They had gone into the drawing room to deliver their decision with warmth and smiles to Bruce Ashley. For a moment he had seemed stunned. When he'd tried to speak he'd been gripped by a prolonged, painful burst of coughing. 'Ada, phone the doctor, please. I'm sure Mr Ashley would benefit from a visit from him.' Louisa had not doubted then, or since, that she was doing the right thing in giving this man shelter.

'I can't thank you enough,' Bruce Ashley had managed finally, wiping at his watering eyes and dribbling mouth. 'I've nowhere to go and very little money. I'm afraid I've no ration books, I found it necessary to sell them. All that I have in the world is what I have with me. All my life I've taken advantage of women, giving no thought to their hopes and expectations, but the generous offer of hospitality from you both makes me feel humble and very ashamed. I'd have you know that my past association in this pleasant little cathedral city of yours was not a happy one. If any of Ursula's family still reside hereabouts they'd see to it that I was hounded out. I also left owing various people money. I have not been an honourable man, Mrs Carlyon. If you still consider it right to allow me to stay, I think it would be wise to keep my presence confidential.'

'You needn't worry about a thing, Mr Ashley. The late Mrs Harvey's family are a snooty lot. They've shunned their own grandson, Jonny, since her death, and as Jonny is a particular friend of mine they ignore me too, and I'm glad to do the same to them. No one but Ada and myself and the doctor will know you're here. He's too young to know who you are. I'll tell him you're an old friend of my aunt's and the same message will go to any curious neighbours.'

Bruce Ashley had found a small, grateful smile. At length he'd said, with a nervous grimace, 'I'll keep nothing from you. It would be a terrible shock for Jonny Harvey to encounter me. The last time he saw me, Mrs Carlyon, I was planning with Ursula to abduct him, and when the game was up, in my cowardice, I pulled a gun on his father and Emilia Harvey. It wasn't loaded but it terrified everyone. And then, of course, I ran out on his mother, leaving her to die. Jonny Harvey must hate me and rightly so. You could be risking your friendship.' He started to weep and this made him cough. 'I'm a dreadful, dreadful man.'

Throughout the years, Jonny had never mentioned his mother's lover. He had been told the significance of the couple's doomed relationship in his youth, to anticipate the possibility of a slipped tongue or a shock announcement from a spiteful gossip. Louisa had studied the weak, pathetic huddle of a man before her. There was no trace of the once dashing young man Bruce Ashley must have been. From the very first moment, he had roused her compassion and a desire to protect him, and she'd said, 'Nonetheless, your welcome here is in no way inhibited. Jonny is currently on injury leave. I'll be careful that when he calls here he'll have no notion of me having a guest.'

Bruce Ashley said now, 'If it's possible, I'd like to go to Ursula this afternoon.'

Louisa glanced out of the window. 'I'm afraid the clouds are building up. It looks like it's going to rain.'

'That doesn't matter.'

'I'm sorry, but it does. Dr Radcliffe said you must keep warm and dry. You have your chest to consider.'

'The doctor confirmed that I'm slowly dying. Emphysema, greatly worsened by my wanton lifestyle and previous smoking habit.' He looked up towards the ceiling, and past it, as if picturing himself in the next life. There was the look of desperate hope Louisa saw in him so often. She was sure he was wishing for what he wanted most, eternity with Ursula. Then came the next expression, of resignation that it wouldn't be so, because, she guessed, as he'd regularly repeated, he'd left it too late to make things up to Ursula. After closing his eyes for a second, he tried to sit up. His voice came faintly but vehemently, 'The sooner I pop off, the less work and bother I'll give to you and Ada. Sorry, that was indelicate of me. I know you don't approve of such an idea. But I really ought to leave your house. I've got nothing I can sell to pay for my burial. I can't allow you to be burdened with that too.'

'I've thought that far ahead.' She steered him gently back to rest. 'I've been waiting for the right moment to broach this to you. Please don't be offended. You see, I've talked to the vicar. I know it was forward of me, but he's a sympathetic person. He's said that if you're willing to confess to him, and to accept, when the time comes, the last rites, he'll arrange for you to be interred fairly near to Ursula. Somewhere where Jonny's not likely to read the name on the headstone.'

'Mrs Carlyon. Louisa, if I may call you that.' His face was an anguish of emotion. A distortion of emotional pain. 'How could you ever offend me? I can never thank you enough for allowing me to die with dignity, hope and peace. Your goodness shames me. But please, my name is unworthy to be inscribed. There should be no memorial to me at all. To be lying close to my dear, beloved lady will be enough.'

'I don't like the idea of you in an unmarked grave, Mr Ashley. Bruce.'

He shook his head. 'Oh, a simple wooden cross, perhaps with my initials on. My first name is actually John. My mother called me Bruce, after her father. If you please, 'J.B.A.' will do me well. No one will know who really lies beneath that scrap of ground. And dispose of me as simply as you can, to save the cost.' He cried, breaking into sobs, making no attempt to stop, despite the agony it caused to his chest and breathing.

Louisa held him. He held on to her. It was the first time in several months he had been this close to a woman, the first time in years he had been held kindly.

The rain fell so heavily after lunch that an excursion to the churchyard, which would have been undertaken with Bruce in Louisa's late uncle's bath chair, was totally out of the question. He tried to read a book, but disappointment and frailty quickly took their toll and he slept deeply, to Louisa's satisfaction. In the kitchen, the warmest room, surrounded by the bric-a-brac she collected for jumble to raise money for the bombed-out, she set about unravelling a bundle of used knitted garments.

She was interrupted by a dripping, ashen-faced Tom on her back doorstep. She took him through to dry off, and while shooting worried glances at him, put the kettle on the hob. 'What is it? It's easy to see something's wrong.'

Tom gazed at her gravely. A tear gathered at the corner of his eye.

Louisa sucked in her breath and clutched her hands together. 'Is it Jonny? Or Will?'

The tear tumbled down from its precarious rest. 'Will,' he replied throatily. 'We've lost Will. Jonny's managed to get hold of some details. He'd been out alone gathering intelligence. One second he was speaking through his earphones, then there was the sound of an enormous explosion. His plane must have been hit, blown apart. There's no chance he'd have survived. At least it would have been over very quickly. I had to get away for a while, Louisa. I told Mum I'd come and tell you personally, rather than you receiving a phone call.'

Her arms outstretched, crying too, she shot across the kitchen to him. 'Oh, Tom, I'm so sorry. Poor Will. Poor Aunt Em. She must be devastated. And Lottie. How are they?'

Tom clung to her. 'Mum's being strong. Lottie's pretending to be. Mum's got Perry. Lottie's got Jill. Jill's been a brick to all of us. And Granddad's there too, of course. I can't believe it, Louisa.' He shook against her. 'I can't believe Will's dead. That he'll never come back to us, jaunty and confident and superior. Chasing girls with me. It's all so bloody awful.'

They drank tea at the table. 'I feel so lost. So appallingly lost.' Tom gulped from the china mug. 'But I've got to buck up. I'm now the eldest son, oh God, I'm the only son. I've got big responsibilities. I promised Will I'd look after Mum and Lottie. I'm scared, Lou.'

She patted his arm. 'You'll manage very well, Tom. I've every confidence in you.'

'I wish Mum wasn't having this baby. It's not that I don't welcome a little brother or sister. It's Mum's age, and this wretched war.'

'Aunt Em's strong and she's still young. Some women have babies much later in life. She'll be fine. I know Perry's got no midwifery skills but he's an experienced surgeon. He'll be keeping a close watch on her. And she's got three women at the farm.'

'Yes, you're right.' Tom sighed out some of the tension. 'I suppose everything will turn out fine, but I'd hate for Mum to lose another child.'

Louisa cradled her hand over his. He laid his other hand on top. His hands, large and work-roughened, hers, small and pale and soft. 'Tom, how's your Uncle Tristan taking the news about Will?'

'I went over to Tremore myself. He was dreadfully upset. Had to sit down. Of course, he'll have Jonny on his mind more than ever, especially now he's flying ops again. I hope Faye will be back soon to keep him company.'

'I had a quick phone call from Jonny two days ago, just to say hello.' Louisa reflected on the dinner she had shared one night with Jonny at Opie's Restaurant, in the town. 'It's bad enough thinking about myself,' he'd said at one point, 'but I've got all the young novice pilots under my care to look out for. Just boys some of them are, straight out of school. I've waited in vain for a lot of planes to come back. Seen too many blasted into oblivion or hitting the drink. I've seen some horrific burns. It's what we all fear the most.' It was the only reference he'd made to the dangers he constantly faced. The rest of the evening had been spent reliving happy childhood memories, laughing, enjoying each other's company. Neither had mentioned the future, sharing the motto *wait and see*.

They'd walked along the dark, quiet streets and up the long hill to her house, arm in arm. Jonny had declined a cup of coffee and straddled the bicycle he'd borrowed. 'Hope you don't mind me shooting off. I'm meeting one of Uncle Ben's land girls. Can't keep her up too long, the dear darling. Bet you think I'm awful.'

'The poor girl probably thinks she's in love with you, but I'd never think you awful, Jonny. You're my special, wonderful friend. Please take care.'

'You too. And you're very special to me, Lou. Curious, isn't it? Why you and I have this distinct bond. I mean, I adore you but I'd never think of trying anything on with you.' He'd kissed both her cheeks and she did the same to his. They'd indulged in a lingering, tender embrace.

'It's you I think of when I'm up in the clouds,' he'd whispered, with some emotion. 'You I look forward to coming back to.' He'd cycled off.

She'd prayed it wouldn't be the last time she saw him. She repeated that silent, lonely prayer now.

'You're very close to Jonny,' Tom said. 'I'd always thought you'd get together, that you had an understanding. I was surprised when you married David.'

'Jonny and I will never include romance in our relationship. I can't explain it, we have some kind of unique connection. Rather like a brother and sister, I suppose. Why did you mention it?'

'I don't know really.' There was a noise overhead. He looked ceilingward. 'What was that? Is Ada home?'

'I, um…' Louisa reddened. She was no good at telling lies, particularly to someone as close to her as Tom was.

There was another thud from above. Tom saw her discomfort. 'Someone is upstairs. It's not a…? Have you got someone up there?'

'Tom Harvey! What do you think I am? No, it's nothing like that. I have a guest. He's not well. In fact he's very ill. He was sleeping when I last looked in on him. A book or something must have fallen off the bed. Will you excuse me? I'd better slip up and see if he wants anything.'

'He? Who is he?'

'Oh, you wouldn't know him. Stop looking at me like that, Tom. He's the same age as your Uncle Tristan but his illness makes him look much older.'

Louisa looked in on Bruce. He was still sleeping, fitfully now, breathing heavily and jerking about. She picked the book and a newspaper up off the floor and laid a cold, wet flannel over his feverish forehead. She'd check on him again in half an hour and if she thought it necessary, she'd summon the doctor.

When she closed the bedroom door Tom was there on the landing. 'Anything I can do?'

'No. He's sleeping.'

'But who is he? It's nothing new for you to do someone a kindness, Lou, but why are you being mysterious about this chap?'

'I'm not!'

'Why the protest?' Tom eased her away from the door. 'I think I'd better take a look at him.'

She clamped a hand over his on the glass doorknob. 'No! Don't you dare. I mean, you mustn't disturb him.'

Tom pulled his hand away, taking hers with it. Then he clutched both her hands in an indomitable grip. He stared into her eyes, trying to read her thoughts, her reasons, her anxieties. 'We've been friends all our lives. I don't like this, Lou. If you have a lover, well, it's none of my business, but otherwise I can't understand this secrecy. Are you in any kind of trouble? You would tell me if you were?'

Because his pleading was out of friendship and affection, and in view of his recent grief, she couldn't leave him in a state of worry over her. 'All right, Tom. Take a peep into the room. You'll see a frail, middle-aged man who's succumbing to a fatal disease. Reassure yourself that he's in no position to threaten me. He doesn't want any visitors but to be left to die in peace and dignity. Please, Tom, I'm asking you to keep his presence here to yourself.'

Tom did as she said and saw the fragile individual with a heavy breathing problem slumbering uneasily in the bed. After she'd shut the door a second time, he asked, 'Is he someone to do with Ada?'

Louisa had been offered a reasonable explanation but she couldn't involve Ada in a lie. 'No, he isn't. He's a poor dying man I came across quite recently. He'd returned to the area to… to seek out an old friend.' For good measure, she added, 'The vicar knows all about him.'

'He will have someone to come to collect him in due course though?'

'The arrangements have all been made.'

'That's something, I suppose. You're such a good person, Lou. If the whole world was full of people like you then terrible things like this war wouldn't happen. You still haven't told me the chap's name.'

Louisa had thought forward to this question. 'It's John Ash.'

Tom was thoughtful. 'You were right. I haven't heard that name before. Tell me if there's anything I can do to help. We're well into autumn, it's very chilly. I'll bring over some logs for your fires.'

'I'd be very grateful.'

They returned to the kitchen. Tom picked up his raincoat but didn't put it on. The weight of grief, of new responsibilities, was suddenly too heavy to bear. He needed the physical nearness of Louisa again, so he dropped his coat and went to her. 'I don't want to go home yet. Can I hold you again?'

She was happy with this. The embrace led to Tom placing his face on her shoulder, his warm breath gliding over her neck. 'You smell nice,' he said. Her perfume was so purely feminine. She gently ruffled his hair. She stroked his back. It was soothing for him, wonderful. 'I wish I could stay here like this but I have to get back to Mum and the others.' He broke away reluctantly.

'Yes. You mustn't have them worrying about you. It's stopped raining, you won't get wet on the ride home. I'll see you to the front door.'

There, she said, 'Pass on my condolences and my love to Aunt Em. I'll come to the farm tomorrow.'

'Good, good.' He gave Louisa one last hug. He made it a long one.

Louisa allowed him to hold her. Her arms were wrapped around his neck.

He snuggled her into him. His lips were near her neck. He kissed her there. It just happened but seemed a natural thing to do.

She was surprised that the brotherly affection had turned into something else. Tom shouldn't have kissed her in that way. But she didn't mind. She leaned her head away, to get a good look at him. Their eyes met. Something, a spark of something, flared between them. It was more than a momentary thing. Snap. One second they were as usual, close friends. Now there was something more.

He put his hands on her shoulders, worked his fingers and thumbs in a gentle yet intimate manner. She put her palms on his chest, watching the backs of her hands as she smoothed over the lapels of his jacket. It was normally the womanly way of making sure a man was tidy. She did it possessively. When she looked up, he gazed straight back into her eyes.

There came a cough, a loud cough that echoed down the stairs. Louisa turned worriedly in that direction. There was another, harsher cough. She returned her attention to Tom. 'I must go up to him.' He hadn't moved or changed his searching expression.

She reached up and brought his hands down off her shoulders. He gave his head a little shake as if coming out of a daydream. 'I'd better go.'

'As soon as Ada gets off shift tomorrow to watch over Mr Ash, I'll come to the farm.'

'I'll look forward to that.' He usually kissed Louisa goodbye. He wanted to now, so badly, but he was afraid he might move the kiss on from her cheek and kiss her mouth, kiss her from the reserves of the new feelings for her that were building up inside him, now that the boundary of their former familiarity had shifted. He was afraid he'd step over a line that would lead to them being alienated. Louisa was decent and honourable, and loyal to her husband's memory, and too aware that his usual responses to women rivalled Jonny and, once, Will. 'Cheerio then. I'll let myself out. You go up and see to this Mr Ash.'

'Bye, Tom.' She understood why he hadn't given her his customary kiss. A barrier had been crossed and there was no going back to the old way between them. It was as well that he hadn't stooped to her, for if his face had come close to hers, if his lips had been aimed near hers, she might have turned her head and kissed him fully, with passion and need. She didn't want him to go. This kind, unselfish man, so desirable to women. She was articulating in her head short sentences to ask him to stay, to come back later, and she was afraid she would actually say them.

The man upstairs started up a nasty bout of coughing and retching. Louisa headed for the stairs. Tom remembered the duty of care and protection he must return to and he opened the door. When she reached the top stair she looked down to the bottom. Tom was still there, having watched her mount every step. They both lifted a hand in a small farewell wave, which was also a gesture of something deeper.

Chapter Fourteen

Jill was on her own in the kitchen, wearing an apron, peeling vegetables for a mutton stew. Land Army members weren't required to do domestic work but she was pleased to be doing this today for the people she had come to see as her family. They were all at the church for Will's memorial service. Her mind crept often to Will and she'd blink on her sorrow. And think about Ronnie and ache to hear from him.

She had asked Mrs Em if she could use the telephone to ask news of Ronnie from his mother. Mrs Trenear didn't know about the engagement, only that she and Ronnie were penfriends. With the house empty it was the perfect time. Afraid of what she might hear, it took a few more minutes to summon the courage and go to the den. The operator connected her to Melvill Road in Falmouth surprisingly quickly. The breath caught in her chest as she plunged in, 'Hello, Mrs Trenear. It's Jill Laity.'

'Jill? Oh, hello, dear. How are you?'

'I'm fine, thank you.' Not wanting to waste the precious time allowance, Jill didn't dither too long getting to the point. 'The thing is, well, you see, I haven't heard from Ronnie for ages. I was wondering if all is well.'

'Why, yes, dear. We had a letter from him only yesterday. He manages to ring us occasionally. Mr Trenear and I will remind him to drop you a line. Of course, you understand that he's very busy. There's so much training going on. We never get a minute's peace here, as you must remember. I spoke to your Uncle Stanley the other day. He told me roughly where you are. It must be so much quieter there.'

'It is,' Jill said, aware again of the comparative cocoon she lived in. 'Cheerio, Mrs Trenear.' There was no point in asking her any more questions.

'Cheerio, dear. You take care.'

Jill dragged her feet back to the mutton stew and put it on the range to simmer. Why was Ronnie ignoring her? It couldn't be anything else. But surely he still loved her? He wouldn't have given her an engagement ring if she'd meant nothing to him. It didn't make sense.

The dogs started up a commotion in the yard. Surely the family weren't back already? Someone was entering through the front door. Jill went into the passage to see who it was. 'Faye! You're back.'

'Hello, Jill, give me a hand, will you, please?' Faye was trying to cope with bags and bundles.

Jill took a large bundle from her. She had a small shock when the bundle moved. 'Good heavens! It's a baby.'

'Carry him into the warm for me. I'll drag the rest inside. Babies need so many things.'

Jill took the baby close to the range, unwrapping the thick tartan blanket from its upper body. She gazed at it, instinctively cooing, and was thrilled to be rewarded with a coy smile from the chubby, pink-cheeked face. The baby's dark grey eyes were watery and nose snuffly as if it had a cold. From the edges of its white woollen bonnet tendrils of black hair were escaping. 'He's beautiful, Faye. Where did you get him? Or her?'

Putting the baby's double-ended bottle of milk on the table, Faye trudged to the little armchair Emilia used and collapsed into it. 'Phew! I'm exhausted. I thought I'd never get here. It was a devil of a job to get travel passes. The train journeys were horrendous, every carriage was packed with servicemen and anxious passengers. When we finally arrived in Truro I practically had to sell my soul to get a lift here. A smallholder from Mitchell was returning home. He put us down at Henna Lane. I've walked the rest of the way, praying that the rain would hold off. The first drops were falling when I reached the yard.' She yawned and stretched her aching limbs. 'Where's everyone got to?'

Jill explained.

'Oh, I'm just too late to join them. Dear, dear Will. Uncle Tris sent me a telegram about him to the croft where I was staying. Has it been awful for Aunt Em and Lottie?' She held out her arms. 'Here, I'll take him.' Once the baby was handed over there was instant eye contact between him and Faye. 'Has my father gone to the church?'

'He's not back yet.'

'Oh.' Faye made a face. 'Do you know if there's been any word from him?'

'None that I know of.' Jill hadn't taken her eyes off the baby. She had little knowledge of infants but reckoned this one was about a year old. 'He's very sweet. What's his name?'

Faye removed his bonnet and held him up so Jill could get a better view. She went a defiant red. 'I hope you're not going to be too shocked. Meet my son, Simon. His full name is Simon Harvey, because I'm not married to his father.'

A few months ago such an announcement would have made Jill looked hurriedly away, embarrassed for the mother, worried for her and her baby's future. Living among a down-to-earth family that kept no secret of their past indiscretions, where she had gained an understanding of why women slept with the men they were drawn to, she merely repeated, 'He's a beautiful child. I can see the Harvey resemblance now. Is there anything I can get you?'

'If there's any dregs in the teapot I'd welcome a cup. Simon will need his bottle warming quite soon. Jill, thanks… you know what I mean.'

Jill smiled. It was good to have formed another friendship. 'I can make you a cup of coffee, Nescafé. Corporal Nate Harmon, Lottie's young man, brought over a big box of treats last week.'

'I've got a lot of catching up to do. Everyone will be wondering about Simon's father. The truth is I've been very foolish, Jill. Sidney Eathorne's going to have a field day when the facts get about. I know I could pretend I was a widow but I've found one lie leads to another and I hate deceit. My baby's father is the laird of the estate where I'd been working. He told me his wife had died years ago. He's got a grown-up family. When I told him I was pregnant, he admitted that his wife has lived in Florence for years with her lover, that he has no intention of getting a divorce as the scandal would bring the estate down. Sorry, I ought to shut up.'

'I don't mind.' Jill made the coffee. 'I was brought up so quietly, in an atmosphere where real life never really entered. It's been so refreshing living here.'

'Thanks. You're easy to talk to, Jill. The farm's lucky to have you.' Faye took a sip of coffee and then the words spilled out of her. 'Despite my circumstances I consider myself very fortunate. Fergus settled a very generous sum on me. He arranged for me to live with a warm-hearted woman in a remote part of the estate for my confinement. I talked to her often about my life, my father. Mrs McPherson was a good listener. Finally she said that I'd turned to Fergus out of the need for love and affection from an older man rather than the desire for a love affair. I agreed with that. I haven't been left with a broken heart. Mrs McPherson encouraged me to see to my father before I made the decision where to settle with my baby. So I came down here after I'd weaned Simon.

'I was hoping I might build up a relationship with my father but I felt he owed me and Simon a home. I was feeling really mercenary about it. I had to wait longer than I'd planned bringing him down after he developed a bad cold. But up there in the peacefulness of Scotland, I found I couldn't resent my father as much as before for his lack of interest in me. He's a very mixed-up soul. I talked it over with Mrs McPherson, agreeing that I had to at least let my father see his grandson. I could be risking rejection in even stronger terms if my father is ashamed of me and refuses to accept Simon. If it turns out he's not interested, then I'll go back up to Scotland and wait out the war. One day I'm hoping to take Simon to Washington to meet my mom. She knows about him, by the way. She's disappointed I'm not decently married but she's happy to receive us both.'

'I'm sure everything will work out, Faye.'

'I hope you're right, Jill. You got on with quite well with my father, didn't you?'

'I could see Ben's always had a lot on his mind. Perhaps he's gone away to sort himself out.'

'I do hope so.' Faye sat forward and grew earnest. 'I came here first today because the instant I reached the village and saw the filling station with my father's name painted on it, I lost my nerve. I thought I'd find the courage to go to Tremore after I'd spoken to Aunt Em. I was going to ask her if I could come back here if things were too awful. Now I'll be able to go on to Tremore with Uncle Tris. I can't see him being too horridly judgemental. I'll be able to get Simon settled in before my father makes his reappearance. I wonder where he is. I hope he's all right. He was in such a strange state the last time I saw him. Can't help worrying – he is my dad. I suppose you know he had a phone call. Wish I knew who it was from.'

Simon pushed two fingers into his mouth and sucked on them contentedly. She kissed him. 'Well, my little man, won't you be a surprise for your grandfather? I'd better see about getting you changed and fed and making you presentable. You're about to be introduced to a lot of your family.'

–

Lottie had stayed dry-eyed throughout the memorial service. A young-looking figure engulfed in black, she was in the churchyard, at the graves of her father and sister and weeping as if she'd never stop. She'd told the others to go on without her, that she wanted a little time alone. She became aware there was someone close by. Tom probably, keeping watch over her.

She sniffed and swallowed and brought herself under control. 'I'm all right. You needn't stay.'

'Honey, it's me.'

'Nate. Oh, Nate.' She eased into a weak, watery smile. 'I thought you couldn't get away.'

He went to her, making to hold her. 'It took a lot of bribery and pleading but I managed to change duty. I didn't want to infringe on your family grief but I had to see you, Lottie. Make sure you're OK. I'll go if it's what you want.'

'No. It's good to see you.' In her despondency she was pleased to have him here, delighted with his thoughtfulness. It was typical of him, he always put others first, and did so in a humble, sensitive way. Leaning against him, arms wrapped round his waist, she gazed down at the graves. 'I can't make sense of it.'

'What exactly?' His voice was soothing, telling her to take her time.

'Everything. Life. Death. The world. The purpose of it all. Does everyone go through this, do you think?'

'I guess they do. You've known a lot of sadness, Lottie.' He read the inscribed words. 'Alec, aged forty-two. Your father was only a young man. Jenna. She was just twenty-five days old. Your sister was hardly here at all.'

'And now thousands of ordinary people are dying before their time every day. Innocent civilians, and young men like Will with his life in front of him, sacrificing their dreams. I suppose it's all for a reason and it will become clear to us one day. I wish the war wasn't happening, Nate.

Yet if it wasn't I wouldn't have met you. I don't like that thought.'

'Nor do I.'

They intensified their embrace, making the precious moments last, creating a memory.

'I'd better run you home, then I'll make myself scarce.'

'Mum won't expect me back for a while longer.' She pulled off her felt hat. 'I want to make the most of this time together.' God only knew how much longer she would have him as hers, locally, alive. As a medic he stood a marginally better chance of lasting through the brutal reality of a battlefield, but the dreadful possibility of him being killed was all too vividly true. They had found they could talk to each other in total honesty and had bravely faced the subject.

'You mustn't grieve over me for always, honey,' he'd said, placing a gentle hand over her heart. 'Never forget me in here, I'll ask no more of you than that. Then you must get on with your life. Live, Lottie, live the time you have to the full and you'll be living for both of us.'

'I will, Nate,' she'd promised. They'd touched briefly on the gulf of their differences, like the two thousand miles of Atlantic Ocean between their homes. If there was ever going to be anything permanent between them, one of them was going to have to make a major sacrifice. Nothing like that mattered for now. If it proved possible for them to make such a decision, they'd be happy to face it then.

He said now, 'Let's go to the little valley.'

In their special place, he led the way to the patch of wild grass pressed down by the previous meetings. They sat, kissed and kissed again. Nate encircled her lovingly in his arms and eased her to lie down with him. 'Keep your eyes closed, Lottie. Let the earth hold us, link us together. There's just us. For now there's no one else but us in the whole world. Good ground beneath us, the beautiful sky above us, creation all around us.'

'I wish we could stay here for ever.'

'We will, in a way. This afternoon in October 1943 will never come again. It's ours. It belongs to us and always will.' He leaned over her. Touched one of her pearl-drop earrings. 'Can I have this? I'll take it everywhere I go and look at it every day. It'll be great having a part of you with me.'

'Of course you can. You can take them both.'

'I want just the one. I'll bring it back to you one day, when the world's safe to live in again.'

It was exactly at this moment that Lottie's great fondness for Nate turned into the deepest love. It was such a strong sensation, so exquisite, infinitely overwhelming, making her body leap into a new way of being, and she let out a bewildered, needy cry. 'I want something of yours, Nate. I want you.'

'I've got something for you.' He reached inside his tunic and pulled out a box. 'It's a necklace made of local freshwater pearls. Wear it often, and wherever you go I'll be right along there with you.'

Lottie sat up so he could fasten his gift round her neck. 'It's the most perfect thing in the world.'

He smiled deep into her eyes. They moved in at the same moment for their next kiss. After a long time, it was he who pulled away. She tugged him back to her. 'Don't stop.'

'We should think carefully before getting into something we, you I mean, might regret.' He kept a distance although his voice was raw with desire.

She lay down again and gazed up at him, loving him even more for the anxiety he showed for her. 'I could never regret loving with you, Nate. Where could be better than here in our special place?'

'You're so young, Lottie. I've got to be responsible.'

'Darling, we don't know how long we'll have to be together.'

'I know, but right now you're upset over your brother. Making love and the possibility of babies is a serious matter, Lottie.'

'I know what you're saying, Nate. It's good and noble of you. But what does a wedding ring matter?'

'It would be everything to you if I end up dead and you with a baby. It'll ruin your life, Lottie. I've seen it happen to other young women. I can't do that to you. I won't risk it.'

She traced her fingers along his frowning brow. 'You really are the most wonderful of men. You don't mind if I tell you that I love you?'

'Not if you don't mind me saying the same to you. I love you absolutely, Lottie. Now let me get you safely home.'

–

Out in the lane, by the light of a dim torch, Tom opened the back-seat door of the taxicab that Louisa arrived in. He helped her to alight and pushed a ten-shilling note at the driver and told him to keep the change. He'd gone back to work shortly after the memorial service and was still in his work clothes but had been careful to scrub himself fresh and clean.

He made his voice nonchalant, as if it was the same as every other time she had come here. 'Glad you could make it, Lou.' *Glad the day is over and you're here at last!* He'd spent the days since taking her the news of Will's death wondering if the birth of the intense attraction between them would die a natural death. It hadn't. Not at all. It was the reverse. It was getting stronger all the time. So strong it was almost painful. But it was the way he wanted it.

'How are you, Tom?' she asked, as always. *Have you been waiting for these moments as much as I have?* She had gone over and over the strange beauty of their new relationship. Was Tom's grief part of the reason for the new ground they had covered? It must be. She still loved David. Had never thought to care about another man. She couldn't possibly feel the same way about Tom. Good old, considerate Tom, her former playmate. Yet it seemed she did. For the nearness of him was wonderful. And now he had taken her arm, pressed it inside his, and fantastic little shivers were racing up and down her flesh. 'And the family? I was so upset that I couldn't be at the church, but there was no question of Ada getting time off and I couldn't leave Mr Ash alone. I feel bad about fibbing to Aunt Em about my reason.'

Tom had escorted her to the front door many times before. One did this to Louisa, so dear and sweetly refined and seemingly delicate, leading her to the front door rather than through the dirt and smells of the farmyard. Louisa brought the protective nature out in a man. Inspired the desire to treat her as a princess. God above, she was special. Utterly special and utterly divine. Why had he never seen it before? Wasted so much time dallying about like a he-goat?

Louisa was glad to be taken the long way round to the front door. It gave them more time to spend alone. She had been alone with Tom many times, but not until a few days ago had she enjoyed the masculinity of him. He was powerfully built, good looking, eligible, vital and virile. It was no wonder women flocked to be with him. Now, she wanted to be the only woman he'd ever be interested in again.

They got to the door. He turned his back to it. 'Louisa?'

'Yes, Tom?'

The door was opened. Disappointment cut into them both. 'Saw you coming. Well, bring Louisa inside, Tom,' Emilia said.

It was hard for him to obey his mother, to relinquish Louisa to her, to watch them hug and kiss cheeks, to hear his mother thank her for coming, to even hear them cry for a while over Will, when all he wanted to do was to be alone with Louisa. Alone, and to lay a claim on her.

Louisa stared into the almost empty sitting room. Only Perry was there, a black armband on the sleeve of his white shirt, and Lottie, in her coverall, sitting astride a chair and leaning dreamily on her arms. 'Is your Uncle Tristan here?' She peered anxiously into each corner, as if he would suddenly loom out at her and besiege her with disapproving looks.

Emilia ushered her to a chair. 'Don't worry, he's gone back to Tremore. You're hardly going to believe who with.' She launched into the family's surprise and delight about Faye and her baby. 'We've told her not to hide

147

herself away. She'll have to face a lot of tittle-tattle and some outright criticism, but she's made friends since she's been here and they won't be judgemental. She's proud of her son and shouldn't be shy in showing him off.'

Louisa hoped the distraction of Faye's baby in his life at Tremore would detract some of Tristan's antipathy from herself when next they met.

It seemed an age to Tom before he got his wish, when Lottie went upstairs to chat to a very subdued Jill, and Perry insisted on escorting his mother up for an early night. 'I bet you wish my Uncle Tris wasn't in Hennaford at all. You mustn't mind him anyway.'

'It's not important what he thinks about me.' Louisa aimed a convincing smile at him.

He imprinted that lovely smile in his mind. 'Is it important what I think of you?'

Asked a question like this before and she would have lowered her gaze. Not this time. 'Very important.'

'Your taxi's not due yet. Lou, we need to talk. Don't you agree?'

'Yes, Tom, I do.'

'We can't stay here. Someone might come down for a glass of water or something.' He clenched his hands nervously. 'Will you slip up the back stairs to my room? No one will know if we creep carefully past Jill's room. Just for a while. Is that all right?' Louisa was dressed too well to suggest somewhere outside and it was very cold. He'd never expect her to suffer discomfort.

She fiddled with her handbag. 'That will be fine, Tom.'

Tom preferred to have his room in the older part of the house, where he had greater privacy and could keep a better eye on the yards. He lit a lantern and Louisa looked around the messy confines. 'I've never been one to stand on ceremony,' he explained, chewing his lip.

'I know. That's what I like about you,' she smiled into his eyes.

He paced the rug, for the first time shy with a woman. 'Well, this is all very strange. I never thought this would happen... I mean, us. There is an us, isn't there, Lou?' He was so anxious she'd answer otherwise.

She stretched up and stroked his burning cheek. 'Yes, Tom. I rather think there is.'

They reached for each other. The first touch of their lips bred love and a desire that was urgent and fierce and unstoppable. Louisa had made her husband wait for intimacy until their wedding night, but with Tom, while keeping her lips against his and kissing him hungrily, she was pulling off her cardigan and kicking off her shoes. Tom would have been happy just to have her with him, to talk to her, but her need for him caused him to be consumed with need. As they opened up more and more to each other, dragging off clothes, mouth hard against mouth, they couldn't wait to be entirely naked and fell down on the bed and quickly found each other in the deepest places.

They didn't know if they were being noisy. During their joining, every exquisite, writhing moment of it, they thought about nothing else except the other. Loving and living and being in the most precious and fulfilling way. It seemed they were united and moving entirely together for minutes and for eternity.

Panting, laughing softly, Tom lay over her body, supporting himself on his forearms. 'I thought I might fall in love one day but not for some years, and not with you, darling Lou. It frightens me now that I might have missed out on being with you. I love you. I've said that to girls before, just to get my way with them, but I really do love you. You do believe me? You do want me to be in love with you? You do want me too? Please don't say this is a mistake.'

She pushed a damp muddle of his thick hair, turned a burnished reddish-brown in the lantern light, off his forehead. 'The only mistake I could have made was not going along with my feelings for you, Tom. I love you.'

Replete and content he lay beside her, jamming her between his arms. 'I think Will would have been very surprised but happy for us. With you at my side, I feel able to take on whatever life will throw at me. I wish you could stay all night.'

She snuggled into him. 'Me too, but apart from shocking everyone I must get back for my guest.'

'Oh, yes, Mr John Ash. I'm most eager to meet him.'

Prickles of unease made worms wriggle in her stomach. 'He's a very private man, Tom.'

He kissed the crown of her head, caressed the soft skin of her neck. 'It won't hurt to say a quick hello. Will it?'

'I suppose not. But I insist that only you can speak to him, Tom. I'm asking you again to keep his presence in my house a secret.'

Chapter Fifteen

In the cold early hours, Ben lay on the narrow camp bed, smoking, trying to unwind. He studied his hands, hands now trained to kill in two rapid shots if necessary. He marvelled that they were steady, for it wasn't at all how he was feeling. He was in a state of exhilaration, nervous anticipation. His greatest hopes were about to be realized, to serve his country, to play a part in freeing Europe of Nazi tyranny, to help open up the Second Front.

He would have liked to write to Tris, just about general things, but secrecy and security was paramount. Tris had to be wondering where the hell he was and what he was up to; although he might have taken a guess from the small clue he'd left behind on his desk prior to departure – old correspondence from a vineyard he'd had dealings with in Bordeaux before the war. Tris had been an officer of many years standing, he knew about the machinations of war; perhaps Tris had surmised that he'd been asked – due to his extensive personal knowledge of the French countryside – to join the French Section of the War Office. If he had, hopefully he'd tell Faye not to think too badly of him over his long, silent absence.

He wanted to write to Faye. It was nearly Christmas. He didn't want her to believe he'd abandoned her again and had no wish to contact her at all during this family-orientated time of the year. He wanted to telephone Faye, hear her voice. Ask her to call him Father. He had developed a fondness for her in the long, lonely hours of rest following the rigorous daily training, of scaling assault courses, learning how to pass on coded messages, the horrors of mock but realistic interrogation, and how to adopt a totally new personality, all for operations behind enemy-occupied lines. The training was tough, it required strong mental application, a positive attitude, a passion to do the job, and learning to care for his daughter hadn't been difficult in comparison. He couldn't altogether say he loved Faye, and yet he had to. He kept thinking about her. She was his child. His flesh and blood.

Merely because he'd longed for a son he hadn't loved her enough. What a shallow man he was, if he could call himself a man. He had hoped for glory in the last war, but through one unfortunate occurrence, a silly little happening really, he had sought refuge in hurt and bitterness. How cowardly of him. He had forsaken his dear, good-natured wife by setting her hopes and aspirations aside, and then he had looked again at Emilia. In another act of small-mindedness he had chosen to hate Emilia simply for not loving him again. During his clash with her she had hurled at him how he had once been. It cut through him like a sword now to remember what it had felt like to be truly happy and content.

He had sought a contentment of sorts up here in a secret location in the Highlands, unaware that, although many miles away from Faye, how much closer she had been. Other training had involved learning the preparation and setting of explosives, picking up weapons dropped from a plane. There had been a short parachute fall off a high tower; tomorrow would come the real thing. He could never become a soldier but he was to operate as an SOE (Special Operations Executive) agent, a member of 'the Firm'.

There was no contentment now. He felt he was disintegrating. Pain and confusion was fragmenting him. He'd missed out on the greater part of Faye's life. If he was killed he'd never see her again. He sat up on the edge of the bed and stubbed out the cigarette. God, how he wanted to see Faye. To throw his arms round her and tell her he loved her. She'd said she was leaving Tremore for a while. She might never come back. She probably hated him. *Oh God, why did I waste my life?*

In the terrible dark void of total loneliness he wept blisteringly hot tears, rocking, hugging himself. He pictured Faye in the hallway of his house, saying goodbye. Goodbye perhaps for ever. If he got back, if she wasn't there, he might spend the rest of his life searching for her, only to find she'd reject him… If that was to happen, he hoped, he prayed, he'd serve well in France and be killed.

'*Dad?*'

What was that? It was as if someone had spoken. Faye? It was a memory of her. In the hall, the last time he'd seen her, yes! Dear God, yes! She'd called him Dad! She'd asked him if he was all right. For days after the clash with Emilia, everything had been a blur. He'd forgotten what Faye had said to him. Forgotten those wonderful words. She did care for him. Faye cared for him! He was laughing and crying now. 'I love you, Faye. Please, God, let me live so I can tell her.'

He'd been told that in the event of his death, some time afterwards, his next of kin would be informed of his service. He had already lodged a letter to Tristan with his solicitor. He could tell Faye he loved her. He still had time to write a letter. Leaping up, without bothering to mop his face dry, he went to the room of a fellow trainee to beg some stationery.

Chapter Sixteen

Jill, Lottie and Emilia were busy in the flour house plucking poultry, most of which would find their way on to the festive plates of the local hotels and restaurants, the infirmary and cottage hospitals, and as soup in military canteens. The birds were hanging up outside by their legs in a long line; the heads of the hens and cockerels newly pulled; the geese, ducks and turkeys newly decapitated; a swift, merciful end at Tom's mastery.

Lottie had insisted Jill be excused this task. Then Tom had baffled Lottie by insisting on seeing to it all himself. 'What are you talking about, Tom? Mum and I have killed many a bird or beast.'

'Let Tom do it. It's his way of looking after us,' Emilia had said, quickly looking away. 'Since Will…'

Lottie had choked back a lump of grief. Sometimes she didn't know how she'd get through if she hadn't met Nate. Sometimes, as now, she didn't know how to look at Jill – there was still no news from Ronnie. The not knowing was beginning to drag Jill down. Now that she had Nate, and Tom and Louisa were courting, Lottie thought it must seem doubly hard for her. She had hugged her mother. 'Are you sure you're up to this, Mum? Perry says you need to rest. You're so big now. Why don't you go inside into the warm and put your feet up? We can manage here.'

'Go inside and darn a few socks, you mean?' Emilia had smiled. 'I might be waddling around like an old duck but I've not turned into an old dear, Lottie Harvey. I'll sit down here out of the draughts.' She headed for an old circular-seated chair. Tom had put a cushion on it. It helped ease her crushing sorrow, having her remaining children fussing over her.

As the women worked, they chatted about mundane things, normal things, putting in nothing about the war, the subject so often on everyone's lips. The boxes for the feathers and down, which would be saved for other use, were steadily being filled. When a dozen birds had been plucked, Emilia said, 'You girls can carry these along to the kitchen. Tilda will help me with the cleaning and trussing.'

'Poor Mum,' Lottie said, when she and Jill were back in the flour house. With deft wrist actions, she started denuding a duck of its soft white down. 'She must be remembering all the fun we had in the old days, times like when Will pushed handfuls of feathers down the back of my dress and threatened to tar and feather me, treacle being the tar. I was a right little pest to him back then. Once, Tom nearly choked on a mouthful of down. Will dragged him outside and thought he was doing the right thing by pumping cold water over his face. I think it was the only time I saw Tom cry. He couldn't breathe and he said he'd been very scared. Will called him a baby. Mum took Tom inside and dried him off and gave him a big slice of saffron cake. Will was disgusted. He called Tom soft for that and he was bloody furious with him for not sharing the cake. Mum and Tom have always had a special closeness. So have I with her. Will always seemed a little remote from us, like my dad. I wonder if Mum feels guilty over it. She's got no reason to, of course, but death does that to you, makes you feel guilty about things you wish you'd done or hadn't done, things you wish you could change. Mind you, Will could be an awkward so-and-so. Bless him.'

'It's good that you're enjoying memories of Will,' Jill said, working on a hen at a slower rate than Lottie, her inexperienced fingers and thumbs aching, her nose clogged with the coppery smell of blood. 'I wish I had brothers or sisters.'

'Well,' Lottie reached out and tickled her cheek with down, 'you've got some now. You might be getting a niece or nephew soon, the way Tom and Louisa behave. There might be a rushed wedding. Just the occasion for you to wear your new frock.'

'Lottie!' Jill could never get used to her friend's direct-ness.

'Oh, so we're Miss Prim now. You know what they do, don't you?'

Jill knew. She had nearly died of embarrassment to suddenly be faced with Tom and Louisa coming out of his room, glued together, eyes bright, with the telltale flush of passionate intimacy on their faces. 'They may only have done it once, Lottie. They may not have done it at all. They're obviously deeply in love. It might have been just the excitement of discovering their feelings that made them… made them… oh, Lottie!'

'Oh, don't be a fool, Jill. I was on my way to you, remember? I saw them disappearing down the back stairs. I looked in Tom's room and his bed was a mangled mess. It's easy to tell by the way they sparkle together that

157

they're lovers. I never thought I'd see Tom become moon-struck over someone for many years. I'm glad it's Louisa, although how she'd fit in here as a farmer's wife, I haven't a clue, but there's no point in thinking about that unless it actually happens.'

Jill paused to think. 'Louisa is a widow. She's used to intimacy. Tom's a responsible man, he probably won't get her into trouble. They're planning to get married, I'm sure. Mrs Em seems pleased they're walking out together. Do you think Mrs Em knows? About them…?'

'Of course she does! The last thing she is is stupid. I think Pappa's had a word with Tom.'

'How do you know?'

'Well, he's had one with Nate. Warned him that he'd break his neck if he tried anything on with me.'

'Gosh. That's a good thing though, isn't it? You don't have to worry when you're alone with Nate. I think it's wonderful that you have a stepfather looking out for you, protecting your honour.'

Lottie laughed as she laid the duck down in the box for the kitchen. 'Honour? You're so old-fashioned, but it's exactly how I like you.' She kept her face side-on to Jill, blushing. 'Have you sometimes wished that you and Ronnie… got to know each other a little better?'

'Yes. Sometimes.'

'Yes! Yes? I wasn't expecting that. I thought you'd tick me off. Don't let this upset you, Jill, but you must be pleased now that things didn't go any further, due to his long silence.'

Jill stared into space, trying to picture Ronnie at his desk, pointing to areas on foreign maps while delivering lectures, inspecting troops on parade, sharing a drink in the officers' mess. A photo of her tucked lovingly inside his breast pocket. She hoped he remembered all the wonderful times they had spent together, the future they had planned. She hoped he remembered her at all. Her voice came thick with tears, 'Sometimes I don't know what to think. I keep writing but get nothing back. He could be on some sort of secret mission, I suppose. I can't really ring his mother again. I'll send her a Christmas card and hope if Ronnie gets leave he'll see it and get in touch.'

Lottie hated seeing her so strained. Jill must be feeling a strong sense of rejection. All she could do was try to cheer her. 'There must be some kind of simple explanation. He might just turn up here one day and surprise you.'

Jill's eyes widened in hope. 'Do you really think so? That would be wonderful. Thanks, Lottie.'

'Don't give up hope.'

'I won't give up. Not until there's a final word of some sort.'

They resumed work. Soon they would be able to take the last of the poultry into the kitchen. The plumpest goose was for the farm's Christmas Day table, to which those from Tremore and Nate had been invited. Jill asked, 'Lottie, are you in love with Nate?'

'That's a first.' Lottie's dark brown eyes crinkled merrily at the corners. 'You asking a personal question.' She hadn't told anyone how she felt about Nate or shown off the necklace he'd given her, fearing comments or counsel would spoil everything, dull or lessen its significance. 'Yes, I love him very much.'

'I couldn't be more pleased for you, Lottie.'

They were joined by Perry. 'Hello, Pappa, have you come to see if we're nearly finished?'

'No darling, I've come to bring this to Jill.'

'It's a letter!' Jill dropped the goose in her hands and wiped them down her dungarees.

Lottie stood at her side. 'Is it from Ronnie?'

'No.' Jill couldn't hide her crushed hopes and then her fear. 'Oh my God, I've seen this handwriting before. It's from his mother.'

—

Nate didn't know that children could make so much noise, that they could shriek shriller than a prairie cat, that they could work up the energy to outrival a cattle stampede, but he was having a whole lot of fun. He had not been particularly looking forward to this afternoon. Children from all around the area of Devoran, which was four miles from Truro, seven miles from Falmouth, had been collected by a convoy of trucks and brought to the village hall for a Christmas party. Used to wide open spaces and very few people at home, the lack of privacy and constant activity at the camp was often a bind, but to see the joy and delight on these kids' faces made every second worthwhile.

He'd help lift them down off the trucks. Families of kids sharing the same features, clutching hands, apprehensive, some tearful, in woollen balaclavas and pixie bonnets and white ankle socks. Some spoke with different or foreign accents, signifying that they were evacuees or refugees. 'Poor kids,' Herv had said, handing out fistfuls of chocolate. 'Some have never seen a candy bar. It's a cold winter ahead for most of them. Guess some have lost their daddies. Hey, kids! We've got Santa Claus coming to see ya, and the Old Man from the North. You haven't heard of him, have you? There's no need to be scared. He'll be wearing a big hat and will have a nice long black beard.'

The children's eyes had grown wide in amazement over the wealth of food, roast turkey and trimmings, although one or two hadn't been sure about putting cranberry sauce on their meat, unshakeable in their belief it was really jam. They had devoured basins of traditional pudding and mock cream. Afterwards, Nate had sat with two children on his knees, the hall in silence at first, while Herv had run the film *The Reluctant Dragon*. Then the sighs of enchantment had been replaced with lusty screams of glee as the story unfolded of good overcoming evil.

'You going to help us overcome Hitler, mister?' a little boy asked Nate when he was stacking the chairs away. 'Like the dragon got rid of the evil people?'

Nate knelt down to him. 'I sure am going to try, sonny.' He gave the boy a packet of Wrigley's chewing gum, thinking about how the coming huge operation he and his comrades were training for would take him away from Lottie. Some time, not too far into the future, he would be called on to use his skills not in the comparative safety of the field hospital here, where he saw only cases of accidental wounds, routine operations like an appendectomy, and cracked heads from the occasional drunken brawl, but he'd be launched into the theatre of battle.

His hands were suddenly filled with smaller ones and he was hauled off to dance around the eight-foot-high decorated fir tree. When it was time for the children to be buttoned back into their coats by the willing army of local women that were helping out, he watched as they each received a bag of goodies to take home with the presents Santa Claus had distributed. The families regrouped, each brother and sister making sure their siblings had its share. No one had come alone, everyone had at least one friend. Life must be like this for Lottie, he thought, envying her her way of life. She had parents, cousins, aunts, uncles, a grandpa. Sadly, only one brother now, but there was another sibling on the way. He was happy to see the mischief shining out of the little faces as the kids filed reluctantly out of the hall. Mischief. Lottie had told him about some of the mischief she and her brothers had got up to. And their deeds of daring. She had such a great home life, an assured future as she was to inherit half of the farm.

He was falling ever more deeply in love with Lottie. He loved her simplicity and confidence, her loyalty and toughness, her gentle femininity. He wanted to be with her all the time. He could never unsettle or hurt Lottie. If events proved they had a future, what would happen then? She had a lot going for her. It would be wrong, unkind, to try to take her away from all that. Everyone else she loved was here in Cornwall. He had no one back home.

'You're staring at nothing again,' Herv chuckled, nudging him so hard he was nearly unbalanced. 'Got your little farm gal on your mind again? Thought you'd know better.'

'There's nothing or no one I know better than Lottie.'

'Yeh? Got it bad, eh?'

Nate grinned. 'As bad and as wonderful as it gets.'

'Well, you shouldn't risk losing a sweetie like that. You gotta do something about it.'

'Herv, I intend to. I just want her folks to get to know me a little more first.'

'Uncle Tris, what's going on? Where did these children come from? I don't recognize them from the village.' Faye was in the hall getting Simon's pushchair ready. She was wearing her raincoat and leather boots, about to walk to the village to catch the bus into Truro, to show off Simon to Louisa. Both had been busy for some weeks and had only been keeping in touch over the telephone. She was taken aback to find herself facing a brood of sulky little strangers. In ill-fitting, shapeless coats, tattered mufflers and mud-lagged rubber boots, the two boys, twins of about eight years, and a girl roughly half their age, clamped between them, stared out from pale, grimy, tired faces.

'They're evacuees.' Tris had just come back from the farmyard and had left his boots in the vestibule. He went to gently ease the children forward but together they veered away from him. 'Someone from the WRVS has literally just dropped them off at the front door. There's so many rooms here – we have no choice, apparently. Ben would have been approached to take in evacuees before, but the authorities weren't too sure because of the fierce manner in which he'd refused to give work to a conscientious objector. You don't mind, do you? These poor little tykes have been put through a terrible time.' He waved a folder he was holding. 'Got the details here. And their ration books.'

'I don't mind them being here at all.' Faye knelt down to the trio. Now she would have a more particular way of participating in the war effort. The children seemed comfortable with her nearness. On closer observance a knot of horror caught in her throat. All the children had runny noses and smelled offensively, the girl of urine. 'Hello there. My name's Faye, and this is my Uncle Tristan. I'm sure he won't mind if you call him Uncle Tris, as I do. Will you tell me your names?'

All the children kept their mouths clamped in a tight, straight line.

Faye turned to the twin on her right. 'Would you like to start? Then we can all trot along to the kitchen to Agnes, the housekeeper, and we'll find you something nice to eat and drink.'

The promise of something for his and his brother and sister's woefully thin tummies made the boy find his tongue. 'I'm Bob. He's Len, and she's Pearl. Are you going to work us? The last people we was wiv worked us hard.' Bob displayed his hands and Len and Pearl followed suit. All six palms were raw and blistered. Their nails were torn and blackened, skin scratched and bruised. Their skinny legs were mottled from the cold and there were bruises on their shins that looked as if they'd been brutally smacked. 'Our mum'n'dad's dead. Mum got a letter about Dad. Then a bomb got her. We got no house left. Our cat got blown up too.'

Anger grew in Faye against the perpetrators of the abuse. 'Well, we'll be pleased if you keep your rooms tidy, but don't worry, we won't be expecting you to work at all. Will we, Uncle Tris? You can stay with us and my baby, Simon. All we want is for you to be warm and happy.'

'We want you to feel safe and comfortable.' Tristan hadn't been given time for much reaction as the WRVS member had rushed off to some more urgent business. He was as outraged as Faye about the way the children had been treated. He rubbed his hands together in the way he did when ready for action and confident he could deal with the situation. Running Ben's concerns, being a father figure to Faye and Simon, had given his lonely life fresh meaning; sheltering three deprived little children shouldn't prove too difficult. He liked it here at Tremore. When Ben came back he'd ask if he could stay on for good. *If* Ben came back – he had a good idea what Ben was doing…

He put on the bright cooing voice he'd used with his own children when they were young. 'Well, children, Faye will get you settled in. I'm sure you'd all like a lovely bath. I'll run along to a nice lady I know, Mrs Killigrew. She works for the Red Cross, she should be able to fix you all up with some clothes and shoes, perhaps even a few toys.'

'Toys? We've never had much toys before. Have you got real soap, mister? Hot water?' Len asked, amazed at what seemed like his family's sudden turn of good fortune, although he was still in suspicious retreat. 'We gotta wash from a tin bowl?'

'No, old chap.' Tristan knelt down to his level. 'Faye and I have got a nice surprise for you. This house belongs to Faye's father, and it has a proper bathroom, with a porcelain bath big enough for all of you to get into together. And we've some real soap.'

'I've got soap that smells of the sea and fresh air,' Faye said. 'The water will be lovely and warm and we've got big fluffy towels to dry you off afterwards. Pearl, sweetheart –' she was longing to reassure the trembling little girl, who was clearly overwhelmed with the situation – 'I can make your hair all pretty for you and put a ribbon in it. Would you like that? Uncle Tris and I will have lots of treats in store for you, but first things first. Food. You're hungry. Come with me and you can all eat as much as you like.'

She put a tentative finger on Pearl's tiny, ill-treated hand. 'Will you come with me, darling?' The girl seemed as if she needed to cry a stream of tears but they were dammed up inside her by great misery. She pulled in her mouth and nodded. A picture of her being too afraid to disobey an order came into Faye's mind. She got up to give Pearl and her brothers space, to show them she was not a threat. She took off her raincoat. 'Follow me, children. Come and meet Simon. He's with Agnes. He'll love the extra company.'

She led the way and they trooped after her, keeping in a pack.

'I'll cycle over to Ford House, see what Elena Killigrew can do for us, Faye,' Tristan said.

He was soon on the doorstep of the woman who was known as owning the most charitable heart in the village. Elena Killigrew was the daughter of Hennaford's former Methodist minister, a mother of two adopted orphans from twelve years ago, and she had an evacuee and foreign refugees in her home. She worked tirelessly for several charities. Tristan hoped he wouldn't have to stay here long. He hated coming to this place. It had belonged to him years ago, it was where Jonny had been born, and also his secret half-sister – it was where Ursula had died.

'Mr Harvey?' Elena Killigrew raised her softly sculptured brows. 'Is something wrong?'

'I know it's a surprise for you to see me here, Mrs Killigrew,' he said apologetically. 'Nothing's wrong. I was wondering if you could help me.' He outlined the purpose of his visit.

Elena seemed to have a cold and she dabbed at her eyes and nose. 'I'm very sorry. All the good used clothes and the toys that I'd taken in recently were only collected this morning. I'm afraid I really haven't got anything to spare. You could try Mrs Louisa Carlyon in Truro. She gathers in far more than I do, living in a larger area.'

Disappointment made Tristan fight the urge not to screw up a belligerent face. Coming here had churned up raw, sordid memories. The last thing he wanted was to ask a favour from the woman who had been the illegitimate, birthmarked baby born here and destined to haunt his peace ever since. 'Yes, thank you anyway, perhaps I'll do that.'

'I'm sorry I couldn't help you, Mr Harvey.' Elena sniffed, raising her hanky again.

Tristan became aware that a cold wasn't her problem. 'Mrs Killigrew, is all well with you?' He was fearful for her husband, Jim. 'You've not had bad news, I hope.'

'Good and bad, Mr Harvey. Jim's ship was hit by a torpedo in the Bristol Channel. Not all hands were lost, thank the Lord. Jim was picked up almost at once by a British frigate and then passed on to a fishing boat. He's alive. He'll be coming home quite soon, but he's lost an arm.' She was sobbing her heart out now. 'I'll have him back for good, Mr Harvey. I know it's not the way I should be thinking but I'm not sorry he'll be out of the constant danger. He'll find life hard with only one good arm but he's alive and for that I shall always be eternally grateful.'

Tristan touched her arm. 'I understand. I've great respect for Jim. He worked hard during his time at Ford Farm. He built his business up from virtually nothing.

I'm sure he'll find the enterprise to carry on and lead a worthwhile life. Does Emilia know?'

'Not yet.' Elena dried away her tears.

'I'll call in there. She'll come down, and I'm sure that Perry, as a fellow amputee, will be able to offer advice to Jim.'

Tristan went on his way, his heart as heavy as lead. Emilia would drop whatever she was doing and rush to comfort Elena Killigrew. While being relieved that Jim was alive, she'd be wishing Will had shared a similar fate. He was wishing one of the same for Jonny, rather than the awful, not unlikely, alternative of him being blown to smithereens or burned alive.

It seemed churlish not to cycle on to Chy Lowena, Louisa's house. Good men were being killed and maimed every minute – what did a sordid secret from the past matter when some neglected and frightened children needed the basic necessity of clothes on their backs?

The horror of his appearance reflected on Louisa's face greatly surpassed the surprise that Elena Killigrew had shown. 'What on earth do you want? Couldn't Faye make it here today?'

'I...' She was so like Ursula at that moment, Tristan lost his words. There wasn't a strong physical resemblance, thank goodness, or people would have noticed it, but he, as Ursula's husband, had been close enough to her to be aware of the little things, a twist of the features, a particular tiny lift of a hand, a certain unconscious flicker of eyelashes.

Louisa didn't like the way he was staring at her. He was searching her. Seeking familiarity. A light shone from his eyes, a light misted by some sort of emotion. Did he have a hankering for her? It could be the reason why he had so inexplicably asked her to dance with him. Did she have reason to be afraid of him? If so, how would he react if he knew she had his late wife's lover under her roof? She prayed Bruce, who was sleeping more and more, would remain quiet. Then she was scared, but not for herself. 'Have you come to tell me Jonny's been killed?'

'No! Nothing like that. Jonny's well, as far as I can possibly know. No, it's this. I want some clothes.'

'What?' Had he gone mad? She began to close the door.

'Please, don't be alarmed.' He felt the biggest fool. 'Let me explain. It's about some evacuees. Faye and I have been given the responsibility of taking care of three children. They've nothing but a few raggedy things to wear and they've nothing to play with. I went to Mrs Killigrew but she couldn't help me. She suggested I try here. I hope you don't mind. The children are in urgent need. Have you anything? For two little boys and a girl.'

This man was the last individual she wanted to pass over her threshold but she had no choice. Her expression as hard and as unfriendly as her tone, she muttered, 'You'd better come in.' In the hallway, she snapped, 'What are their ages?'

Tristan stepped no more than an inch inside the door. Humiliation made his cheeks feel they were about to combust. He had treated Louisa coldly for years, and now, as during their last encounter at the dance, he was behaving in a peculiar manner. 'Um, the boys, I—I think are about eight or nine, their sister a lot younger. Three years perhaps. They're short and thin. They need shoes. I'm afraid I've no idea what size their feet are.'

Louisa was coolly unimpressed with the information. 'I think I'd better phone Faye and ask for some details.'

All he could do was to nod in belittling compliance.

She walked to the other end of the polished tiled floor and with her back towards him engaged Faye in a brief call, making notes as she listened. She put the white, gilt-decorated receiver down. She gave Tristan the smallest glance. 'I have to look through a few boxes. I'll be as quick as I can.'

He acknowledged with a polite cough.

'Would you like to come through?' She pointed to the kitchen.

'What? Oh, no, thank you. I'll keep out of your way. Would you be kind enough to form some sort of parcel which I can carry across my back? There's no basket on my bicycle.'

'There's no need to stay here as if out in the cold,' she said in challenge, impatient with the whole thing, the bad feelings he had created, and now the confusion. 'As you've made me feel all my life.'

'Louisa, I'm sorry I came.' He dithered on his feet, looking down. 'If we could just get on, I'll get out of your way.'

'Give me a few minutes,' she said tersely, her temper rising.

She came back shortly afterwards with a large parcel; due to the shortage of paper its wrapping was a baby's shawl. 'This should do to start the children off. When I've had time to look out some more things I'll let Faye know. I'm sure you won't want me turning up with them at Tremore.' She pushed the parcel at him.

Tristan put his hands on it. 'Louisa…'

She did not relinquish her hold. 'What? What can you possibly say to me, Tristan Harvey? What is it that you have against me? I used to think you were afraid that Jonny and I would get together, but you were just as hostile when I married David. I bet you hate it that I'm seeing Tom. Do you think I'm not good enough for him?'

'Of course you are,' he said lamely, tugging on the parcel to gain it from her.

'Then explain to me why you hate me!' She let go of the parcel, hurried past him, and leaned her back against the door. He wasn't escaping yet. 'For years I've pondered on the reason for your beastly attitude. There's one possibility. I demand to be told! Do you know who my parents are?'

Caught by the worst question she could ask, Tristan's shame at hurting her turned to defensive anger. He needed to escape her beautiful, accusing eyes. *Ursula's eyes.* 'I know nothing about you!'

'But you do! You must.' Fury made her birthmark glow a dark red. 'You've always been known as a kind and generous man, except where I'm concerned. Do I remind you of someone, is that it?'

She had no idea how near the truth she was. 'No! Look, this is ridiculous.' He had to think of a way out of this, something, anything! 'I—I... Louisa, just forget that I was ever uncivil to you. The last war left me with some strange emotional wounds. I'm sorry. I'm sorry that I've been cruel to you. Can't we make a fresh start? Be friends? After all, if you and Tom marry, you'll become my niece.'

'And you wouldn't mind that?' She examined him closely.

'No. Not at all.'

'I don't believe you. As far as I'm concerned we're back to square one,' she spat. 'Because I'm adopted and undoubtedly from a disadvantaged background, you didn't think I was ever good enough to be Jonny's friend. Who the hell do you think you are?' Flinging her hand wide, she slapped him hard across the face. Before he could recover from teetering steps, she swung the door open. 'Get out of my house!'

Tristan found himself on the other side of the door, his face stinging, eyes smarting, the parcel dangling precariously in his grip. 'Bloody hell,' he uttered under his breath. The repercussions of Ursula's affair and the local adoption of her baby were still going on. Louisa would never try to be civil to him again, and Tom, Faye and Emilia would want to know why. And so would Jonny.

—

Tom joined Jill in the dugout, the place she had taken to slipping off to when seeking total privacy. She was sitting in the pitch blackness on a camp bed, the clues to her whereabouts the glow of her cigarette and her light perfume.

'You've had a heck of a day,' he said in understatement.

'I was expecting something but not that.'

'It's tough on you.'

'Tough? That's hardly the word for it.'

He joined her, smoking, his long legs trying to find enough space to spread out. 'You talked to Lottie and Mum. S'pose all the usual things have been said. Anything I can do?'

'You already have just by being here. I'll get over it. The hurt isn't quite as unbearable as it might have been, because all the respect I had for him has been swept away. He was my first love, my first, naive love. Would you like to know exactly what the letter says?'

'If you'd like to share it with me.'

By the light of a small torch she produced Mrs Trenear's letter. *'Dear Jill, I must apologize that news of my son has been a long time coming to you. I can only say how very ashamed Mr Trenear and I are of his behaviour. He came home on leave today and I mentioned you to him. He confessed that you and he were closer than we were led to believe and that he had even given you an engagement ring. You know Ronnie's sweet nature, but he's also a bit of a dreamer. He likes you, Jill, but anything more, he says, was a mistake on his part. All he wants to do is get through the war, get his degree and concentrate on being a scientist. He just couldn't raise the courage to tell you, he didn't know how to put things right, so it's been left to me to perform this sad duty and inform you of his real feelings. I'm so very sorry. I hate to ask, but the ring was once my grandmother's – I had no idea he'd taken it – could you please send it back to me? You have mine and Mr Trenear's wishes for a happy and deserving future. Once again please accept my apologies. Ronnie's too. Yours sincerely, Mrs Ethel Trenear.'* She had read the words in a disbelieving monotone. 'Well, what do you think of that?'

'The chap's a bloody coward. He's been cruel. You're well out of it, Jill.' Tom moved in and gave her a resounding kiss on the cheek. 'How can anyone treat such a lovely girl like you like that? Well, you've got all of us now. Will you send the ring back?'

'It's already packed to be posted tomorrow, with his photograph. I just want to forget the whole humiliating thing. It's better than losing Ronnie in the war, I could never wish him any harm.'

'And I suppose you'll forgive him in time. You and Louisa are two of a kind. I'm damned lucky to have you both. I know you've got Lottie looking out for you, but never forget there's always me too.'

Chapter Seventeen

'That was a lovely meal but I should have taken you out somewhere, darling,' Tom said across Louisa's dining table. 'St Valentine's Day is supposed to be a special occasion for lovers.'

'It has been special. We can go out on the town next year.' Through the rosy-orangey glow of twin candles in ceramic candlesticks, Louisa gazed at him hopefully. She hoped she and Tom would be on the same terms in twelve months' time. Tom had remained loyal to her for four months, the longest time he had ever shown interest in a woman, but she fretted that despite the loving things he often said that he'd tire of her and go back to his old ways. She had engineered this evening alone with him, suggesting to Ada that she spend the evening with her family. She had begged a little extra steak off the butcher and opened the bottle of champagne she'd been keeping for when or if peace was proclaimed. She was wearing her loveliest dinner dress, made seductive by taking in extra nips at the waist and lowering the neckline. It hadn't mattered Tom had arrived in sweater and sports jacket. She was trying to provoke some form of commitment from him. It was she who had first mentioned that this was the most romantic day of the year, and she took heart at his reply. 'We can be just as close here.'

'Of course we can. We could slip out for a drink but I don't suppose you want to leave Mr Ash unattended.'

'I'd better not.' Wild horses or even Tom wouldn't drag her away from her duty.

While she was on her feet stacking the dishes, Tom encircled her waist from behind and kissed her neck. 'That's what I admire about you so much, the way you care about others. How is the invalid?' Louisa had allowed him to speak briefly to her guest a couple of times. On the second occasion the mysterious Mr Ash been much the same as on the first, polite but virtually uncommunicative.

'He's very slowly going downhill. I'm hoping he will get through to spring.' Bruce was hoping the weather would be warm enough soon, so he could visit Ursula's grave at least one more time. She wanted to say, 'I've been in love with you, Tom, since the first time we were together. You don't say it back very often. Just how do you feel about me?'

'I'll help you do that,' he said, joining in clumsily, making cutlery slide noisily off plates. He wasn't allowed to touch a thing in this way at home; Tilda didn't approve of men doing 'women's work', and her decisions regarding domestic issues were sacrosanct. 'The washing-up can be left till tomorrow, can't it? I want you all to myself before Mr Ash needs something.'

'All right,' Louisa said. She had put two hot-water bottles in her bed. Tom sought to make love as often as possible. She enjoyed his passion. He had great knowledge and endurance. He was always mindful of her needs. He never failed to give her the utmost pleasure. With so many people at the farm and Ada living here, times for intimacy usually had to be kept brief and Tom used every minute for loving. Afterwards, if he spoke at all, it would be to mention the farm or someone from it. She longed for just one occasion when they could just lie in each other's arms and discuss themselves. She wanted him to open up his mind to her, to find out what the chances were for something permanent. As wonderful as it was – and she found him irresistible – their continued familiarity went against her nature. His family were undoubtedly aware of their closeness, and Ada, although an innocent where men were concerned, was careful with her expression, obviously uncomfortable, after Tom had been here, so she also knew. Afraid of their affair becoming public knowledge, afraid that she would feel herself to be cheap, she was determined to press Tom over his intentions soon.

When the dishes were piled up on the draining board in the kitchen, she said, 'Would you like a cup of coffee? Nate gave me a jar of Nescafé.'

'S'pose you've had chocolates too.' Tom's tone was disapproving.

'You're a one to talk about someone giving out luxuries,' she joked, reaching for the kettle. 'You get lots of goodies off Nate's friend, Herv. Has Nate done something to upset you?'

'Not specifically. I was hoping his friendship with Lottie would fizzle out. Goodness knows where it's going. He makes every endeavour to endear himself to the family and our friends. Now the danger to our shipping has been lessened with the U-boats practically knocked out, the invasion of our troops on Europe is getting ever closer. The county's bursting at the seams with our own men and even more of Nate's countrymen; travel in and out of it is getting ever more difficult. I'm worried about

Lottie. Perry reminds him to behave himself and he says he wouldn't dream of compromising Lottie. A strange sort of fellow, if you ask me, if he's serious about a girl and happy keeping himself to himself.' Lounging against the display dresser, he sipped his coffee. 'He could be playing crafty, biding his time. But what if Lottie gets carried away and something happens anyway? What if he goes off leaving her heartbroken, or worse still, pregnant? Faye finds the gossiping hard but she doesn't seem to worry too much that she hasn't got her baby's father with her, but it wouldn't be the same for Lottie. She's besotted with Nate. She was heartbroken he couldn't join us for Christmas because all the Americans were put on a blanket operation. She ought to take note from Jill, who's suffering over her chap's deception. I've got worries enough about Mum with her going way past her due date. I suppose you're going to tell me I'm probably worrying over nothing.'

Louisa was gazing down into her cup, watching the black liquid swirl. She was smarting about the talk turning to his family. One or more of them, or Jill, was always there inside his head, in between them. When she had told Tom about her spat with his uncle, he'd shrugged and said, 'Well, Uncle Tris has always been like that with you.' It seemed he was taking her for granted.

She said, thin-lipped, sitting at the table. 'No. I think Lottie's romance is really none of your business.'

'What?' Tom dumped his cup down and threw out his hands. 'Lou, how can you say that? Lottie's my little sister. It's my place to protect her.'

'Lottie is a woman. She's shrewd and level-headed. I can't see her doing anything she shouldn't. She's not the sort to get swept away. And she has your mother and Perry and your grandfather to look out for her.'

Louisa was refusing to look at him; instead her gaze was aimed above the rim of her cup. He went to her, and with his hands splayed out on the table he leaned towards her. 'You said that as if you're jealous of Lottie.'

'Perhaps I am. I was hoping this would be a special evening for us.' She met his eyes.

'Oh, sorry.' He smiled in the way that made her love him, want to lose herself in him. Bringing his face close, he kissed her lips. She closed her eyes and he kissed the lids. His mouth was so warm, so strong, so gentle. He moved in on her and brought her to her feet. Drew her body against his. With one arm around her, the other hand spread along her face, his forefinger caressing behind her ear, he kissed her with ardour. Then he took her hand. 'Let's go to somewhere more comfortable.'

He was going to take her upstairs. Sometimes he carried her all the way to the top. Sometimes he stopped on a stair and started making love to her there. He'd stir her, fluster her, drive her wild, or keep her simmering, teasing her, tormenting her. He never failed to bring her to triumph.

All the way along the passage he kissed her, opening her lips up to his, probing inside her mouth, tasting her; a connoisseur of love. He stopped and eased her against the wall. He wasn't going to transport her any further. He couldn't wait. He was going to have her here. He began a fiercer round of kissing. Slumped against the wall, she kept her eyes closed, her lips parted, waiting, longing for him, sighing for him.

He eased back a little. He was gazing at her. A new look was written on him.

Tom was in awe, in wonder. He'd been so since he'd first held and touched her in the man-to-woman way. He couldn't get over this sudden turn in his life. Louisa. She'd been his playfellow, a soft, shy little girl, worried constantly about her birthmark. In later years he'd found her as someone he was fond of, whom he respected. Always, he had felt duty-bound to defend her, cherish her, she the epitome of decency, honour and fragile womanhood. Their first kiss had shattered him. The turbulent response he had invoked in her had stretched his imagination beyond its limits, all his preconceived ideas had disintegrated as she had given all of herself to him, satisfying him in ways he'd never believed of her.

'What is it, Tom?' Louisa said, clearing her throat of its huskiness. Now he'd stopped, she felt vulnerable with some of her clothes hiked up, some of them pulled down. Quickly, she regained her modesty.

'We ought to think about getting engaged or something.' His desire had not lessened and he closed in on her again, aiming his mouth at hers.

Louisa shifted her head to the side. It had been a vague proposal and nothing at all like the romantic declaration of love and hopes of marriage, delivered with a desperate pleading, from David. She was left feeling flat and somehow offended. 'Let's go back to the dining room.'

'Why?' Tom was disappointed there was to be no lovemaking but it was obvious her feelings had taken a swift dive. He escorted her, in the reserved manner of one taking a lady in to a formal dinner, back to her seat at the table. 'What have I done wrong? I suppose I've shocked you. You'll want time to think about it. Perhaps discuss it with someone.' She kept silent, toying with her empty wine glass. She was making him feel foolish. He lit a cigarette, took a long, heavy drag. 'Lou, you look so miserable. Aren't you the least bit happy?'

She wouldn't offer anything to make him feel more at ease. 'It was hardly the time and place to ask such a thing, Tom. If you were asking me to marry you.'

'Marriage? Of course I meant marriage.' He stroked one of her fingers, cold and unyielding on the stem of the glass. 'I know you wouldn't sleep with me unless we intended to make it legal. Oh, hell, forgive me.' He stubbed the cigarette out. 'I'm making a right mess of things. That's because I'm not any good at this romantic stuff. I'm sorry, Louisa, darling. I love you. Please will you marry me? Think about it for as long as you like.'

'Thank you, Tom. I will, think about it, I mean.' She gave him a half-formed smile. After all, he couldn't help his prosaic nature, and so much else about him was good.

'You could ask Mr Ash what he thinks about it,' Tom said, hoping the suggestion would lift the mood. It was the first time things had gone badly between them and it was horrible, like being dunked in icy water and left to shiver all night.

'I might do that,' she lied. She had introduced Tom to Bruce as an old childhood friend of hers. Knowing already that Tom was her Aunt Emilia's son, Bruce had taken him only as her friend and had shown no more interest in him.

'Good,' Tom relaxed, feeling he was beginning to win back lost ground. 'Now I'm likely to be your husband I think it's reasonable that you tell me soon all about him.

You keep him shrouded in mystery. Why are you so keen to keep him a secret?'

It was all she could do not to tear her eyes away from him. She was afraid he'd read that she was hiding something that concerned him personally. Tom was one of the most pleasantly natured people she knew but he was unlikely to ever approve of whom she was sheltering or the fact that she was doing it. 'You don't need to know this very minute.'

'No, I don't. I've spoiled the moment, I mean, about us and… you know… There's some champagne left. Shall we cuddle up on the sofa and finish it off? I'll stay quiet and you can think about my proposal.'

Quiet he was, assessing what the future would be like as a married man. It would be very strange, but everyone settled down eventually. It wasn't as if a wedding, if there was to be one, was going to be arranged straight away. He held Louisa, caressing her, stroking her long, scented hair – he'd never stop enjoying being close to her.

Louisa found herself too raw to think about marriage to Tom. It hadn't been sensible of her to think about it: nothing could be settled anyway until after Bruce had died. Her hopes had been scattered and right now she was incapable of reforming them. But they intruded in different ways, all bringing heavy emotion with them. Each thought had a name. An identity. Bruce. Tom. Jonny. Tristan Harvey. The first she was inevitably going to lose. She could have the second yet she feared she'd lose him because she wasn't confident he'd really thought what his proposal would really mean to him. And she feared she'd lose the third because of the last.

She was keeping a secret. It was obvious that Tristan Harvey was too. In a moment of panic she knew that her happiness, her whole future, centred on what his secret might be.

Chapter Eighteen

The wind was thrashing through the trees and practically blew Jill across the yard from the milking shed. Now expert at using the milking machines and cleaning down, she was the last to leave the parlour, carrying a bundle of white coats, hats and aprons to the wash house. She put the bundle in the giant-sized basket by the copper. She wasn't thinking about anything except a warming breakfast of porridge. One of the best things about working on the farm was the quantity and quality of food. There was more meat and eggs to be had, cake was put out nearly every afternoon and cream made the puddings yummy. 'Yummy' was a word Lottie used often. Jill smiled. The silly, happy little word had come to her automatically. The hurt and rejection of Ronnie's cowardly silence was losing its grip on her. She was free to find love again but would be content with her life if love didn't bother her again.

Although Lottie had been downhearted back at Christmas over Nate's cancelled leave, Jill had enjoyed the best Christmas Day of her life. She had been overwhelmed with presents and now had a well-stocked toiletry drawer. Edwin Rowse's gift of a few clean pages from an old exercise book placed in a box he'd carved himself from scraps of wood had particularly touched her. 'For when you can start writing to someone again, maid.'

Jill sauntered along to the house and saw a familiar van in the yard. Next instant, she was assailed by the village butcher.

'Morning to 'ee, my luvver. I've come for the pig Tom put away yesterday. How are you, then?' he asked in his demanding loud voice, looking her over as if she was a prime piece of meat, and he like a bloodhound on the scent. 'Got a spring in your step. Nice colour in your cheeks. Love life going well, is it?'

'I'm very well, Mr Eathorne. I haven't got a love life any more.' There was no point in letting people believe she was still engaged and she might as well get the news spread round Hennaford all in one day. 'How are you?'

'Oh, I'm just perky. What happened then? Someone else, was it?' Sidney always shot straight to the point in the hope of as much drama as possible. He held her up, determined to pump her of every bit of information, before going inside and inviting himself to breakfast.

'He simply felt he wasn't ready.'

'Not ready? For a fine young maid like you? How could he think that? The man's a fool! He must be mad. You're taking it well, if you don't me saying so. Well, you won't stay alone for long, but for goodness sake pick one of our boys. Not like young Lottie, dallying with a blooming Yank. They drive too fast, have made our roads dangerous. Isn't one of our lot good enough for her?'

'Of course. You can't help who you fall in love with, Mr Eathorne.' Jill tried to dodge round him, but Sidney was expert at keeping his prey exactly where he wanted them.

'Love? As serious as that is it? Well, the maid's not a dallier like her brother, although Tom's mended his ways a lot lately. Seeing someone in particular, is he?'

'I've no idea what Tom gets up to, Mr Eathorne.' Tom had been unusually subdued for the last two days, offering various irritable excuses, that he was going down with a cold, or had indigestion, or was just plain tired. He had made Jill ponder on his mood by declaring to her privately, 'You might come to think you were better off before, Jill, when it was just you and your grandmother. There's no getting away with the slightest little thing here with so many people always around.' If there was anything wrong with Tom it had nothing to do with illness or fatigue.

'Faye Harvey came into my shop yesterday. 'Tis a brave thing she does, bringing her baby along everywhere she goes. She had the little evacuee maid too. She done wrong but she's a natural mother, I'll give her that. People are still talking about her – they should mind their own business! You'd think they'd have something better to do.' He nudged Jill as if they were used to sharing confidences. 'Was her young man taken before they could get to the church?'

'I don't know the circumstances.' This time Jill walked on resolutely, her ear turned away from him.

He just as resolutely dogged her steps. 'Married man, was he? Left her in the lurch? Some men can be cruel and irresponsible. Don't know what Mr Ben will make of it all when he comes home. Any word about he?'

'None that I know of, Mr Eathorne.' Jill smiled sweetly. She was taking off her boots to go inside. 'You can ask Mrs Em all you want to know now.'

'Ah, ah, uh,' Sidney blustered. Jill grinned maliciously to herself. Mrs Em was one person Sidney Eathorne never got the better of when rooting for gossip. She was likely to accuse him of being an old busybody. He'd be wary of Lottie too, she wouldn't hold back at being rude to him. 'Can smell the porridge from here. You lead the way in, my handsome.'

They found the kitchen in uproar. Emilia was clutching the table with one hand, gripping her side with the other and wincing. 'No, Tilda, I haven't got time for breakfast. This isn't the *start* of a long labour. The baby's coming right now!' Suddenly she was standing in a pool of water.

'What?' For a second Perry was thrown into a dither, then he took charge. 'Right. Don't worry, darling. Everything's under control. Tom, help me to get your mother upstairs. Lottie, phone for the district nurse.'

Emilia leaned forward, panting. 'No time to do that either. Take me to the sitting room. Bring the maternity things down from our room. I'm giving birth almost at once, like I did to little Jenna. Perry, you need to hurry!'

Jill squeezed her way into a corner, out of the way but ready to spring into action if she was called on.

White-faced, Tom opened the passage door so Perry and Lottie could rush his mother through.

'Hot water. Hot water,' Tilda muttered, shaking visibly.

Only Edwin was calm. 'Em's used to all this. She won't panic.' He filled his pipe for an expected celebratory smoke.

'Anything I can do?' His lips pulled back, revealing his big teeth in anticipation of dramatic news, Sidney peered down the passage after the sitting-room door was shut. Delight at coming straight into some excitement was written up and down every quivering, prying inch of him.

No one answered. Taking Jill with him, Tom went to listen outside the maternity door. Edwin joined them. Sidney crept after them.

'Ow, ow, ow, owah!' Emilia was heard yelling at the top of her voice.

'Oh my God...' Tom glanced anxiously at Jill. He had never heard his mother in such pain. He was scared.

'Nearly there!' Perry exclaimed.

'She'll be all right,' Jill whispered to Tom, but she was worried too, praying that this wonderful family wouldn't be hit by another tragedy.

Five minutes passed in which Tom sighed and shook his head and stamped his feet, like a handsome proud hunter restrained from the chase, in which Jill increasingly touched him, gripped him, held on to him to reassure him. She wondered how Lottie was holding up – she was probably too busy to think about anything more than what she was helping with. Lottie suddenly cried, 'Go on, Mum. Push!'

Tom, Jill, Edwin and Sidney jumped in their skins in unison, then gave a joint noisy exhalation of breath.

'What's happening?' Tom pleaded.

'Shush, boy,' Edwin restrained him.

There was the sound of a lusty cry. A baby's cry. 'Is it all over?' Tom whispered, still fearful.

Edwin was grinning broadly. For a short man he suddenly appeared six feet tall. ''Es, 'tis. Another grandchild. My dear Em's done it again, bless her. Your gran would have been some proud to see this day. Come on, boy, we'd better make some tea.'

'But I want to know what it is.'

'Aw, they'll need a little while yet.' Edwin dragged him along to the kitchen.

For once, Sidney was drooped-mouthed and speechless.

A short while later Tom was holding his baby brother, wrapped in the shawl that he and all his siblings had first been kept warm in. 'He's a good weight, fine and healthy stock. How do you feel, Perry?'

'This is the happiest day of my life, but it wasn't me who did all the hard work. Are you sure you're all right, darling?' He was holding Emilia's hand, kissing it, kissing her flushed cheek.

She gentled a finger down his face. 'I feel strong enough to go tattie-picking. Don't worry, I'm only joking.'

Lottie was hopping round Tom. 'Let me have him. That was the most amazing thing I've ever seen. I hope all my babies come as quickly as that.'

Emilia welcomed the tea Edwin brought her. 'It can be a bit of a shock, Lottie.'

'He's absolutely beautiful.' Jill gazed at the baby.

'All these years and now we're back to nappies, Mrs Em.' Tilda was sniffing into her hanky. 'I couldn't be happier.'

'I'll give Uncle Tris a ring. He'll be delighted. And then I'll let Lou know,' Tom said.

'You might be holding one of your own soon, eh, boy?' Edwin thudded on his back. 'We're all expecting an announcement from you and Louisa, you know.'

Tom made no reply, instead tossing a helpless look at Jill.

'Tom?' Emilia eyed him quizzically.

Sidney was noting yet another juicy morsel to pass on. 'Oh? More need for congratulations then, young Tom?'

'There might be.' Tom dropped his eyes to his baby brother. 'We'll concentrate on him just for now.'

Emilia was satisfied with the answer. She reached out. 'Can I have my baby now?'

Tom handed him over. Perry put his arms around Emilia and their child. The room went quiet.

Lottie asked, 'What are you going to call him? William?'

'Perry and I have spoken a lot about the baby's name,' Emilia said, stroking her son's pink, downy cheeks. 'Perry had suggested William as a second name for a boy. It was a lovely thought, but I think the name should remain with his older brother, and my brother, his Uncle Billy. We hope he'll grow up in a world very different to the way it is now, a new world. So we've decided on names new to the Boswelds, the Rowses and the Harveys.' She kissed the baby's cheek. 'Welcome to the world, Paul Michael Bosweld.'

Jill stood back and surveyed the joyful scene. A lump of emotion high in her throat.

Emilia beckoned to her. 'Come closer, Jill, and take a good look at him. You're an aunty now.'

'Well, I couldn't have come at a better time,' Sidney deliberated. He tapped sharply on Tom's shoulder. 'Now then, young Uncle Tom. The wind's picking up mightily. There'll be rain any minute. Help me get this pig aboard.'

Chapter Nineteen

Like a shadow, Ben slid out of the woods and scrambled down the banks of brambles and concealed himself among the long-deserted farm buildings. He longed for a smoke but waited patiently, knowing he wouldn't be disappointed. The person he was waiting for rode along this way every day to the village, a few kilometres from St-Lo. Five minutes later came the sound of a creaking pushbike. Stepping out of his hiding place, Ben placed himself directly in the path of the rider.

The man, middle-aged, his plump cheeks threaded with red veins, a beret tight over his balding head, a heavy black topcoat flapping round his legs, brought his conveyance to a wobbly halt. 'Ah, my dear Jean-Claude. I haven't seen you for these past seven or eight weeks. How rugged you look.' He spoke with eloquent turns of his puffy brown hands. All the while his small, deceptively vacant eyes were darting at Ben and the vicinity.

Ben's hair was long under his wool hat and he had a full beard. His clothes were dark and they were crumpled because he slept in them. He strode forward until there was barely a foot's space between him and the Frenchman. He answered in fluent French. 'Maurice. That's because I'm living in what my countrymen would call the great outdoors. My field name is no longer Jean-Claude. I can't take on another SOE identity, the scar across my eye is too much of a giveaway following the detailed account given by the betrayer of my appearance. There's a price on my head. I now fight the guerrilla way. Patrice, my wireless operator, was betrayed too. Vichy scum turned him over to the Gestapo, they tortured him to death.'

'That is unfortunate.' Maurice pushed out the flesh of his lower lip. 'You have my sympathy for your compatriot.'

'Your sympathy's not required.' Ben's hand strayed inside his rough jacket. 'Those responsible have all been hunted down. Today they will be put to death. In fact there's only one left to die a traitor's death.'

Maurice's face hardened. He reached to his waistband but Ben pulled his gun out first. In panic, he licked his lips. 'Jean-Claude, I don't understand what this is all about.'

Ben stared him in the eye. 'Collaborator.' Ben's shots entered cleanly between Maurice's eyes. Man and bicycle clattered to the ground. Blood spread over the dirt; he should have had blood on his conscience.

As quickly as he'd emerged from the trees Ben re-entered them, leaving the body as a warning to others. He had no qualms about dispensing with the life of Maurice. He was a savage, who had readily betrayed his countrymen and women, not out of cowardice but out of greed, for money. Twelve innocent villagers had been lined up in the village square and shot because of his betrayal. Ben joined those waiting for him, fifteen men and three women who lived without papers and an identity, members of a non-political Maquis. Most were young, living in the woods, the hills and the mountains to escape being gathered up by the Germans and taken away to work in labour camps. Ben kept in touch with the SOE circuit leader. The war was turning a little more to the Allies' favour. The most important work for him now was to make things as difficult as possible for the enemy invader. The RAF and the American 'heavies' – many planes, he was sure, from his home county – were daily bombing German strongholds, a softening up for the Allied invasion that was to come from the sky and the sea. Ben's task with these resistance workers was to stop German troops, tanks and ammunition getting to the front line. Although he lived every moment on the edge of his nerves, he did so with a calmness and cunning and expertise that had earned him the nickname *le loup*, the wolf.

Deep amid the trees, he lit a cigarette, indulging in that short moment to think of Faye, to love her. Then he put her out of his mind. He needed to concentrate. To plan and make the explosives for the next bridge he and his comrades were to blow up.

Chapter Twenty

Lottie had the engine of the Ferguson tractor stripped down. This she did every three months and she was more skilled than Tom at servicing and repairing the vehicle, known affectionately as Old Chugger. She thought about Nate and his careful driving, which wasn't usually the case with the Americans – Sidney Eathorne was right – they were apt to throw their heavy vehicles foolishly round the inadequate roads, gouging chunks out of hedges and risking collisions. Nate was a steady man, but now and then he'd show a reckless streak, scaring her the time he'd clambered up a tree to rescue one of the silly barn cats and had swung down to the ground with it, branch by branch, using one arm. If one of the branches near the top of the ancient oak had snapped off or he'd slipped, it would have been curtains for him. For a quiet man he had a wicked sense of humour, laughing when poor embarrassed Tilda had tried to hide her voluminous underwear from him on the washing line. In a dry, Bob Hope-style quip, he'd said, 'Don't worry, my dear, I've seen hammocks before.'

It had been ten days since she'd last seen Nate. He was involved in more serious training exercises, often on the coast by the telltale residue of salt water left on his jeep. She imagined him somewhere now, perhaps on the north coast, where the beaches were larger, the seas heavier and needing more precise navigation, perhaps at Perranporth or Newquay, setting up mock casualty clearing stations and enacting the treatment of badly wounded casualties.

She had asked him once why he had chosen to be a medic. 'Don't get me wrong,' he'd replied. 'I don't think myself above taking out the enemy. I was good at nursing sick critters back on the range, and the hands and I often had to see to our own first aid. Seemed obvious that was what I'd do. I think I've got the strength of mind to deal with the wounded and dying. It's a sorry thing, there's been more than one fatal road accident over here with our troops. Sure isn't easy finding the way round your tiny country lanes. Now that seems a dreadful waste to me, men being killed and not ever setting foot on a battle-ground. Most of them are only boys, Lottie. Seventeen, eighteen years, just left their momma's sides. There's so many young ones in the British ranks too.'

'Don't go on, Nate. I don't want to think about what's coming.'

'Don't fret, honey. I'm sorry. I don't like to upset you. I'll try my darndest to get back to you as quickly as I can.' It was the only reference they'd ever made to the forthcoming plans for European liberation.

Every time he went back to base she had no idea when she'd see him next. He rang as often as he could. Sometimes, precious times, to say he was on the way over. Occasionally he'd just turn up. He'd spend time talking to her mother and Perry. Each time they seemed a little easier about him, but she refused to discuss Nate with either of them, not wanting to hear their inevitable words of caution. She knew well enough that she might not have Nate for ever.

She longed for Nate to ring or come soon. To hear the news about Paul, to see how beautiful her baby brother was. She'd been anxious for the birth to be over, not caring too much about the baby, just wanting her mum to deliver without complications and be all right. She'd had no idea how much she would love the little mite, enjoy watching him stretch and ball his tiny fists. Her late-night habit meant she'd often give him his last nightly feed from her mother's expressed milk, giving her more rest, then she'd lay him down in the nursery, asleep and content, innocent of the death and destruction going on to provide him with a safer world. She wanted a large family of her own. *Please God, spare Nate. I love him so much.*

Rubbing at her brow, making herself black and greasy, she set about wiping the spark plugs with a rag. A vehicle swept up ridiculously fast beside her, sending small stones and mud scattering over her coverall trousers. 'Hey! Nate! You startled me.'

'Hmmm.' He got out of the jeep with its familiar star and identity number, its unique name, *Tumbleweed*, chosen and painted on it by Nate. He studied her with a grin. 'I know that look. Anyone but me would've had their head chewed off. Sorry, honey. Couldn't resist it. You look gorgeous! Come here and give me a kiss.'

She ran to him and, holding the greasy objects out of the way, offered her lips for a loving kiss. 'You don't usually swagger about. You look very happy. Why?'

'I've got a whole twenty-four-hour pass. A whole day and night to spend with you.'

'Oh, damn it! I can't really get any time off. Mum can't help with the spud planting – oh, you don't know the wonderful news. I've got a baby brother! Paul Michael.

He's seven days old. He's brilliant. You must come inside and see him. I watched him being born. Oh, Nate, it was so much more special than helping with an animal birthing.'

Nate squeezed her until she thought she'd burst. 'I didn't expect you to be free. I'll work with you. I'm sure Tom can lend me some old togs. That should be worth some time alone with you. Do you think your mom would mind if I bed down in the barn?'

'You can share with Tom, silly.' She gazed at him, drank him in, thrilled beyond words that he was here. 'This is going to be a wonderful day.'

'I'm counting on it.' He kissed her soundly, taking her breath away. 'You finish off here. I'll go in and say hello to the folks.'

Emilia was in her chair in the kitchen. She had just finished feeding the baby and had him up on her shoulder, patting his back. 'Hello, Nate. Have you seen Lottie?'

'Yes, ma'am.' He came close enough to gain a view of the baby's face. The few babies he'd seen before were practically bald and he was taken aback to see this one had a mop of black hair. 'I wish I'd known about the little fellow, I'd have brought him something. He's really cute. Looks like his father. Lottie sure is excited about him. Excuse me, ma'am, why are you beating on his back?'

'I'm bringing up his wind. All babies get wind when they're feeding. Would you like to hold him?'

Nate was a little scared and fixed his eyes on his hands as if they were useless objects. He no longer felt strong and capable but like wobbly rubber. 'Um, yes, I guess. I might hurt him.'

'Babies aren't made of china.' Emilia laughed. 'Take my chair. You'll find it easier the first time if you're sitting down.'

They exchanged places. Nate wiped his hands down his shirt then lifted his arms up cautiously for the baby. Emilia eased Paul down into a comfortable position for him. Except for Lottie, never had he felt anyone to be so warm and soft, who smelled as sweet. 'Gosh, ma'am, this is really nice. Congratulations. I forgot to mention it.'

'Thank you, Nate.' She met his smile with one of her own, thinking as she made coffee how boyish he looked. Nate was twenty-three years old. Emilia was saddened that he, like Will, like so many thousands and thousands of other young men, might be deprived the pleasures of fatherhood. She had grown fond of the Texan, but things weren't, as she'd heard another American say, 'all peachy'. It was time something was said.

She put a mug of coffee on a shelf close by him. 'Nate, I'd like to have a serious word with you.'

'Please, ma'am, Mrs Bosweld.' He looked up from caressing Paul's minuscule ear, from watching his dark eyes trying to focus. 'I think I know what you're about to say, what you've got the right to say. About Lottie and me. About my intentions and so forth. Well, I want you to know I love her very much. I cherish every last little thing about her. I guess you've been worrying about me taking Lottie away from you. I got to be honest and say that before I left home there would've been nothing to stop me going back. I'd planned to do the usual things, look for a wife, rear a family to carry on the Harmon name. There's been Harmons on that piece of land for five generations. They first farmed there with the cost of their own blood.

But when I met your daughter, the instant I set my eyes on her, everything I held dear no longer looked the same way. I was so scared of those feelings, I took off. The next time I saw her in town, I drove off to think it through. But I had to seek her out, ma'am. It seemed a foolish thing to do, getting involved with a girl so far away from home, at a time when the war means I might not be able to give her a future.

'So what I'm saying is that I'd give up everything for Lottie. It's been hard, but I've kept my distance from her, ma'am, I swear. I've been mindful of her, if you take my meaning. But I can't live without her. That's the most terrifying thought of all. Please, I beg you, let me and Lottie get married. I got to go across the waters soon. I want to go knowing Lottie is my wife. That she's my next of kin. If you want, I'll make the arrangements to sell the ranch today. I'll do anything, you just give me the word. Please don't just turn me down, at least think about it, please, ma'am. Will you speak to Mr Bosweld or shall I? Say something, ma'am.'

During his speech, Emilia had sat down. There was no doubt in her mind that every word he'd spoken was true, but there was a lot to consider. 'Have you asked Lottie to marry you?'

'Not yet. I wanted to speak to you first, do it all proper.'

'But Lottie's so young.'

'Pardon me, ma'am, but I understand you were even a little younger when you married her daddy.'

'Well, yes, that's true, but… well, Nate, you've taken me by surprise, although not totally, I have to admit. It's easy to see you adore Lottie. I need to speak to Perry.'

'Of course, you do that, soon as possible, if you please. I'm sorry if this is difficult for you but I'd like to ask Lottie to marry me today. I'm praying this will be one of the happiest days of our lives.'

Emilia wanted to say all manner of things. Issue warnings and advice. Ask him to think again. To at least wait until the end of the war. But Lottie had a right to her own life. Lottie wasn't keen to talk about Nate, yet it was obvious she loved him. She had the right to consider if she loved him enough to marry him sooner rather than later. 'Ask Perry if you can talk. Let Perry have his say. If he agrees, tell him, although I have reservations, it's fine with me.'

'Darling, I'm back,' Perry called out from the front door. He'd returned from visiting a sick tenant in the village, a grouchy old woman who had taken to his chivalrous charm. 'Mrs Couch is still laid up, still refusing to move in with her daughter, but she's made these little bootees for Paul.'

Nate stood up with the baby and passed him to Emilia.

Perry's face fell a fraction. 'Oh, Nate, I didn't expect to find you here.'

Nate was horribly nervous but he jumped straight in. 'Would this be a good time to speak to you, Mr Bosweld?'

'I've got to get back to the garden. Got cabbages to plant.' Perry's whole bearing was uncharacteristically uncivil.

'Perry. Give him a few minutes, please.' Emilia smiled wanly.

'Oh, very well.' Perry did something she had never seen him do before, he scowled. 'You'd better come to the den.'

Emilia put Paul down in his pram and he slept peacefully. She left the door open to listen in on the men. There were many loud exclamations from Perry – he was giving Nate a hard time. Nate seemed to be saying little. When the voices died down low, she strained to hear the tone of the interview. Very serious, she decided. She was rolling out pastry for a meat and potato pie when the den door was thrown open.

Nate hurried into the kitchen. He had a huge grin. He straightened his tie. 'Do I look all right, ma'am?'

'Very handsome.'

The interview had obviously gone his way: he was like a whirl of sunshine. 'Here goes. Wish me luck.' He sped out the back door.

Emilia didn't know if she felt happy or sad. Ten minutes ticked by. A bad sign. Perry was taking his time coming in from the den. Emilia had the pie in the oven and she was carrying the heavy wooden board and other utensils into the back kitchen when he appeared. He was awkward on his legs, limping, the prosthetic evidently chafing him. He hauled the things out of her hands, strode off with them and dumped them down on the draining board. It was rare for Perry to get into any sort of bad mood. Right now he was shaking with anger. Calmly, Emilia wiped the flour off her hands. Perry was glaring at her, dark with resentment, but he looked so gorgeous all she wanted to do was kiss him. He never failed to stir her passion for him.

'Why are you doing that?' he asked in clipped tones.

'It needed to be done.'

'Where's Tilda?'

'In the village. Queuing for food.'

'Damn it, Em! Paul's only a week old. You know you should be resting. Why am I surrounded by headstrong women?'

'Because you love to be. I take it you've given Nate your blessing to propose to Lottie?'

'Blessing?' He curled his fists. 'Hell, no. I couldn't think how to refuse his bloody stupid damned request because you didn't do so beforehand. You're Lottie's mother. I haven't got the right to go against your wishes.'

'You've got the right to have your say.' She went to him, only a breath away.

'Oh, I had that all right. Had the chap standing there quaking. For all of five minutes! He knows as much as I do that you can't win against a determined woman. For goodness sake, Em, you should have sent him away. Threatened to set the dogs on him. Don't look at me like that. You know I can't hold out against you when you look at me like that. You're being wilful. Unfair. Em, don't—'

'I don't want her to marry yet, Perry.' She reached up and put her hands either side of his face. 'At least she won't be going to America.'

Capitulating, he put his arms round her and they cuddled up close. 'What if she wants to go? Lottie's so adventurous. She might like the idea of a new challenge. He's giving up his home and country for her; I've got to give him that. What if she decides she'd like to make the sacrifice instead?'

Emilia was quiet, worried about this new possibility. 'Let's wait and see. Will and so many young people won't ever get the chance to marry. Nate might not come through and Lottie's going to need all our support.

Darling, let's be happy for them. Make it a happy time. It might be all they're going to get.'

He sighed long and hard. 'You're right as usual. It's no wonder I love you so much.'

—

Nate found Lottie, with Jill close by, up to her ankles in mud, planting seed potatoes down near the woods, in banked-up ground that had once been left gloriously to the wild. Tom was working in the next row, a little ahead. 'I've come to help,' Nate called across to him, 'but is it OK if I take your sister off for a little while?'

Tom saw his excitement. He knew at once that this was going to be more than the American asking Lottie if she'd like to go to the pictures. He felt a sense of loss, an instinct to protect her. 'We've already had our crib.'

'I promise it won't take long,' Nate persisted.

Curtly, Tom nodded and carried on working. Oh God. Will was dead. He, himself – if Louisa ever made up her mind – might soon be engaged to be married. He had a new brother. Faye was an unmarried mother. Uncle Ben had disappeared. Life was changing far too much for comfort.

'We ought to get on, Nate,' Lottie said, for once not as perceptive as her brother. 'Rain is on the way.'

'Honey, I really need to talk to you. Now. Can we slip off somewhere alone? I promise it won't take long.'

He was too cheerful for there to be any serious news. Making a puzzled face, she straightened up and massaged her aching back. 'We could go just inside the woods.'

They strolled hand in hand. Lottie could feel the buzz, the tension, in his fingers. 'Are you planning a surprise for

Paul's christening? Is that why you want a private word, to make sure it would be agreeable to the family before you mention it?'

'Nothing like that.' The second they were out of sight, Nate gently hauled her round to him. 'Darling, this is about you and me. Us. I thought to take you somewhere nice. Book a table at the Red Lion Hotel. But I couldn't wait, and now I'm here I'm glad I didn't.' With a fingertip he ran a tender path along her chin. 'I think I love you the best just like this, your sleeves rolled up, earth on your face and under your nails. Healthy, glowing and beautiful.'

'Nate?' She clutched his hand, hope and excitement filling up the reaches of her body and soul.

'I'm asking you to be my wife, Lottie. As soon as it can be arranged. Your mom and Perry have given me permission to ask you. I've already taken the liberty of talking to my commanding officer and have applied for a special licence. Before you raise any objections, let me tell you that I'd like to sell up so we can buy a farm of our own over here. You won't have to live far from your family. I love you so much. What do you say, darling? Please don't let me wait for an answer.'

She had been hoping Nate would ask her to marry him, that they'd become engaged before he had to go off to fight. This was far outside her greatest dreams. She'd thought it all through. She would have been willing to go to America and let Tom inherit the farm alone. Nate loved her as much as she loved him; she had found the depth of love she'd always wanted. 'I won't do that to you, Nate, darling. Yes! My answer's yes. I love you with all that I am and I don't want to wait either.'

Tom heard Nate's whoop of triumph and Lottie's delighted scream. He fell down on his haunches but moments later, after making a wry face at Jill, who was smiling towards the woods, he carried on working, resigned to Lottie's happiness. At least Lottie was sure she wanted to be with the man she loved. It was a long time before there was a full workforce in the potato field.

Chapter Twenty-One

Bruce Ashley was up and out of bed, slumped on the couch. Dressed and shaved, he was ready and eager to go to Ursula. He was recalling the first time he had seen her. It had been 1916, in a Truro tea shop, and she had been with her child. He'd taken little notice before of women with young children unless they had a nanny; not rich enough for him to live off. There had been nothing provocative about Ursula. She had been leaning across to wipe the boy's mouth with a napkin, the picture of a loving, attentive mother and someone's chaste wife. He had been rooted to the spot. Something about her sparkled like a star. Her dark eyes were full of light, her hair was glossy ebony, her skin pure and translucent and white as snow. She was as beautiful as a child from a fairy tale, yet she was all woman, a goddess. It was the greatest physical attraction he'd ever had for someone and he'd ached to have her.

At the time he was in lodgings, looking for prey, confident with his good deportment and well-honed, healthy, fair looks he'd quickly find a more luxurious place to rest his idle bones. Women thought him beautiful and fell for his raffish charm. They liked his roguish, cultured voice, his white-toothed smile, his touch of irresponsibility. They overlooked the fact that he was a lounge lizard and they queued up to win him, and when they had him, they sought to do the usual female thing of changing him, getting him to settle down, to stay exclusively theirs. This young woman would make a pleasing distraction, on the side, to the wealthy widow he had set his sights on.

As she was a maternal sort, he played a trick to attract her caring side, pretending to have a headache, to be feeling a little faint, in great need to sit down quickly at a nearby table. A furtive glance. Yes, he had grabbed her awareness. 'Forgive me.' He'd piled on an apologetic smile. 'It's these wretched migraines.'

As he'd wanted, she'd called for the waitress to fetch him a glass of water. He had admired her son. His fun-loving side made four-year-old Jonny respond well to him. By the time Ursula had left the tea shop he knew where she lived, that her lieutenant husband was away fighting at Ypres, and enough of her routine to engineer a seemingly chance meeting with her the following week in the town. Ursula loved her husband but she was bored. At first Bruce offered companionship. An expert at knowing when to tug on a woman's heart, to make each move, he drew her in, and by the time he'd first got her into bed, to her having an affair with him was as natural as breathing. Ursula said, inevitably, that she loved him, that he made her happy. Just as inevitably, mechanically, he'd said it back. It had been strange to be caught unawares with her on his mind, missing her. Missing her dreadfully. Against his calculating nature, he had found himself planning to take her and Jonny away. He had had to get out of Truro anyway: too many of his debtors, including a crooked business associate of Ben Harvey's, were after his blood.

As he let the memories play on, they turned sad, difficult to cope with, and tears of remorse splashed down his now raddled face. He would have got both Ursula and Jonny away if not for the intervention of Alec Harvey. Harvey had given Ursula a hard choice. To let him raise her son until his father came home, to hide away and give her baby up, then ask for Tristan's forgiveness, or to go off as planned and leave Jonny behind. Alec Harvey was taking Jonny either way and Ursula had chosen to go with Bruce so she could keep their baby. They'd left on the next train for Bristol. It was a shady, backstreet life he had taken Ursula to, and when the cruel landlord had come knocking for the overdue rent, he had run out on her. With no other choice, heavily pregnant and starving, she had made her way to Hennaford, begging all the way, turning up at Alec and Emilia Harvey's wedding. Tristan Harvey was recovering at Ford Farm from battle wounds and she had pleaded for his forgiveness. He had taken her back but wouldn't accept her child. Ursula had wanted the child so much. Again she had been faced with a terrible choice of either keeping Jonny or her baby.

'If only I hadn't really loved you and come back for you,' Bruce whispered in despair.

His reappearance and second plan to abscond with Ursula and abduct Jonny had been thwarted by Tristan Harvey and Emilia Harvey. His cowardice in running off again had led to Ursula's death. If not for the distress he had caused her, Ursula might have lived and watched Jonny grow up. And her daughter, *his* daughter, might be well and alive somewhere.

He checked his weeping, not wanting to upset Louisa. Soon he would make atonement for what he'd done, paying with more than just bitter regrets. He wasn't long for this world and in the next one he would deservedly rot and suffer hell's fire. 'If I could just see you one more time, Ursula,' he choked and coughed on the words. 'And catch a glimpse of our little girl…'

–

'I always think March is a cold, windy month,' Louisa said, already in her coat and scarf. 'I'm going to wrap you up as warm as toast. Now, let's take our time getting you down the stairs.'

They were nearly at the foot, Bruce taking one slow, energy-leaching stair at a time, when they were startled by a knock on the door. 'We'll stay quiet,' Louisa whispered. 'Hopefully, whoever it is will come back later.'

'Sorry, I'm disrupting your life.' Bruce leaned heavily on the banisters.

There was another knock. They waited. All went silent. They carried on down.

'Hello! Louisa? Where are you?'

'Oh, no,' she gasped. 'I forgot to lock the back door.' There was no time to get Bruce back up to his room. 'But we might not need to worry too much. It's Faye Harvey. She won't know who you are.'

Faye appeared, carrying Simon through to the hall. 'Oh, there you are. Oh, I'm sorry, I didn't know you had company. I've brought Simon with me. Do you need a hand there? I'll put Simon down somewhere.'

'It's all right, Faye. We can manage. I'll just get Mr Ash into the bath chair.'

'I should have rung.' Faye gazed curiously at her friend's guest. 'You're about to go out. I shan't be staying long. I need to pop into the town to get some cod liver oil for the Smith children.'

'I need to catch my breath before we venture outside,' Bruce said, keeping his head down. 'Do stop and speak to your friend, Louisa. I'm pleased to meet you, Mrs Harvey.'

'And I you, Mr Ash.' Faye thought it very strange that Louisa, even for one so modest about her charitable works, should not mention she was nursing someone. Louisa was obviously uncomfortable with her sudden presence. 'Actually, it's Miss Harvey.' She was getting slick at correcting the taken-for-granted assumption on her status. The man didn't even raise a brow over it.

'Let's all go along to the kitchen,' Louisa cheeped brightly. 'I've been baking bread and it's lovely and warm in there.'

When they were settled, with Bruce wheeled at a discreet distance by Louisa to where he couldn't easily be focused on, Louisa said in bright conversation, 'Simon is a dear. Can I hold him? How are the Smith children?'

'They're all really well.' Faye handed Simon over. 'I couldn't imagine life without them now. The twins are excelling at school. Pearl is a quiet little soul.' To Louisa's dismay she went to Bruce. 'Do you have any children, Mr Ash?'

He was keeping his head down on his chest. Slowly he looked up then glanced down at once. 'No, I don't, Miss Harvey.'

'Has there been any word from Uncle Ben?' Louisa cut in loudly. She was opening the biscuit barrel to get a treat for Simon.

Realizing how weak Mr Ash was, that a friendly conversation would be too much for him, Faye drew back.

'Not a word. Uncle Tris thinks he's doing some important war work, hush-hush stuff. I think it must be something like that after the mysterious call he received just before he took off. I'd so like to hear from him, just to know he's all right. He was in such a state after his quarrel with Aunt Em. Whatever went on disturbed them both very much. Aunt Em said that she told him some home truths. I'm sure he needed it. Perhaps it'll do him some good in the end. When he comes back he might be more open. I'm hoping he'll accept Simon.'

Louisa was now sitting with Simon bouncing on his sturdy legs on her lap. He was grinning and gurgling. There was no hint in him of what his father might look like: he was a Harvey through and through. 'I'm sure Uncle Ben will be delighted when he sees Simon. I'm pleased you feel better about him.'

'I want nothing more than for us to be one big happy family.' Faye would have included Tristan in her remarks but it wouldn't be kind to mention him here.

'So all's going well with the Smith children?' Louisa was trying every ploy to keep Faye's mind off Bruce.

'They're a bunch of little sweeties,' Faye enthused. 'Once they trusted us not to work them half to death, like they were in their last billet, it's all been plain sailing. Eliza and the land girls dote on them. They're a great help about the farm, specially with the animals, and bless them, they've taken it upon themselves to collect paper and other salvage round the village.'

'I suppose Pearl likes to help with Simon?'

'Yes, but she's so taken with…' there was nothing for it but to add, 'with Uncle Tris, she's like a shadow at his side.'

'Excuse me, is his son safe?' Bruce asked.

'Jonny? All was well quite recently,' Faye replied. 'You know him, Mr Ash?'

Bruce shook his head. His deathly pale face turned a distressed red as he was seized by a terrible burst of coughing. Louisa passed Simon to Faye and fetched a drink of water. When the coughing stopped, Bruce's breathing was noisy and hard won.

'If you don't mind, I think I'd better be running along.' Faye withdrew sympathetically. Louisa went with her while she put Simon in his pushchair outside the back door. 'I'm calling in at Aunt Em's on the way home. There's to be a discussion about Lottie's wedding plans. I hope you'll be able to come to the wedding on Saturday, Louisa.'

'Hopefully, if Ada will be able to change her shifts around.' Louisa half turned away, anxious to return to Bruce and not talk about him.

Faye walked round her. 'So she can be here with Mr Ash? Louisa, who is he?'

'Oh, he's just an old friend. Of Aunt Polly's.' Her face was tight over the lie.

Faye saw she was on the defensive but said no more. Louisa looked paler than usual and weary. Faye didn't know her well, but something was wrong. She was stalling with a reply to Tom's proposal. 'She's very busy these days,' was the only response that could be got out of Tom. It didn't appear there was going to be another Harvey wedding in the immediate future. She gave Louisa a peck goodbye. 'Well, let's hope we can catch up properly soon. Bye. Take care.'

Bruce was taking tiny, careful sips of water with a trembling hand. 'Please don't try to stop me going to Ursula.'

'I wouldn't dream of it.' Louisa took the glass from him. From the look of him it might be the last chance he'd get of saying goodbye to his long lost love.

To the few neighbours who had seen her out with Bruce, she was taking him along the popular churchyard walk for an airing. As before, she left him alone beside Ursula's grave, keeping watch in case someone came along so she could move him quickly away. It wouldn't do for him to be seen viewing this particular resting place. All was peaceful, with pale yellow and pink primroses making their first gentle show on the hedgerows and the banks, and the trees were unfolding their leaves. Twenty minutes later she went back to him.

'It's time to go, Bruce,' she whispered gently, reaching for his hand.

'She's never got any flowers,' he wept. 'She's never had any flowers. I can't give her any, people would wonder about it, and even Jonny has never left her some. Ursula loved flowers. She loved pretty things, and I took it all away from her. I deserve to burn in hell for what I've done.'

'Bruce, don't think like that. Ursula loved you. She wouldn't wish that on you.'

Stuttering and gasping he went on, 'It's how I left her. She must have been in hell giving birth to our child, knowing Tristan wouldn't take her back again, that she'd only be able to see Jonny occasionally. She died a painful death. Even if she'd lived, there would have been so little to go on for. Just loneliness. Isolation as a fallen woman. Oh God! Oh God!'

Louisa knelt down and, not caring if they were seen, she put her arms around him. 'Bruce, please don't get in a state. You'll make yourself worse. There's every chance you and Ursula will be together again. Don't give up hope.'

After a while he brought himself under control. 'I'd like to go back now. Louisa, can you ask the vicar to call on me? It's time I made a proper confession, to find peace, if I can.' He lifted her hand to his lips and kissed it and held on to it for a moment. He had grown to care deeply for this lovely young woman, who was so much more than bountiful. She had taken him in, continued with the commitment with grace, humour and true kindness. Doing things for him that even a close relative wouldn't care to do. If not for her, he would already have died in misery and been resigned to a pauper's grave. He didn't want her to grieve or worry after he'd gone, to bear regrets. He'd see the vicar for her sake. No matter how wretched he felt, from now on he'd keep it to himself. He wanted her to believe he'd died content. The last memories of him to be good. 'Thank you so much for bringing me here again. I hope Tom Harvey appreciates what a lucky young man he is. He doesn't call on you as much as he used to, I've noticed.'

'He's very busy on the farm.' Louisa pushed thoughts of Tom ruthlessly out of her head. She was getting good at it: it was too complicated to consider becoming Tom's wife. There would be time in the future to consider if she wanted to spend the rest of her life with him, if she loved him as much as she had David. She had conceded to herself that their differences stretched to something on the same par as Lottie's to Nate Harmon's. They were making things work, but it seemed the spark, the burning need had gone out of her and Tom's relationship. Perhaps when there was the chance it would all come back.

She felt she should stand back and give Bruce another quiet moment.

Bruce gazed down at the lonely name on the headstone. 'Goodbye, my darling. Wherever I end up, you'll have my love for ever.'

When Faye got to Ford Farm, everyone was there. The arrangements for the wedding were made during a quick break. It was to be an occasion shared by the whole community in the Methodist social rooms. 'Well, that's all decided,' Emilia said. 'The rector's only concern is that the bridegroom and his best man's leave aren't cancelled on the day.'

'We'll make it a good do for you, Miss Lottie.' Tilda dabbed her moist eyes with her apron. 'With the whole village chipping in and bringing a plate of something, there'll be plenty of food to go round. It's just what we all need during these hard times. Oh, Miss Lottie, I can't believe you're getting married!'

Lottie laughed and hugged her. 'Neither can I. Well, we'd better get back to work.' She glanced at Tom, who was swigging down a bottle of ginger beer, so eager to get outside again he was at the door.

'If I had my way I'd make it a double wedding.' As the words left his lips he wasn't sure if it was what he wanted. Louisa kept her distance from him in every way.

Sometimes he sensed she wasn't pleased when he was at her house. Then he remembered how good things had been between them, how passionate and exciting. She must simply be worn out nursing her gravely ill guest.

'That would be a little difficult,' Faye said. 'Louisa's got a lot on her plate. Tom, you must know about Mr Ash, who's staying with her. Why have you never mentioned him?'

'Because Louisa asked me not to,' he barked, turning bright red, dribbling drink down his chin.

'Mr Ash?' Emilia frowned at Tom. 'Who's he then when he's at home?'

Tom was saved from answering by Sidney Eathorne sticking his head round from the back kitchen. No doubt he'd got wind of the discussion. 'Hope I'm not intruding.' He winked conspiratorially. 'I'd put back a bit of sausage meat for you. Just thought I'd pop in with it. Any tea left in that pot?'

'Come along in, Sidney.' Perry got up from the table and offered him his chair.

Flourishing his white coat and striped apron as if he was wearing dress tails, Sidney sat down. 'Did you know that pair of evacuee rascals are running about your front garden, Mrs Em?'

'The twins are very well behaved,' Emilia said crisply. 'As you already know.'

Not liking the look of the butcher, Pearl, up on Tristan's lap, hid her face against him. Every other pair of eyes in the room was turned charily on Sidney.

Sidney wasn't fazed at all. A lifetime of being a busy-body had rendered him immune to impatient glares. 'May

I ask what the bride will wear? Something run up from butter muslin?'

'My mother's wedding dress,' Lottie gave the information loftily.

'How nice. If you're looking for something old, the wife's said to say she's got a very nice three-strand pearl necklace. It has a diamond clasp. She wore it on our big day.'

As haughty as she knew how, Lottie breathed, 'No, thank you. Everything's been taken care of.'

Sidney smiled at her as if he were nothing more than a dear old village character. 'I'm so pleased, but I don't envy you starting out on married life at a time like this. Well, mustn't hang about drinking tea when there's deliveries waiting to be made. See you all in church.'

'He'll be there bright and early to give it an inspection,' Lottie seethed. 'The old bugger had better not make any remarks about Nate and his friends.'

'Steady on. Language,' Tristan reprimanded her.

Tilda, the most faithful churchgoer among them, shook her finger at Lottie. 'Yes, young lady. Don't forget there's a child present. But although I would never use such a word myself, I agree that his runaway tongue has been known to cause trouble.'

'The man's gone now, poppet.' Tristan kissed the top of Pearl's head. He was enjoying having lots of company in the house, especially a little girl who reminded him of Adele. He was excited over the news that his daughter would have leave from Portsmouth for the wedding. If Jonny could make it, it would be the icing on the cake. He grinned to himself: there was no icing sugar to be had nowadays and cakes were either covered by a white cardboard façade lent by the baker or a tasteless, gooey sort of chocolate. He could make these little musings because he was happy and needed, no longer lonely. Strange that Tom could be described as being lonely and unhappy now. 'Well, we'd better get back, Faye. We'll need to butter up the children to get that cod liver oil down them. Let us know if there's anything we can do before Saturday, Em.'

As the Tremore people drifted away and Perry went off to hoe the garden, Tom fronted Lottie and Jill. His expression was implacable. 'Do you girls think you can manage with Granddad and Midge for the rest of the day? I need to see Louisa.'

'I suppose.' Lottie shrugged amiably. 'It's about time you and her came to a firm decision together.'

'I don't mind,' Jill said. Tom was her second best friend, she hated seeing him so downcast, and it was a little disconcerting, as if her security here was being threatened.

'Why the rush, Tom? Can't you ring her?' Emilia said. 'We're a bit pressed for time now.'

'Mum, I really need to see her.'

Tom looked as if he was going anyway. It was rare for him to be this stubborn. 'Go along then. I'll feed Paul, then help out too. Tilda can watch over him.'

He shot away to the back stairs to wash and change.

'What's got into him?' Emilia said. 'You don't think he's put out because Perry's going to give you away, do you, Lottie? Your granddad is happy for him to do it. I never thought about Tom.'

'It can't be that,' Lottie replied. 'He's always taken it for granted that Perry would walk me down the aisle.'

'He was all right until Faye mentioned Louisa's guest, Mr Ash,' Jill observed.

'Oh, yes,' Emilia recalled Tom's earlier discomfort. 'I wonder what it's all about. Not trouble, I hope.'

Tom flew along the lanes on his bicycle and was on Louisa's doorstep within twenty minutes. He was puffing and sweat was trickling down his back. He wiped moisture off his brow. The house was quiet. There was no sign of his intended fiancée in the downstairs rooms and he crept up the stairs. He found her sitting at Mr Ash's bedside, watching him sleep. She didn't know he was there. She was looking down at the sick man so tenderly, she was even holding his hand. Tom watched from narrowed eyes.

'Has he taken a turn for the worse?'

'Oh! Tom! I had no idea you were there. He's very tired. Is something wrong? You look so serious.'

'Come downstairs, Lou. We need to talk.'

He stood back so she could lead the way, then he kept close to her heels, breathing down her neck.

Louisa was unnerved. She knew what this was about. Faye had mentioned Bruce's presence and Tom wanted to confront her about it, to be told the whole truth. Still she hedged, putting the kettle on for tea. 'Have you come about the wedding?'

'I think you know why I'm here,' he said in a grave tone. 'Faye asked me about Mr Ash. Why I was keeping him a secret. Now I want to know why you're keeping him a secret. I won't be fobbed off any more. Who the hell is he? Were you once involved with him?'

'Don't be silly! What exactly did Faye tell you?'

'Nothing. She was interrupted. Well?'

She swallowed the constriction in her throat. 'You aren't going to like it.'

'I've already worked that out.'

His sarcasm made Louisa flinch. 'Please don't glare at me, Tom. This isn't going to be easy. I took a poor suffering man into my house knowing who he was and that I could not reveal his true identity. After I fell in love with you, I wanted to tell you who he was but I couldn't.'

'Why on earth not? There should have been no secrets between us. I've had enough, Louisa. Tell me who the bloody man is.'

Louisa looked him straight in the eye. 'I'm going to, but first let me warn you that I will not let you challenge or upset him in any way. In a sense it's really none of your business, and I'm only going to tell you the truth because we've been so close and we might have a future together. His real name is Bruce Ashley.'

Tom had heard the name only a few times over the years when family history was being discussed. It was a name that brought hurt and shame, quickly followed by silent tongues. 'Bruce Ashley?' He stormed about the room. 'The man who ripped my Uncle Tristan's life apart, who took Jonny's mother away from him, as good as killed her? No wonder you didn't want to tell me.'

He bore down on her in quick, hefty steps, forcing her to move back until she was trapped between him and the larder cupboard. 'Well, thank you very bloody much, Louisa! This shows exactly where your loyalty lies. You've admitted you even took that bastard in knowing full well who he was. It's not as if he tricked you and then you couldn't find the heart to throw him out. How dare you be so sly! How dare you keep this from me!'

Louisa was angry too, and indignant. 'I was afraid what your uncle would do. Don't forget that I owe Tristan Harvey nothing. He treats me like an outcast. He frightened me the last time he was here but you didn't even care!'

'Fair enough.' Then Tom started to shout. 'But Jonny's your friend. According to you a very special friend, yet you thought nothing about betraying him. Have you no idea just how vile that man is? He pulled a gun on Uncle Tris, Jonny and Aunt Em. He could have killed them.'

'The gun wasn't loaded. I know the whole story and he's genuinely sorry. He's eaten up with remorse. The reason he came back was to visit Ursula's grave because he still loves her. He's trying to make amends.'

'He's left it years too late for that. He deserves to die in the gutter. That's where you should have left him.'

'I thought you loved me for the very reason I couldn't ever do such a thing.'

Tom looked at her with pure distaste. 'I don't think I know what I fell in love with. I don't think I know you at all.'

'And I can say the same about you. You may not approve of what I've done but you haven't got the right to attack me so viciously over it. Are the Harveys the only people who matter in this world? Have you never heard of forgiveness and letting go of the past? Your family isn't perfect. I could throw a long list of scandals about them in your face, but I choose to overlook others' shortcomings. I think you'd better go.'

'You've got very fond of that old cad, haven't you?' Tom sneered.

'Yes, Tom,' she hissed. 'Very much so.'

He pulled back from her. 'I can only thank God that I've been saved from making the biggest mistake in my life.'

'And I too! Get out. I never want to see you again.'

Tom hurtled out of the house. He made to mount his bicycle but he was so frantic he let the handlebars drop and fell down on the doorstep. For several long moments he had no control over his limbs and felt sick and dizzy. *How could this happen?* In a few short hours, his life had fallen apart. And to the woman he had so admired and thought he'd loved, had banked his future on, he had said the most terrible, unforgiveable things.

When Bruce needed attention he rang a little china bell. He was ringing it urgently now. Louisa went up to him, forcing her watery legs to work. 'My dear, what's happened?' he croaked, trying to sit up. 'Who were you quarrelling with?'

She sat on the bed, close to him. 'It was Tom. It was terrible, Bruce. We're finished.' The shock and numbness left her and she started to cry, the huge, bitter tears of the heartbroken.

Bruce lifted his weak arms to her. She leaned forward and carefully laid her head against his shoulder. 'Was it because of me? Does he know who I really am?'

'Yes, he knows all about you, but the way he reacted… I never thought Tom could be so beastly,' she sobbed. 'He was hateful. He turned, it was as if he hated me.'

'I'm so sorry.' Bruce found the strength to stroke her hair. 'You didn't deserve that.'

After a few moments of his comfort, she whispered, 'Bruce, don't leave me yet. I need you.'

Chapter Twenty-Two

The sun was golden, dazzling and bright, as if paying homage to her wedding finery when Lottie stepped down from the trap, which was decorated, like the iron lychgate of the church, with wild flowers and ribbon. Perry had scraped enough blooms from the garden to make bouquets for her, and for Jill, in her new hat and frock, and Adele Harvey, fair and prepossessing in WRENS uniform.

'Are you sure you want to go through with this, darling?' Perry couldn't help a twinge of disappointment at seeing the verges packed with ribbon-bedecked American vehicles.

'Pappa…' She laughed blissfully. 'I hope Tom won't be too miserable and Louisa will come.'

'Never mind them,' Jill said, unfolding her long veil. 'It's your day. Enjoy every minute of it.' Repeating for the umpteenth time, 'You look so beautiful.'

Lottie felt herself floating through the church towards Nate, so handsome in his dress uniform. The small stone building was packed to bursting, with family, friends, and GIs, a couple of American officers, and ooing and aahing villagers in the back pews, many on their feet.

While the vows were being exchanged, Jill glanced at Tom. Sometimes he stared ahead, sometimes he looked at Lottie and forced a smile. Sometimes he kept his head down, sometimes he turned round and gazed through the crowds, no doubt looking to see if Louisa had turned up. He wouldn't tell anyone why he and Louisa had finished. Everyone was dying to know who her mystery house guest was, surmising Tom's misery could only be something to do with him. Faye had been questioned, but her description of the man wasn't that of a love rival. 'I've phoned Louisa but all she'd say was that she doesn't want to talk about it.' Poor Tom. He was so miserable. What was it all about? Louisa didn't seem the sort to simply throw him over, particularly as she had been sleeping with him.

Tristan was wondering about Tom too. When he had asked him if there was anything he could do, Tom had snapped, 'You've done enough already!' What did he have to do with Tom's and Louisa's broken romance?

Pearl tugged on his jacket. 'Do I give it now, Uncle Tris?' With Faye's help she had made a cardboard, tinsel-covered horseshoe to give to the bride.

'Not yet, poppet. When we go back outside.'

Faye was next to them, with Simon. She had thought to leave him with Agnes, knowing that otherwise she would be in for a lot of whispers behind raised hands from the gossips and the righteous, but she was proud of her son and refused to hide him away. Some people were kind, assuming her sweetheart had been lost in battle before they could marry. I'm happy enough for now, she thought. I don't envy Lottie the possibility that she might soon lose Nate.

It was hot and stuffy in the church and the doors had been left open. Excited gasps broke out as someone came in. Everyone looked round, including Lottie and Nate, hoping it was Louisa. The person coming up to the front, full of smiles, was Jonny. 'Sorry I'm late,' he said gaily. 'Do carry on.' To Tristan's delight, he squeezed in beside him. 'Brilliant to see Adele here.'

Lottie thought she would die with joy. Perhaps Louisa would arrive and run up to Tom and they'd make it up here and now. She wasn't given to romantic fancies but today she'd believe in anything.

Mr and Mrs Nate Harmon left the church under an American guard of honour.

Sidney Eathorne stood aside with the crowd when the family photographs were taken. Inclining his head here and there, he let forth exclamations of loud admiration and stage whispers. 'Doesn't the bride look a picture? It's the dress her mother wore when she married the squire. What do you call that colour? Pink? Coral? Course, her mother was two months gone… I wonder… Understandable why Mrs Em's so weepy, she must be thinking that Will should be here taking the pictures. God rest him.'

With Edwin driving the pair of ponies, Lottie and Nate entwined their fingers and kissed all the way to the Methodist rooms for the reception, only stopping to wave to well-wishers. Nate jumped down and lifted Lottie off the trap and kept her in his arms. 'Are you thinking what I'm thinking, honey?'

'That it's here where we first met.' She kissed his lips.

'I love this place. We'll have a party here for the baptism of our first baby.'

'Hey, mate!' A lorry load of squaddies drew up. The driver leaned out of the window. 'We don't like you stealing our women.'

Nate grinned back at the frosty face. 'Sorry about that. You and the rest of the guys want to come inside for a drink?'

'You've twisted me arm,' the driver called back. There was hoots of cheerful agreement from the others.

Lottie gasped as over a dozen young men in khaki birthed from the canvas at the back of the lorry and landed on the scrap of pavement. The driver drove the lorry off out of the way. 'Nate, we won't have enough food and drink to go round.'

'Don't you worry, Mrs Harmon. Herv and I dropped off a few things before we went to the church.'

The squaddies hurried to the social rooms' doors and raised their arms to form a guard of honour. Lottie was thrilled to enter the reception with her husband in this way. The soldiers stayed there until everyone had filed in to be greeted by the bride and groom.

'You all right, Mum?' Lottie asked Emilia. 'I wish Will was here too.'

'I'm fine. At least we've got Jonny.'

Jonny was badgering his father. 'What's all this about Tom and Louisa? I couldn't believe it when Sidney told me. What went wrong?'

'I don't know, son. Perhaps they realized they just weren't suited.'

'We're not,' Tom blurted out over Jonny's shoulder. He was unsteady on his feet. He had got hold of some black-market single malt and had already drunk half the bottle. 'She's not what she seems to be.'

'What does that mean, old chap?' Jonny demanded.

'Don't "old chap" me. I'm not a bloody Brylcreem boy.' Tom lurched and Jonny grabbed him and held him upright.

'I'm not going to allow you to wallow in bitterness like Uncle Ben over a lost love. Outside. Now. No arguments. You're not going to spoil Lottie's day or upset Aunt Em.' Jonny dragged him out of the back door.

The field at the back of the social rooms was where the village held most of its annual events. Owned by Ben, it had been ploughed up, currently planted with turnips, but there was enough grass left for those at the reception to spill outside, to lay down picnic rugs and eat and drink in the sunshine. Jonny frogmarched Tom to a quiet corner. 'What the hell's going on? You might be my cousin but I swear if you've done anything to hurt Louisa I'll give you a bloody good thrashing.'

Tom had not struggled against the humiliating ejection from inside. He fell back against the hedge, ignoring the hawthorn bushes scratching his back and ripping his suit; defeated, utterly wretched. 'I said a few harsh things to her, out of jealousy, I admit, but because she hurt me. God, Jonny, she's been keeping secrets from me. She left me out of one of the most important things to her. How can I ever trust her again?'

'What secrets? Damn it, Tom, I can't believe Louisa could ever do anything to cause you this much misery. She's too good, too pure. You're not saying she's got another bloke?'

Tom fought to clear his vision, then stared at the man so directly involved in the mess. 'I can't tell you. I won't, not even if you beat me into the ground. You must ask her. It's up to her if she tells you the truth.'

'It's that serious?'

'It should never have happened. I'm sorry for you, Jonny.'

'For me? This is getting silly.' Jonny chewed his lip. 'I'm going to see her. Do you promise to sober up and behave?'

'You have the Harvey oath. Now bugger off!'

'I'm beginning to wish I'd never got leave.' Jonny strode away.

Left alone, Tom straightened up and saw to his askew tie. Someone was gazing at him. Jill. She was about the only one he could tolerate right now. 'You look lovely,' he said, making the effort not to slur his words.

'Do you want me to keep you company?'

'Yeh. Thanks. Better get some food or something. Don't want to put a dampener on things for the happy couple, or Mum making a fuss.'

'I'm sorry about you and Louisa,' she said, as she strolled inside on his arm.

'Typical Jill.' He found a real smile at last. 'This is the first time you've mentioned it. You never pry. You're just… you. A really good friend. Perhaps I ought to snap you up. Take you and this lot back to the church in double quick time.'

'It's not me you're in love with, Tom.'

'Perhaps I never really was with Louisa. Well, I've blown it with her now.'

'You don't know that. Perhaps when you've both had a little time and space everything will work out.'

'It's not as simple as that.'

Jill was burning to know more but as always stayed discreet. 'The band's warming up. There will be some music and singing soon. Let's try to enjoy ourselves today.

We don't want to give Sidney Eathorne anything else to talk about.'

Chapter Twenty-Three

'Surely we're close enough friends for you to tell me what went wrong between you and Tom,' Jonny urged Louisa. 'It's upset you so badly you've even stayed away from the wedding.'

'It's personal.' She was in the kitchen, sorting out used clothing into piles for washing and reuse or unsalvageable stuff for the rag and bone. It made the room smell musty and seem Dickensian bleak.

'So you keep saying, Lou, but I don't buy it.' He didn't like seeing her so pale and fragile, as if a single unkind word would snap her in two. There was no doubt she was very tired, but it was as if her youth had been drained out of her, as if the vital ingredient that made her so ineffably lovely and gentle was in danger of being all used up. 'Tom was a ladies' man and my first thought would have been that you'd caught him out with someone else, if not for this business with your lodger. What's the deal? Are you going to tell me who this Mr Ash is?'

'I can't.' This was the worst fix of her life. She'd already lost Tom. He was furious and disgusted with her, as she still was with him over his attitude. Jonny would probably see her actions as a betrayal too. If she could think of something to fob Jonny off he'd never need to know. Bruce had very little time left. He was peaceful at last.

She wouldn't allow his last days to be thrown into turmoil and possibly shortened. If Jonny got as angry as Tom did he might even try to throw Bruce out.

'Tom said the same thing. Lou, darling, I'm worried about you. Won't you let me help you?'

'If you want to help, then please, Jonny, stay out of it. Just remain my friend.'

'All right, if that's what you want. Perhaps you'll feel able to tell me about it one day.'

'Perhaps.' She never would.

'Want a hug? You can trust me, Lou. I'd never do anything to hurt you.'

She answered by going to him and resting in his warm embrace. There was nothing she could say. She had helped one person and by doing so risked losing the love and respect of nearly all those she cared for. She couldn't bear to lose Jonny too.

–

While offering round tiny pieces of un-iced wedding cake, Emilia had been thinking about Jonny's sudden exit after Tom's mention of Louisa's mystifying Mr Ash. Even allowing for how close Jonny and Louisa were, it was unexpected that he'd choose now to hurry off to her. It kept bothering her that somehow she should know who the wretched man was. Ash? Ash… She knew of nobody of that name. The closest to it was someone from the past. Bruce Ashley… whose lover happened to be buried in Kenwyn churchyard… Louisa had met someone close to her home by chance… Emilia stopped stock still. Had fate played a cruel trick?

She rushed off to Tilda. 'Here, take this. I need to slip out. Paul's just been fed. He's with Faye.'

Tom was dancing the Palais Glide with Jill. Emilia interrupted and drew him aside. 'I'm going to ask you something, son, and I want a truthful answer. 'Do you know the full identity of the man staying with Louisa?'

'Do you think you know who he is?' Tom hedged. The last thing he wanted was more trouble for Louisa – he had sworn that he'd protect her.

Emilia wasn't going to be put off. 'Someone from the past. Your Uncle Tristan's past. Am I right?'

He nodded miserably. 'I've known she'd had a secret guest for some time. I couldn't cope when I finally got the truth out of her. Sorry, Mum, I should have told you, but I promised I'd never mention it to anyone.'

'Never mind that. There's more to the story than you know. It's time everything was revealed. Stay here and make sure everything keeps running smoothly.'

Next, she located Perry and Tristan, enjoying some banter with the squaddies. 'Sorry to break things up. Perry, Tris, you have to come with me. Now.' She hurried them out of the front entrance.

'What's going on, darling?' Perry knew all her moods. Rarely had he seen her so grave and intense.

'What's wrong?' Tristan hung back. 'I was about to see if Pearl's tickety-boo.'

'She's fine playing outside with the other children. Come on, we've no time to lose. I'll tell you on the way.'

'Hey. Your mom, stepfather and uncle have run out on us,' Nate whispered lovingly into Lottie's ear. 'They're probably going to tie some old boots and cans to the trap to see us off. Or to prepare the marriage bed.' A wicked twinkle played in his eyes.

'I suppose so.' Lottie was ponderous. It was usually the younger element that got up to that sort of thing. Jonny had shot off somewhere too.

Tom made to go after the rapidly disappearing elders. Jill tugged him back. 'I couldn't help overhearing some of what was said. Whatever it is, let them see to it. Mrs Em told you to stay here. Louisa may need you afterwards.'

'I don't know about that. Jill, I'm frightened. Look, you might as well know what's up. If there's to be ructions and it spills over back here, you'll be the best one to find a way to tell Lottie. Let's find somewhere private.'

–

'If you're right about this, I'll kill him!' Tristan reverted to some choice soldier's language. He had the ponies pulling the Tremore trap at a fast trot.

'Violence isn't going to help,' Emilia stated, squeezed in between him and Perry. 'You've got to think of Jonny.'

'I am, but if Ashley's come back to haunt me, if he destroys things between me and my son…'

'Don't forget the chap's dying,' Perry said. 'You've got to stay calm.'

'I've been dreading this day might come. I should have told Jonny years ago,' Tristan cursed himself. 'I had plenty of openings, every time he asked me what I had against Louisa. I should never have taken out my hatred of Ashley against her. Jonny will hate me for it.'

'Not if you keep cool and tell him sensibly,' Emilia said. 'He might understand why we kept the secret. He's got no respect for Ben but he had a lot for Alec. Alec never wanted him to learn about what really happened that night. We'll point that out to Jonny.'

'Let's hope after the initial shock both Jonny and Louisa will take the news gladly,' Perry said. 'They'll be gaining a lot. Louisa's in for the biggest shock when she finds out it's her father she's been nursing under her roof.'

—

Louisa came down from upstairs.

'How is he?' Jonny stubbed out a cigarette. 'I've made tea, afraid it's like gnat's pee. What have you got in the pantry? You look as if you haven't eaten for days.'

'He's sleeping. He sleeps all the time now. He didn't eat anything yesterday.'

'It can't be long now then.'

'No.' She hugged her cardigan in tighter round herself. 'I'm going to miss him so much. Funny really, I haven't known him long, yet I feel I've known him all my life.'

'I'm sorry, Lou.'

'Don't be. I don't regret meeting him.'

'Well, that will bring you some comfort after he's passed away. I wish I could be around for you then. You do regret finishing with Tom though? You do want to make things up with him?'

'I don't know if that's possible. I don't allow myself to concentrate on how I feel about Tom, though for a while it seemed so right between us. I have to keep strong to face the death of my friend.'

'Well, perhaps you and Tom weren't meant to be.' Jonny was recalling Tom saying he'd never trust her again. He'd never seen him so upset. And now it was the same with Louisa. She broke into tears and rushed to his arms.

234

'Louisa? Can we come in?'

'Aunt Em!' She broke away from Jonny. 'What are you doing here? And you, Perry? Why have you left the wedding?' Her brow knotted and her upper lip turned into a snarl when she saw the further person who had taken the liberty of walking into her house. There was such a compassionate look to her aunt, a mixture of gravity to the two men. Her gut twisted in fear. There could be only one reason why they were here. If only Jonny had already left.

'Don't be afraid, Louisa,' Emilia said. 'We should all sit down. Why don't you come and sit by me?'

'But he mustn't stay.' She stabbed a finger towards Tristan. 'He'll make a scene.'

'I promise I won't.' Tristan raised himself stiffly on his toes.

'I'll make sure he won't,' Jonny said, throwing a warning at his father, who looked as if he was suffering from all kinds of plagues. 'At last we'll get to the bottom of what's been going on all these years.' He shuffled Louisa, who had grown frozen, towards Emilia. They sat down either side of her. He took her chilled hand. He could sense she was hardly daring to breathe.

Tristan stayed on his feet, clasping his hands behind his back, his chin up, military style. Perry retreated circumspectly to a window.

Seconds went by in wrought silence. Emilia steadied herself with a deep breath. 'Of course the past events happened before Perry came to Hennaford, but as my husband, he knows all about it. I am sorry, Louisa and Jonny, that the two of you have been kept in the dark but please believe that the decision made so many years ago was felt by all of us, and that includes Alec, Ben, Polly and Julian, to be for the best.'

'You included Jonny, Aunt Em. How is it that both of us are involved in the past?' Louisa said, her voice breaking up.

'Yes, let's get it over with.' Jonny was on the attack. 'Father, what exactly has this grudge you have against Louisa got to do with me?'

Tristan emptied his throat but still felt he was choking. 'This is very hard… you must both prepare yourselves for a shock.'

Louisa gripped Jonny's hand until she was digging her nails into him. He didn't notice the pain.

'First, let me say that only Emilia, when the matter was discussed again some years ago, felt that the truth should come out. Anyway, the truth is… the plain fact is… Ursula, your mother, Jonny… was also mother to you, Louisa. You are the baby she gave birth to.'

'What?' Living under extreme stress for so many days, it was too much to take in and Louisa collapsed against Jonny in shock.

'That can't be right.' Jonny shook his head in disbelief. He wrapped Louisa into his body, in protection, as if they were on some collision course.

'It's true,' Emilia said. 'There was never going to be the right time to tell you. Polly was Louisa's legal guardian and she more than any of us wanted to keep it hushed, in fear that Louisa would be shunned in society. We couldn't go against her wishes.'

'Well, this is more than a bit thick!' Jonny threw at his father. 'All these years, Lou and I have been brother and sister and you've worked as hard as the devil knows how to keep us apart. We had the right to know. It wouldn't have hurt after we'd grown up. We could have kept the secret ourselves or faced the world and damn the self-righteous! It wasn't right. It's appalling!'

'Son, please, let me explain—'

'You can't! I've always trusted you to be honourable, worthy of respect. Now I find that your rejection of Louisa wasn't some trifling thing, an idiosyncrasy, your funny little way, as I've always tried to reason it away. You've continually rebuffed her, bewildered her, you've been downright bloody cruel!'

Louisa was struggling to free herself. Reluctantly, he let her go. She got up shakily, staring at Tristan with all the emotions that were trawling through her. Her voice emerged as a stranger's, one harrowed word at a time. 'Then this means that the man upstairs, Bruce Ashley, is my father.'

'Yes.' Tristan was wrought with terror that Jonny would never forgive him. Even now he could not hide his utter distaste at the mention of his old enemy. 'I'm afraid it is.'

'Afraid? Afraid, Mr Harvey? Did you think I'd be disgusted, like you are? I've cared for him these past few months. I've grown very fond of him because he's truly sorry for what he did to her, to Ursula, my mother. He's so sorry that he doesn't think himself worthy of forgiveness. No, I feel more for him than fondness. I love him. Now I know why. He's about to die, and if it wasn't by chance that Faye had seen him that day I'd never have known he was my father. Oh, I've been afraid, Tristan Harvey. Afraid of you finding out about Bruce and turning up here to seek revenge on your wife's lover. And all this time you've been afraid, afraid Jonny and I would find out your sordid secret. I can accept the others thought they were doing the best for me but you've despised my very existence. You think I'm sordid. I hate you for that.'

'I don't believe it.' Jonny was up and pacing one spot like a caged beast. 'I could have been killed at any time and I'd never have known I'd had another sister. This war has changed all perceptions, broken down barriers, moved us to where we acknowledge what's truly important. Why could none of you see that? Especially you, Father?'

'Son…' Jonny threw his back towards him and all Tristan could do was hang his head.

Emilia glanced at Perry, lost at what to do.

Calmly, Perry approached Louisa. 'Please take a moment to listen to me, Louisa. I'm looking at all this from an outsider's point of view. Emilia, Tristan and the others only wanted to protect Jonny. The people who were to adopt you refused to have you because of your birthmark. Emilia and Alec offered to raise you. So did Ben. They had sworn to Ursula that they'd take care of her baby. Try to think of it from Tristan's point of view. It's understandable that he didn't want the baby of his late wife and her lover raised in Hennaford. He allowed Julian Andrews to take you. He and Polly Hetherton wanted you very much. Thanks to all of them, even Tristan, because as Ursula's husband, he could have signed you away to an orphanage, you grew up in a loving home.'

'I can thank you for that, I suppose.' Louisa uttered every word with a bitter-sharp sting in it as she marched up to Tristan. 'I'm sure the option of an orphanage would have been preferable to you! Where my birthmark would have ensured no one ever took me on. I told you once before to get out of my house, now I'm telling you again. Get out! Never, ever come back!'

'Louisa, you've got the right to be upset,' Emilia pleaded, shaken by the strength of her hostility. 'I know you've had a lot to bear recently. But can't you see that Tristan was the only innocent party back then? He adored Ursula. He was battle scarred, he took it all very badly.'

'I'll go,' Tristan said, fumbling towards the door. 'I have tried to say sorry to you lately, Louisa. I swear I truly am sorry.'

'You're only sorry because you're afraid how Jonny will take this. I hope he turns against you,' Louisa hurled after him. 'Don't you want to dash upstairs and hurt Bruce?'

'A short time ago certainly I would have wanted to, but now everything's out in the open, seeing you and Jonny together as you should be, brother and sister, I feel nothing for him. I'm sure, when you've had time to cool down, you'll realize you don't mean much of what you've said. If there's one person who's incapable of hating and desiring revenge, it's you. You're a woman of honour and compassion. Few people would have given succour to a man like Ashley. It's cost you your own happiness with Tom and I'm sorry about that too.' Tristan hardly dared look at Jonny. 'Will you stay here?'

'Of course. I've got twenty-six years to catch up on with my sister.' The eyes on his father were remote and cold. 'I'll come to Tremore before I head back to base.'

'I'm sorry, Jonny. Please don't be too hard on your father. I'm sorry, Louisa. I hope because of Tom it won't stop you coming to the farm,' Emilia said. All she got back was blank faces. It was too soon yet for them to come to terms with the revelations. Linking her arm through

Perry's, they followed on after Tristan's lonely, dejected figure.

Alone for the first time under their new status, the enormity of the affair took its toll on both Louisa and Jonny. The walls of the room seemed to be folding in on her and in a moment of panic she ran to the open window to gasp in great lungfuls of air. 'Hell, I need a drink!' was his reaction. He rooted in the drinks cabinet and poured two good measures of brandy.

'Here, get this down you.'

She took the glass like an automaton, but while he drank without allowing the liquor to warm up, she cradled hers in her hands. 'How do you feel about me taking in Bruce?' she said, in challenge. Closer she might be now by blood to Jonny, but the man upstairs still came first.

'I can't say I like it, but it's just the sort of thing that you'd do, Lou. How can I blame you for that? I suppose it's a relief somehow to know that someone loves my mother that much. My memories of her are mixed and hazy. She was good to me but twice she tried to take me away from my security. I've never resented her, just felt sorry for her. I promise I won't go near him. Go up to him, Lou. Go on. He needs you.'

Suddenly it was as if a terrible, oppressive weight had been lifted off her. She swayed on her feet, then got a grip on herself. 'At least I know who I am now.'

'Yes, you do, and I'm so glad. I'm so glad that you're my sister. Will you tell him? That you're his daughter?'

'Yes. I only hope that it's not too late for him to understand.'

Jonny finished the brandy then went off to the kitchen to find something to pull together to eat. Louisa was going to need her strength. He fashioned a meal to fry up, cold potatoes and carrots, onion, scraps of bacon. He shoved aside a bundle of smelly clothes and laid two places on the table. Discovered the Nescafé and spooned the necessary grains into two mugs. Rambling round the garden, newly tilled with vegetables, he smoked a cigarette. Thinking not about how this affected him, not about his father's silence, only about Louisa and how upsetting it was going to be to lose the man she'd just been told was her father. Damned pity she and Tom had fought over Ashley, he would have been a comfort to her. Planning for their marriage would have been the perfect thing to give her new hope and purpose. After Ashley's death she'd have nothing – he, himself, was almost certainly bound to be killed on one of his next raids.

Jonny wasn't one for praying. Now he joined his hands together. *Please God, let me live through. Let me come safely through right to the end or Louisa will have no one.*

He went back inside. The kitchen was empty. Louisa had been upstairs a long time. He crept up. He heard her speaking quietly in between the laboured breathing of the dying man. The door, just along the landing, was open and he could see her at the bed. At the doorway, he threw a stage whisper: 'Forgive me coming up, but you really ought to eat something. I'll have it ready in ten minutes.'

'Jonny. I can't leave him.'

'Oh. This soon, is it?' He went to the doorway. 'Shall I call the doctor?'

'There's nothing he can do. Would you run along to the vicarage and see if the vicar's at home?'

The vicar came and performed the last rites. Bruce slept all the way through.

Jonny saw the vicar out and took coffee up to Louisa. The patient's breathing was barely audible now. She was a tiny figure of heartbroken resignation. A lost child. His heart ached for her. 'Lou, darling, where shall I leave this?'

'Bring it in if you'd like. Otherwise, leave it on the chest out there.'

He went into the room and passed her the cup. Intending to steal out again, he couldn't resist glancing down at the man in the bed. He saw an emaciated shell, a shadow of a human being. Dear, wonderful, strong Louisa. It would be hard for anyone to watch such a state of deterioration. Now she had to see this through knowing the man was her father. 'My God! I'm sorry, I remember him as such a handsome chap. Fair, like you, youthful, beguiling. He used to play with me, he could be so funny. The memories are coming back now.'

She looked up, tears gathered at her eyes. 'Jonny, will you tell me about them, after he's gone? It would mean so much to me.'

'Of course. Has he woken?'

'No. I'd so like him to, but it would be cruel to wish him back. I've told him I'm his daughter, I hope he understands. He's almost there, with her, our mother. He's mumbled her name twice. He knows she's near.' To forbid the tears she sipped the coffee.

Before this Jonny had not believed in an afterlife. 'Lou, refuse if you want to, but could I stay, in case she comes, in case Mother comes to all of us.'

'I'd so like your company, Jonny. To share something so meaningful with you.'

He got a chair and sat beside her. Holding hands, she holding Bruce's cold, withered fingers, they watched and waited. Louisa whispered through the gathering stillness, 'Go to her, Father. Go to Mother.'

Coming back from the far reaches of a distant plane, Bruce opened his eyes. He blinked. Saw shadows. 'Who… is it?'

'It's Louisa. A friend is with me.'

Jonny hesitated. Should he say it? There was only going to be one chance. 'It's Jonny Harvey. Ursula's son. I'm with Louisa. Your daughter. She's yours and Ursula's daughter.'

For an instant he appeared to be thinking clearly. 'I thought… now I know…'

His eyes closed. The ravaged face was lit for a moment by a smile. The smile faded but the light stayed. A peace filled the room. There was a hint of perfume.

'Mother?' Jonny looked up expectantly. He was touched by something, something like a light tap on his shoulder and something deep and profound in his heart. It made him weep tears of joy and sorrow.

'Mother?' Louisa ventured. Then it was as if she was being held by another pair of arms.

There were four people in the room. The light left Bruce. Then there were two.

Chapter Twenty-Four

Ben was catching his breath on the hard flagged kitchen floor of a bombed-out cafe. It was nearly summer but he was cold and exhausted from lack of sleep and he had eaten little for several days. He accepted a cigarette from the weary hand of one of his French compatriots. They didn't speak. Each of them, now down to seven men and one woman after a recent bloody fight with a small German convoy, knew the importance of gaining a little rest before going out on their next operation. They had taken part in blowing up railway lines, watching locomotives climb the air like crazy caterpillars and enemy troops being blown to kingdom come. They had laid explosives in weapon arsenals and run like hell before everything within blast distance was annihilated. Now the expected liberation was imminent, the group were concentrating on cutting enemy communication lines.

Against the opposite wall, the woman – just a girl, really – a pretty thing from hardy peasant stock, with a deceptively naive gleam to her dark brown eyes, moved, inadvertently revealing a flash of bare thigh. Ben looked away. He hadn't felt sexual urges since the conflict with Emilia, it had drained him of that need, and Josette was young enough to be his daughter. He hated the idea of any man lusting after Faye, taking advantage of her. He believed himself fully capable of killing anyone for hurting her. What would she think of him now he was a ruthless killer, even though he did it in the name of justice and peace? He allowed himself just a few indulgent seconds to linger over Faye every day. More would fill him with anguish, loneliness and a longing that he couldn't bear, and that might make him careless and cost one of these good French people everything.

He'd always believed it to be a privilege to fight for liberation, to shield and protect. It was. Yet the more he went on perpetrating acts of sabotage the more numb and dehumanized he felt, and sullied and vile. He couldn't remember exactly on what occasion when he had shot a particular German soldier. He had been the last enemy in a stand-up fight as he and the others had made their escape after taking out an officer's car and motorbike and sidecar outriders. A cry from the soldier made him stop and look back, kick him over so he could see his face and aim his Bren gun at his head. He'd had every intention of finishing him off.

'*Hilfe mich…*' The soldier had stared up at him out of pain-stricken, frightened eyes.

Ben's guts had lurched and he'd very nearly vomited over his own boots. He had killed a boy, for as surely as the soldier was about to die, he was only about eighteen years old. And the boy was asking for his help. For an instant he didn't know what to do, help the boy out of his misery or leave him to his fate, all alone and far from home.

Then a hand had pulled on him roughly. 'We must go!'

Yes, he had to get away. He went, but not before the next moment passed and he saw the life expire from some German mother's son.

The anonymous boy, whom he would never forget, was no more. And he himself was someone else. Someone else from the brash, self-confident businessman who had roamed this now desecrated country to hunt down new quality wines in its sun-glazed vineyards. Someone without a real identity, just a new name when it was considered wise for a change. He had once lived the high life, dined in the best hotels with the top echelons of local society. Now he crouched like an animal, a savage, dirty and scavenging for food, but while he cared nothing for himself, he felt the same for his country. And Faye.

Anything left in the kitchen had been ransacked after the explosion that had destroyed the cafe. He had half an hour before it was his turn to take over as lookout. He shut his eyes and tried to recall the taste of a dry Chablis with trout, a Beaujolais with chicken, a sweet Sauternes with *pâté de foie gras*, or his favourite, a majestic Burgundy with home-grown game. His imagination failed him. There was nothing on his tongue but ash and nicotine. Oh, to puff on a fat Havana cigar, just once more. To take a hot, soapy bath. He hadn't washed for days, nor had the others and they all stank. In a flash of his typical broad humour, Raphael, the group's leader, a classical music master, had joked that the Bosch only had to sniff the air and they would all be dead meat, just as they smelled.

Something made him snap his eyes open. It was an instinct through continually living on his wits more than an actual noise, but next instant he was sure there was something. Something wrong. In a fast but not panicked fluid movement he got to his feet, listening hard. 'Did you hear that, Raphael?'

Raphael nodded, deadly serious. He had heard the noise.

The others gathered round, hurriedly strapping on rifles and guns and grenades. Ben's mind was on the two lookouts. No alarm had been raised – Ben was convinced they had been silenced. He drew a line across his throat to display his fears. Raphael nodded, as grim as a funeral chief mourner, and led the way cautiously into the cafe. Ben went immediately after him. They dropped low, behind the splintered bar. All was quiet. Arnaud had been stationed at the church and Julien at what had once been the school, places that gave the best advantage to watch the roads. Raphael tossed his head to indicate Ben should steal to the left and he would go to the right. Ben made a sign: OK. Slightly hunched over, nerves screaming tight, bodies taut as springs yet ready to fly into action, they started out, the rest gradually following on. The group would fan out and make sure, as they had done not long ago, that the perimeter of their resting place was secure.

His Bren gun held in position, Ben was nearly at the school, looking for Julien, when the first shot split the air. It was not fired at him. He was aware of a cry as one of the Frenchmen was hit. As he threw himself behind a heap of rubble he caught a glimpse of Julien sitting in a heap, blood splashed down over his dirty shirt. Ben's cut throat illustration had been chillingly true. The group had been discovere,whether betrayed or tracked down, they had a fight on their hands. Across the little dusty road, German helmets were bobbing up from cover in force and it was obvious they were outnumbered.

Raphael tore back from the church. 'Take cover!' Before he could follow his desperate order and take cover himself, he took a bullet in the head and dropped dead in the road, his beret spinning crazily in the air before landing on him.

The day turned into chaos and insanity. In the brutal exchange of fire, bullets from machine guns and rifles whizzed and zapped, hitting buildings and glass, making shrapnel and splinters, thudding into soft flesh and mincing bones. Ben was aware of his compatriots and enemy soldiers falling, in ones and twos, like wheat cut down by an unholy sickle. He was in for it this time. There was nowhere to go but into glory. Death was coming to him but he was resigned to it. He'd been glad to serve his country and this occupied land, he had done what he'd had to do.

'Louis!' Josette shouted to him.

'Run, Suzanne!' Suddenly she was not there any more. She disappeared in a blast.

The rubble of the school was holed in several places, and to avoid being hit, Ben lay nearly flat, firing through a ragged opening. A sharp pain and a curious thud told him he'd been shot in the shoulder. The Bren gun fell from his hands. He rolled on to his back and reached down to his waistband and pulled out a small firearm. He got up, he'd fight in the open. He wouldn't allow himself to be captured and tortured for information. He stalked towards the Germans, firing as he went. His legs buckled as bullets slammed into them and he dropped to the ground with a terrific thump. He must have received a bullet in the spine for he was completely paralysed.

He must have been the last alive in the group – the firing had stopped. In seconds he was surrounded by Germans pointing guns at him. An officer bent to him and yanked the hair back from his brow and exclaimed in delight. The scar had given away that he was the wanted man known formerly as Jean-Claude. Ben thanked God that no matter how much time he had left, no matter what was done to him he was incapable of feeling a thing. His only regret was that he'd never see Faye again. Or Tristan. Or Emilia. He loved them all. However many moments he had left, he'd glory in reflections of them. What were they doing? Did they ever think of him?

He was back in Hennaford. Working Ford Farm's fields with his older brother, Alec. Loving with Emilia. Moving into Tremore. Bringing home Brooke, his lovely American bride. Viewing Faye after her birth, disappointed that she wasn't a son. Then he was filled with a father's love for her, a love that had come too late, yet somehow he knew she loved and forgave him.

Blood trickled out of his mouth. He coughed. 'Faye…' It was on this blessed note that his memory ceased for ever.

Chapter Twenty-Five

'I don't want you to use anything this time, Nate. This is the perfect place to conceive a baby, where we had our first kiss.' Lottie was stretched out dreamily on a picnic rug, gazing up with all her love for her new husband.

'I agree it's the perfect place, Lottie darling, but it's not the perfect time.' His desire fragmented by doubts, he gently rolled off her and pulled her clothes together, but immediately brought her to face him, lying side by side, caressing her face, his tender brown eyes fervently persuasive. 'It's been a long build-up, but I'll be shipped overseas any day now. The whole county's been shut off. It's a miracle I was able to make it here today. Don't go all quiet on me. You know how I hate to disappoint you. I'm thinking of you, honey. When I land in Europe I'll be right up there in the danger zone with the other guys, taking care of them, being where I'm needed.'

'I know all that.' She trailed her fingers through his hair. She was affectionate and earnest. 'I also know that you, like my family, think I'm not much more than a girl and I won't be able to cope if I lost you. I can't bear that thought, darling, but I'm strong enough to say it, and I'm strong enough to carry on alone with your child. I want your baby, Nate. Whatever happens, I want to always have part of you with me.'

'It's a wonderful thought but don't you think a baby should have its father around to help raise it?'

'It will because I'll tell it all about you. How wonderful and beautiful you are.'

It made him smile. 'You're the one who's beautiful. Well...'

'Yes?' She pushed her hand inside his unbuttoned shirt and lingeringly kissed his hot skin. 'Let's not waste any time. I've only seen you twice since our wedding.'

He let her carry on, enjoying her demanding touch. In her bed on their wedding night, after her initial shyness, Lottie had thrown off all inhibitions. She wasn't slow at making the first move on him. 'It's because we're soulmates,' she'd said. 'You make me whole.' He was worried that without him she'd be frighteningly less of a person. If he went ahead with what she wanted, if she got a dreaded telegram, if she had his child, at least it would be a reason for her to go on and rebuild her life.

She was working her way all over him. 'You were saying, darling? I know I might not get pregnant today but we can have a wonderful time trying. I'm determined to have my way.'

'Little madam.' He smiled provocatively.

'What?' She tossed her head, laughing.

'It's what the butcher called you at the reception.' Expertly, Nate imitated the local nosy parker's thick Cornish accent, the sideways glance and the working of his jaw he always gave before departing with something confidential. 'You've taken on a lot for yourself there, you know. Young Lottie can be quite a little madam when she gets started.'

'Well…' Lottie moved about him, catlike. Her glorious wealth of coppery hair was in a mess. 'Usually old Sidney talks a load of drivel but for once he's perfectly right.'

'Show me then.'

'Is that an order, Corporal?'

He reached up and put his hand behind her head, pulling her face to his and kissing her mouth passionately. 'Sometimes I like to give orders. Right now, Mrs Harmon, you're completely in charge.'

–

Jill was bored, even though it was Sunday afternoon, which meant she had precious time off; only help with the milking required. When she lacked her closest friend she'd seek out the next. Tom. He was presently in a tiny secluded tumbledown house, at the bottom of a hill, in Church Lane. An old lady, a tenant of Ford Farm's, had died there recently, leaving no one behind, and Tom was there sorting out her things. Miss Reynolds had been so reclusive Jill had never set eyes on her. She was curious to learn something about her and to see inside her home, which apparently she had rarely allowed anyone to set foot in. Even the oldest villagers knew little more about Miss Reynolds than that she had first rented the house off Tom's great-grandfather as a young woman with a small private income.

One reason Miss Reynolds's little dwelling had been hard to spot was the tall trees that grew out of the high hedge in front of the house. There was no gate. Jill squeezed through the impossibly narrow entrance almost blotted out by brambles, nettles and hawthorn, her bare legs getting scratched and stung and her cotton skirt snagged on the way. The minuscule plot of garden was wildly overgrown. It was said Miss Reynolds had stubbornly, sometimes with hostility, refused all offers of help, seeing it as interfering charity. Mrs Em had mentioned that when Tom had turned up back-along with a saw and scythe, to make way for some daylight to her windows, she had chased him off with a horsewhip.

Jill found herself facing what could be charmingly described as an interesting and neglected doll's house. A one-up-one- down affair, the cob walls were uneven and coated near the ground with moss. The planked front door came as a surprise. It measured no more than five foot high and the words 'Lower Hill' were quite newly painted on it in an exquisite hand. Perhaps Miss Reynolds had been one of the 'small people' who'd had artistic inclinations. She tried the knobbly iron latch, ready to call out Tom's name. It wouldn't budge – must be bolted on the inside. A wall ran round close to the side of the house, over which woody shrubbery loomed and drooped. She eased her way through, noting snapped twigs, no doubt made by Tom's struggle to gain entry. The stable back door was thrown open. She went in, blinded for a moment after the bright sunlight.

Tom had been in the downstairs room since lunchtime, lounging in the one and only armchair, which barely supported his back, his long legs sprawled out almost to the other side of the room. He'd finished what he'd come to do but was in the mood to linger. It was he, prompted by a sixth sense that something was wrong while driving the tractor past this way, who had discovered Miss Reynolds's stick-thin, eighty-nine-year-old body. The doctor said she had died of natural causes in her sleep.

A good way to go. Just a glance around today had shown that the few ancient bits of furniture, there in place at her arrival, were riddled with woodworm, fit only for burning. There was no evidence of Miss Reynolds ever lighting a fire – just as well from the neglected state of the chimney. However had she survived in winter, the little scrap of flesh and bone? Sheer bloody-mindedness, he guessed. What had made her so belligerent, shunning all contact? A lost love? He could understand that. How had she got through all the loneliness? He belonged to a large, close family and had many friends, yet the loneliness since losing Louisa sometimes came down off the walls of his room at night to meet him. So cold and so bleak he could almost see it as a living entity.

His heart gave a peculiar lurch and the hairs on the back of his neck prickled. Miss Reynolds was in the doorway, framed in a golden haze, come back to turn him out for intruding. 'Oh!' His hand flew to his heart. 'It's you, Jill. I thought you were a ghost.'

'You look as lost as I feel. Want some company?'

'Come in. Afraid there's nowhere else to sit unless you care to rest on my lap. I'm wedged in this little chair, not sure if I can get out.'

'What a strange little place.' She delved into every nook and space. The curtains were moth-eaten. Tom had packed the few dust-laden ornaments, of fine quality, and the cream and brown odds of crockery into a box. 'There's not a single photograph. What did the old lady look like?'

'She had snow-white hair in a long plait wound up round her head. Her hands and feet were as small as Pearl's. She spoke like a BBC broadcaster. I used to think she had a vicious streak, but when I looked at her face as she lay dead she looked quite content. Perhaps she knew no one could ever bother her again.'

'It's sad though, isn't it? Wanting that much solitude.'

Tom's eyes grew watery. 'Sorry.'

'Don't be embarrassed, Tom.' She went to him. Their friendship was so close she felt no shyness at sitting on his lap. He rested his face against her shoulder. She put her arms round his neck. 'Cry as much as you want. It's been easier for me. I had Lottie to blubber to.'

'I'm glad she understood your heartbreak,' he sniffed. He wasn't going to cry – he'd done enough of that. 'She loses her patience with me.'

'Don't you think she has a point though?' Jill said soothingly. 'That it's time you spoke to Louisa? According to Faye, she's just as miserable as you are. You might be able to sort things out. You'll continue to find it hard to go on if you don't thrash out your feelings with her. One of you needs to make the first move. Why don't you make it?'

'I'm not being stubborn, honestly, Jill. I don't believe Louisa is either by keeping her distance. We hurt each other badly. I don't think we can get back what we had.'

'You won't know if you don't try. And if you can't, don't you think it would be good to be her friend again? Think about it.'

He did. They stayed wrapped up silently, finding comfort, enjoying the nearness. It was different holding Jill. Her body was just as feminine as Louisa's but he could have her this close without lusting for her. Had lust been the biggest attraction where Louisa was concerned? Had her aura of purity, her great compassion, the hint of unavailability, made him long for something he'd thought he could never have? If he had really loved her, how could he have kept this long silence? He knew then that his raw feelings had been more to do with his hurts than the need to be forever with Louisa. He told Jill these thoughts. 'That makes me bloody damned shallow. I compromised Louisa. I asked her to marry me but I didn't put it to her properly, in a way a woman would want. Then at the first little crisis, instead of trying to understand the motives behind her secrecy, I blew her out. I as good as deserted her. All I've done since is to send her a letter to say sorry about her bereavement – that must have seemed bloody insulting. I do need to go to her, Jill. To say sorry and ask her to forgive me.' He kissed the crown of her head and snuggled her in tighter. 'Thanks. You're everything a chap could wish for in a friend.'

'You too.' She was so comfortable with him she could easily have dozed off into a contented sleep.

'When will you go to Kenwyn?'

'Today. Soon. But not yet. Let's stay like this a while longer.'

–

Tristan timidly approached Ursula's grave. He'd brought flowers, a few carnations, not knowing if he should leave them. He hardly had the right. He was pleased to see there were some there already. 'Hello, Ursula,' he whispered. 'Hope you don't mind me coming. I'm so sorry. I was too hard on you. If I'd accepted your baby, you might have fought to live. If you knew how I've treated your little girl you'd hate me.'

Despite the crows croaking their everyday treetop graveyard dirge, there was an unearthly hush. A sense of isolation. Tristan swallowed. He was infringing, he had no right to be here. Bruce Ashley had come back to Ursula. They belonged together. He'd leave, take his flowers with him. Then he knew another reason for his unease. He wasn't the only visitor to this quiet place. Louisa walked round to the head of the grave and faced him. As grim as death. She was pale and thin, her eyes too large for her lovely face. 'Do forgive me. I shouldn't have encroached. I, um… just wanted to… say goodbye to her.'

'Why did you come?' she asked in the softest whisper.

Her thoughts were unreadable but Tristan feared she'd fly at him. He took a respectful pace back. 'I've wanted to since the day, um, Bruce died. On the way back to Lottie's reception it hit me just how cruel I'd been to you all your life. And to Ursula. I really did love her, please believe that.'

'I suppose I should feel glad about that. You'll always hate my father, won't you? Do you want to see where he's buried?' Accusation blazed in her. 'There's flowers on his grave too. I'll never abandon either of them.'

She expected him to decline, perhaps mumble another pathetic apology and walk away. She was taken out of stride when he said, 'Yes, I would like to, if you meant that as a serious offer.'

'I didn't. I was being sarcastic. Why do you want to go there?'

Tristan shrugged. 'I wouldn't have dreamt of it until you asked. To make a sort of peace, I suppose. I'm not feeling noble, Louisa. I hated Bruce Ashley more for taking Ursula away from me rather than for hurting her so much. Sometimes when I look at you, you remind me of her and I remember how much she meant to me. She was once my lifeblood. I adored her. Her betrayal sliced my heart in half. But I shouldn't have taken it out on you.'

'Since Bruce died I've spent nearly all my time alone, time in which I've examined all the facts and all my feelings. I've tried to understand things from your angle, although I didn't really want to. Ursula tried twice to deprive you of Jonny, during a time when you were going through hell in the trenches.'

'It's no excuse for my years of animosity. Please forgive me.'

She came round the headstone and gazed at the name, so reviled, so tragic. 'You and Jonny are my closest links to the mother I never knew, but Jonny doesn't remember very much about her. If I was to ask you questions about her, would you tell me what I want to know?'

'I might do. Yes, I would. The memories shouldn't be exclusively mine. It would please Jonny if we started to talk, came to a truce. Oh, God, Louisa, you look so frail and alone. You've cut yourself off from everyone except Faye. It isn't good for you. It's time your suffering stopped. I'd be privileged to help you in any way I can.'

She pulled in her face, her chin quivering, close to tears. Concern from the one person who'd always rejected her brought her rawness, all the hurt, to the brink. 'Put your flowers in with mine.' Her voice was scratchy with emotion. 'Then come with me.'

She led the way to the new grave dug at the end of the row of resting places. 'He didn't want his name put on the headstone but I couldn't allow him to be anonymous. I hope you don't mind the words.'

Tristan read the stone. '"John Ashley. 1892 to 1944. Reunited with his love." Was that his real name? Wise of you to leave out Bruce, with people like me around. No, I don't mind the words. After all, I was the fortunate one. I had Ursula for a few good years and then a very happy marriage with Winifred. And I was the one who watched Jonny grow up into a fine man.'

Louisa pointed to the verge, just feet away. 'Bruce liked to sit there. Shall we?'

'I'd be pleased to.' Tristan tentatively offered his arm.

She took it and they walked and sat down. 'Life is strange. I'd never have thought that I'd sit here with you.'

'Before we talk about other things, may I know how you feel about Tom?' Tristan said. 'He's been so wretched. He's genuinely sorry for upsetting you.'

'I believe he is. I don't know why I haven't been in touch with him. I make up my mind to write or telephone, then I just can't bring myself to.'

'Don't take this the wrong way, but is it because you need to forgive him? It's what you did to Bruce, and the others for keeping the secret. You've even forgiven me, haven't you? It's what you do, Louisa. Your deep feelings for Tom, your disappointment in him, his lack of support and understanding, while you were wrestling with the stress of keeping Bruce's identity a secret, was too much for you. You know better than I there is a sweet release in forgiveness.'

She sighed heavily, her whole body sagging. 'You're right. I've known it all along. I just... with Tom it's so hard. Was hard. I'll go to him soon, clear the air.'

'Do you want him back?'

'No. We weren't meant to be together. I've come to realize that I didn't feel the same way about him as I did David. We should have stayed as friends. It would be good to be his friend again. To be able to go to Ford Farm without worrying I might bump into him.'

'And to Tremore? I hope you feel you can go there. You'll be very welcome.' Tristan looked up and was pleased to see someone coming towards them. 'It's Tom. He looks as if he's got something to say to you. I'm sure you'll sort it out. I'll leave you to it.'

'Tristan,' she said, before he'd gone. 'Would you like to wait for me? Come back for tea? Whatever conclusion Tom and I come to, I'd be glad of your company.'

'My dear Louisa, I'd be delighted to.'

'Surprised to see you here, Uncle Tris,' Tom said, his amazement plain, when they met along the path. 'How is she?'

'I've started to make things up to her. You'll need to go gently with her, Tom.'

'I will, don't worry.'

A short time later Louisa walked back to her house escorted on either side by the two men.

Chapter Twenty-Six

On the fifth night of June, just as those at Ford Farm were retiring to their beds they were brought out of doors. They were used to bombers making an outward journey at dusk and counting them back in at dawn. Tonight was different. The drone, the beat, went on and on and on, far louder than ever before due to the sheer heavy number of aircraft heading for the south coast. Pinpricks of navigation lights could be seen, like coloured moving stars.

Half-believing what she was hearing, her heart thundering with awe and pride, every nerve taut with dread, Jill reached for Tom's hand. 'This is it.'

His emotions matched hers. Unable to form any words, he squeezed her hand. He guessed the same thing would be happening up and down all of the south of the country. The bombers were off to make the first wave of assault – for the next twenty-four hours, on average, a bomber would take off in England every three and a half seconds. It meant the ships and landing craft had already left. The massive operation of D-Day had begun.

Clutching a fretful Paul, Emilia clung to Perry. 'May God protect them all.'

Edwin and Tilda had never come into close contact before. Now she was glad to link arms with him.

Lottie moved away on her own. She hadn't seen or heard from Nate for six weeks; intensive training had forbidden it. A week ago, Falmouth had endured its worst bombing raid and there had been many casualties. She had been relieved to hear that Jill's uncle and family had come through safely, but it had been hell wondering if Nate had been in the area and hurt. No tragic news had come. As the terrible expectation of the invasion had hovered in the air, the time had been progressively harrowing for everyone. The horrors of war had been increasingly isolating her from Nate. The whole of the country's mail had been stopped, all travel severely restricted. News had filtered through that the coast was sealed off.

The unparalleled activity above meant that Nate was now most likely somewhere off the edge of the French coast. For the first time, soon to be pitched into the hell of battle.

'Nate…' Her prayer was that simple.

At Tremore, Tristan and Faye stood on the balcony of Ben's bedroom, arms round waists, their minds on Jonny. 'He's made it so far,' she said, leaning her face against his dressing-gown sleeve.

'We can only go on hoping and praying.' Tristan would find nothing to comfort himself throughout this night. The scale of the whole operation was unprecedented in history, the outcome never more vital, but he was proud his son was in the thick of it.

'Simon should sleep through but we'd better check on the other children. If all ends well in the next hours, weeks, months, they can start to look forward to going home, only they won't have a home to go back to. I can't bear the thought of them ending up in an orphanage, Uncle Tris, perhaps split up.'

'Pearl, Bob and Len aren't going anywhere they don't want to. I know you'll probably find someone and get married one day, Faye, but until then how would you like to help me raise a second family? The children like it here. I hope Ben lets us all stay.'

Faye was silent. Was her father somewhere out there, where the aircraft were going to? Was he anywhere at all? 'Do you really think he'll come back?'

'I hope so. Don't you think he will?'

She shuddered. 'I've this awful feeling that he's dead. I suppose we'll find out eventually what's happened to him. Right now, we must pray for Jonny and Nate and all those other young men.'

'Yes. Louisa will be praying for Jonny too.'

–

Jonny and his Lancaster crew were flying in the first wave of bombers in neat wingtip-to-wingtip formation across the rough Channel waters. Their mission, to begin the assault on the strongest enemy coastal defences, extremely tough opposition, but reconnaissance photographs had shown that the German propagandists had greatly exaggerated the formation of the Atlantic Wall – an impregnable barrier their forces had been stated to have built against the expected invasion. The intelligence made him think sadly of Will. He didn't think about his own chances – he was already years older than the average pilot. His crew had mixed feelings about him. The older men considered him lucky because of his long-held survival, the younger ones wondered if his number was about to come up and take them with him. Tonight his squadron was to pound the Normandy coastline, while other planes, along with dummy ships, were to cleverly make it look as if Calais was the intended place for Operation Overlord.

When this mission, God willing, was over, they'd return, snatch a rest while the crate was being bombed up again, and go back to strike targets inland. By then the beaches should have been taken…

-

The long, empty weeks without Lottie had been exceptionally tense for Nate. A sense of unease and boredom had gained dominance of him and his countrymen during the interminable wait for 'something to happen'. The training, with the use of live ammunition, landing on the Cornish beaches, was to prepare the men for landing with heavy equipment, to storm the occupied beaches and hold them. He'd tended mock wounded, and a few nasty real wounds, mainly from accidents on the crafts or clambering down high makeshift walls on nets, in practice for when it must be done from troop ships to the boats and DUKWS. These 'ducks', locally built amphibious crafts, were designed to be driven straight from the boats through the surf to the beaches.

When the briefings had come, the tension had lifted a little. Every man was detailed on his exact duties and was shown a map of the landing beach and allowed to study it for as long as he wanted. Men with some knowledge of the European coastline recognized the small chunk of intended coastline as being French. The code name for the beach they were to storm was Omaha. The order to pack up and move out had been met with relief, disbelief, eagerness to get on with it and get it over with, and a sickly apprehension that made the heart beat strangely, the gut refuse to settle. A few men sank into a fateful gloom. Many felt proudly that this was somehow to be their main purpose in life, what they had really been born for. A few wrote poignant or philosophical or far-reaching words in their diaries. Some just ached to go home to their once ordinary, everyday lives.

The journey on the vehicle-choked roads, heading for where the 'sausages' were to embark, had been frustrating and stuffy, and had taken so long the men had got out of their vehicles to cook meals and make coffee. The embarkation had been at Tolverne, where an American naval base was set up, on the River Fal. A little cottage had nestled there, flanked by overhanging trees, a feature of the pretty estuary waters. After the short journey down to Falmouth harbour, they were out at sea.

After Nate had endured the claustrophobia of being cooped up in the troop ship, a twenty-four-hour stand-down due to poor weather and seasickness, among many other seasick fellows as the sailing got under way, he'd had no idea that a rendezvous of the full invasion fleet had taken place off the Isle of Wight, more than two thousand Allied ships, the greatest meeting of sea craft ever orchestrated. The British Second Army were about to advance on the more eastern end of the sixty-mile stretch of Normandy coastline, their invasion beaches code named Sword, Juno and Gold. The United States First Army was to land further west, and as well as the beach coded Omaha, there was Utah, on each side of the estuary of the River Vire. Mainly Canadians had the assault of code name Juno.

Under last night's darkness, at each end of the invasion area, huge forces of airborne troops, British to the east, American to the west, had landed by parachute and glider, their purpose to protect the flanks of the seaborne forces. In dawn's first reluctant light a great bombardment, the heaviest and most concentrated ever scaled, had begun from the big naval ships and aircraft to 'soften up' the targets. The battleships, cruisers and destroyers quivered and shook as they unleashed the terrible battery, as if they had been brought to a living force all of their own.

Now it was Nate's turn to play his part in the biggest war operation mankind had undertaken. With red crosses on his helmet and armbands, he was now in the first wave of the armada about to land at Omaha. The landing craft rolled and heaved in the waves. Ahead was a stretch of sand and shingle three or four miles long, and steel barriers – some mined – and fences of barbed wire. Up above the sandbanks were heavily fortified machine-gun and mortar posts – fate had decreed that the German 352nd Infantry Division were there on a full-scale practice. A soldier retched and was sick over his boots. Off went a small chain of likewise sufferers. Fighting queasiness himself, Nate was determined to stand tall, keep his balance.

Over the sound of the engine and hissing sprays of seawater, the officer barked orders. Threatened. Encouraged. Herv was praying a Jewish prayer. Todd was a Catholic and was reciting over his rosary. Nate hadn't bothered much these past years with his Baptist background – here was a good time and place to fall back on it. Jeff, Mort and Brad were there. These men he had trained with, lived with, laughed with, his friends, his brothers. Men just like all the others on board. Men who now sweated. Cursed. Chewed gum. Stayed tight-lipped. Cheekbones protruded over clenched jaws. Heaving guts juddered. Eyes widened. Eyes narrowed. The craft rose and fell and with its unmerciful motion it brought up cool spouts of water. No lips tasted the tang of salt. They all tasted fear.

Shells now roared around them. The craft ahead of them was hit. Holed. Screams! Men frantically bailed out the rushing intake of water. In vain. Men in the sea. Trying to swim. Survive. Some bobbing, stained with red.

Five hundred yards from shore. Waterproof wrappings were secured over rifles to protect them as the men waded to the shore. Prayers – that they'd live long enough to use them. Live through. Get through somehow. Todd kissed his crucifix and offered it to Nate to do the same. Nate pressed his lips to it, glancing up at the glowering skies. 'Please, for Lottie...'

Someone: 'Our Father...'

Another: 'Shut up!'

Whisper: 'Christ help us.'

A prurient oath against the enemy.

Family names.

'Mom...'

Three hundred yards. Two hundred. Low tide to avoid hitting obstacles under water. Obstacles that paradoxically were to offer the only cover on the shoreline from enemy fire. Spray soared up round the boat as a shell whistled close. Too damned close. The boat alongside was hit. Burst into flames. All personnel ablaze.

Nate swallowed hard, glad as the funeral pyre was left behind that he couldn't see, couldn't hear, couldn't smell the agonies. His landing craft plunged into the surf. Ramp crashes down. Run off. Hold rifles up high. Try to hold heavy equipment up high. Medical packs too. Muscles already straining. Thrashing through the water. Men felled. Like toddlers just learning to walk, cut down by cruel playmates, tiny black holes appearing, blood spurting crimson flowers and streaming away in the waters. Death and maiming, a harlot of red. On boys who'd not yet had time to learn how to live.

'Medic! Medic!'

'Morphine!'

It was all an ordinary man could do to thread one thought after another. Pandemonium. Helplessness on faces. Dying faces. Sweet, sickly smell of blood and death. Nate. Not yet advanced out of the water, his services already needed. Fall to knees. Keep head down. Press dressing to a gaping leg wound. Artery severed. No hope. Soldier screaming. Writhing. Dies. One among the first destined to lie under lawns and lawns of white crosses on Normandy soil. Men falling into deeper water, dragged down by heavy equipment, the struggle to disentangle and swim to the surface futile – will not even get a grave.

Nate got up, splashing through the surf. Surf only up to his ankles now. Soldier ahead of him. Hole through his helmet. Drops lifeless. Water blossoming inky red. Nate leaps over him. A leg bobbing by. Men scattered. All dead. Jeff dead.

On wet sand. 'Medic! Medic!' All around him, he's needed. Must do what he can. Treat casualty. And another. Stumble on. Blinded by plumes of black smoke rising in the defiled grey air. Deafened. Confused. 'Harmon, get your goddamned self over here!' Answer doctor's summons. Fall on knees beside gut-spilled casualty. Doctor crawls away over body parts of someone, perhaps two someones, to a soldier he might be able to save.

'I don't want to die!' the boy Nate is tending screams. Eyes bulging with terror and agony.

Bullet zips, chews furrow out of Nate's cheek. 'You aren't going to die!' Stabs boy with morphine shot. 'You're going to make it. I promise!' Has to bawl above the thunder and insanity of battle. Works on the chaos, his hands saturated with blood. Blood is up to his elbows. The boy dies. He moves on. Past mutilated bodies and mutilated DCKWs and amphibious tanks, some of the scant few that have made a landing. The defence is pitiless. Most of it was supposed to have been taken out. Calculations were wrong somewhere.

Waves lap up the shore, indignantly wash the bloodied sand. Vainly. Bleeding rivers running down from further up the beach. Soldier down. Nate lifts his head. Too late. Suffocated by sand. Behind a steel barrier a boy is curled up in fear, shrieking, shrieking. In front of him, on water's edge, men have been hit by flamethrower, performing grotesquely beautiful death dance.

It's Nate's task to tend the wounded of the demolition teams, the all-important men needed to blow up the obstacles and make the gaps needed for the vehicles to drive through and press inland – once the pillboxes are taken out, those murderous stations that are killing the troops in great numbers. The demolition crews are losing too many men, their success is being ruthlessly limited.

They're having to plead, cajole, threaten the terrified, the demented, the wounded seeking refuge behind the iron monstrosities, to move out of the way as they scramble to fix their explosives.

There's an almighty blast, men fall and die from the sheer dreadful force as well as being blown up. Clumps of iron form deadly shrapnel – the Germans have inadvertently done the job for one crew. Nate feels red hot stabs of pain as skin is shaved deeply off his lower leg.

Crouching, limping, he makes it to a casualty, a sergeant with a shredded arm. He drags him by the collar to where infantry are pushing on, trying to hurry. Making for the cover of the bank of shingle at the top of the deep incline – close to enemy, it's out of firing range. Nate goes after them. A hail of fire. Dropping with the casualty he uses a heap of dead bodies as cover to bind up the unconscious sergeant's gaping wounds. Stabs in the morphine. Hopes the sergeant stays safe as he leaves him for stretcher-bearers. Gets up, lumbers on and dodges on the run. A soldier is at his side. The soldier is felled, his helmet spins crazily through the air as if in contempt. 'You son of a bitch!' Nate yells at the anonymous German gunner.

He's spun on his feet from a blast. Confused. Disorientated. Shakes his head. Desperately needs his vision to clear. Doesn't know if he's facing the right way. Suddenly he's off his feet. There's no new pain but surely he must have been hit.

'You crazy?' It's Herv who's yanked him down. 'Here. Hold these.'

'What?' He's still in a daze.

Herv shakes him. 'Come on, buddy. I need you to come round.'

It takes all of Nate's concentration and willpower to make his brain work, to see right. Herv directs his hand and he finds himself taking over a pair of forceps clamping an artery in a casualty's chest. The casualty is gritting his teeth. Singing, 'Glory, glory, alleluia.' His arm is minced. He'll lose it, his life too if infection, the next enemy of the critically wounded, makes a play on him. Morphine shot. Bleeding halted. On their bellies they drag him to the bank of shingle. Hope the stretcher-bearers are able to reach him. If he's lucky, he'll be loaded on to one of the landing craft as they return with the wounded. No shortage of a human load.

'You need a dressing on your face!' Herv bawls above the terrible din.

'It's nothing! I'll see to it later!'

Nate and Herv crawl backwards like insects a few yards out of the safety zone to the next casualty. A soldier is choking up blood from an appalling abdominal wound. Ribs stick out of him like claws. A blast shakes the ground. Shakes their nerves. Bullets zoom close to their heads like vicious, venomous bees seeking victims. The blast makes the casualty's heart stop, every effort isn't enough to restart it.

'Next customer,' says Herv. They don't have to go far. Men are being hurtled down all around them. The nearest man has been shot through the heart. Go on to the next one. They get no idea what it used to be – white-hot metal has found a soft target and annihilated it. Crawl. Both stay alive to gain a bit of beach. Next. Tiny rivulets of blood seeping from helmet to chin. Eyes gone. Brain gone. Move on.

Cries for help. Cries for mercy. Swearing. The few surviving officers urging men up the beach. 'Where the hell are we? This isn't right!' Seems the landing had been some way off mark. Purgatory. The enemy up above the shingle got the upper hand. For now. If they get this wave of men, or the next, they won't get the third.

'Herv! I've got to leave. I have to tend the demo crews.' Nate must see to his first duty.

For several seconds there's nothing between them and a hail of bullets but the mercy of the Almighty. Herv cries. Swears. Holds up his hand. It's reduced to ribbons. Nate wraps a dressing round it. 'Get back to cover! Or make for the shore! Good luck!'

He leaves Herv. Run, grunt, dodge, run, grunt, falls flat on his face. A hand there, just a hand with a wedding ring on it – a family destroyed. Is this all real? Or the worst nightmare?

'Help me! Help me!' There's a private alive under a heap of bodies.

'Where are you hit?'

'Don't know. Can't feel anything. Got a smoke?'

'No.' Feel over his limbs. Bullets hitting the dead. Splat, splat, splat, soft entries. Explosion nearby. Sand is hurled up feet in the air. Shuts eyes and throws himself over the casualty. Waits. Clears a little. There's a soldier to the right dragging back a wounded comrade. Not allowed. Against orders. Must run on. But understandable if it's your best buddy. Both fall silently, like a mime act. Never to get up again.

'Get me out of here,' the private pleads.

Nate pushes away the horrible tangle of limp, chewed-up flesh until the private is free. There's blood all over him. 'Where's the pain?'

The private thinks. 'Don't think there is any. Thanks, Corp.' He takes a deep breath, grins, snatches up a jobless rifle and a garland of bullets, then runs on, leaping over the confetti of carnage.

Nate belly-crawls to a man just dropped. Ministers to the gushing throat wound. Casualty doesn't make it. Looks up. Sees the private throw himself against the shingle bank. Safe for now.

'Medic! Medic!' He threads his way again through the fallen, avoiding craters. Comes to another blasted demolition crew member, minus a kneecap, horrifically disfigured. 'Thank God!' Choking sounds. Voice rattles. 'I can't stand the pain…'

Morphine shot. Apply dressing where the soldier's nose once was. Heavy blast! Cloud of smoke and sand. Use this as cover to haul the casualty up to the shingle bank. Lays him in the long, long line of wounded. Wireless operator is shouting above the din, 'First wave ineffective. Cannot hold beach. Say again…'

'Keep still!' It's Brad. Good. They can make a pair.

'It's good to see you. Doc make it?'

'Don't know.' Brad's aiming a dressing towards Nate's face.

'What are you doing?'

'Hold this. Half your cheek's hanging off. It'll need stitches.'

Nate swears, suddenly aware of the torturous, stinging, burning pain. 'Not too hideous, is it?'

'Mmm, reckon your Lottie will still love ya.' Brad winds a bandage round his face to keep the dressing in place. 'You going to be OK?'

'Made it so far.'

The next wave of boats were being launched and following in their wake. Reinforcements might make a better impact. Nate's only concern was to reach those who needed his help.

Chapter Twenty-Seven

Lottie wiped sweat off her brow, then knuckled away the tears forming against her will. She supposed it was like this for most women in the early days. Better get on – she didn't want any comments to be made. The more sympathetic and understanding they were, the harder she found it to take.

The rest of the workforce were hard at it, particularly Jill, so different now to the nervy, eager-to-please mouse of just over a year ago, heaving stooks together like a hardened labourer. Tom was cutting grass in the next field, visible on the rise. When he brought the tractor round and was facing them, Jill waved to him. The pair of them were in thick together, but maddeningly there were no signs of them progressing on to anything really close. They seemed content to stay just as friends, which was a pity. They were just right for each other, had so much in common. Why couldn't they see it? They kept each other's spirits up and were interested in all that the other did. They made each other laugh. They seemed to understand each other completely, anticipating what the other would do or say. There was no competition between them. They looked perfect together. They had no right not to fall in love. Everyone at the farm and Tremore had come to feel the same. It was an unspoken awareness, but no one even as much as hinted this to the couple in the superstitious fear that something so right and lovely, a dream that could become a perfect reality, would be shattered.

Someone was coming through the field gate. Uncle Tristan. Lottie tore off to him. 'What is it?'

'Nothing, my love. Don't worry. There's no bad news. I've come to help with the haymaking.'

'Thank God!' She let her relief out in a rush of breath. She smiled, swept up her head in her usual proud way, but promptly crumpled into a weeping mess.

Tristan took her into a fatherly embrace. He had witnessed her trying to keep herself under control during the past few days but never reduced to a jibbering weakness. 'Oh, Lottie, it's getting to you, isn't it?'

'If only I could hear something. Jonny's managed to pass on messages to you when he gets back off ops, but I haven't a clue about what's happened to Nate. People are beginning to get telegrams, Uncle Tris. I'm so afraid for him.'

'All the beaches were successfully taken and the troops are steadily pushing inland. I can't promise you that Nate will be all right but I'm sure he'll be keeping his head down. He'll be thinking about you every minute, Lottie.'

'I know.' She produced her hanky and used it briskly. 'He'll be counting on me to be strong. To get on with things and make him proud.'

'You're allowed to be human.' Tristan smiled.

The scene of emotion and comfort brought the others in the field running to them, and also Tom, having stopped the tractor and leapt over the hedge. He brought up the rear, then placed an elbow in comfortable intimacy on Jill's shoulder. Tristan explained. Lottie was cross to have embarrassed herself. 'It was nothing. Nothing worth holding up all the work for.'

'I'm about to go home and feed Paul,' Emilia said. 'Why don't you come with me, Lottie? I'll get Tilda to—'

'No, Mum, I'm fine,' Lottie stressed, impatient and edgy. 'It's hard for me right now but I was just being silly.'

'We're only trying to help,' Tom muttered.

'Sorry,' Lottie bit back. Then she blushed and gave a reticent smile. 'Actually, I'm afraid you might have to put up with me coming over all silly an awful lot. I'm pretty sure I'm pregnant.'

'Oh, darling, I've had my suspicions about it for some time. It's wonderful news,' Emilia said, kissing her. 'Why didn't you mention it before?'

'I was so afraid it would be a false hope.'

'Lottie! Congratulations!' Jill gave her a bear hug. Then she returned to Tom and threw her arms round his waist. 'Isn't it brilliant?'

While holding on to her, he leaned forward and kissed Lottie's cheek. 'Well done, sis. You'd better take over on the tractor rather than lugging heavy weights about.'

'Thanks, I will, but don't you dare treat me like I'm made of china.'

Emilia laughed. 'Uh, as if you've ever listened to anyone's advice.'

'You're both much of a muchness,' Tristan said. 'Congratulations, Lottie.'

'My first great-grandchild. Good on you, maid.' Edwin saw this as an occasion to light up his pipe. He glanced at Tom and Jill and muttered under his breath, 'Time others got settled down too.'

'I think I will slip back with you for a few minutes, Mum,' Lottie said. 'I'd like to tell Pappa and Tilda the good news myself.'

During the midday break, Tom dragged Jill up off the ground before she'd got her last mouthful of hevva cake down. 'Come for a walk.'

Taking water with them, sharing a cigarette, they ambled alongside the curving hedgerow. Jill tugged at protruding stalks of wild parsley and vetches. A blackbird vented a chattering alarm, '*chak-chak*', at their approach. When out of sight, they flopped down on a green patch away from the rough stalks, she leaning her back against his solid, muscle-bound arm. 'It'll be nice for Paul and Simon to have a little playmate, at least until Lottie and Nate set up somewhere on their own. Do you think they'll go far?'

'Lottie likes to think she's a trailblazer but she's a homebody. Can't see her going very far away.'

'Are you excited about becoming an uncle?'

'Of course. Hope it won't be a little brat like Lottie was though. I was quite patient with her but she used to drive Will up the wall, always whining to join in with our games. She'd do anything to get attention. Broke up one of his matchstick models once. He'd complain to Mum. Lottie would scream the house down. Mum usually took Lottie's side. She spoiled her. I suppose now she's pregnant, Lottie's going to be a right teasy little cow.'

'Tom!'

'I know she's got the right to be worried about Nate, but her moods have always been ruled by her monthly cycle. You're not at all like that.'

'Tom! Some things are best not mentioned, thank you.' She hid her burning face. It might be a farm they worked on, where the most intimate things of nature couldn't be hidden, but it was shocking to have the subject of 'the curse' brought up.

Unrepentant, Tom reached up in the hedge and snapped off a dog rose and used it to tickle her neck. It dislodged her turban scarf and she pulled it off. It would need to be retied. Lottie would have bawled at him for the inconvenience. He closed his eyes and relaxed. The best thing about Jill was she never minded what he did. She was the best of company. He enjoyed taking her out and about. They'd gone to an ENSA concert and the pictures in Truro; the town now, like everywhere else, strangely quiet since the troops had pulled out. He walked down to the pub two or three times a week for a drink and usually asked her to join him. He traced his fingers through her hair.

Jill was happy to let him do this. She was totally at ease with Tom. Last night she had come out of her room with the intention of taking a bath. She was in her flannel dressing gown and worn-down fluffy slippers. Tom had come up the stairs, took one look at her and fell about laughing.

'What?' She'd frowned at her sliver of soap and flannel. 'What's so funny. Oh no!' Too late, she'd realized she had three curlers in the front of her hair and cold cream making a shiny film over her face. Then she couldn't see a reason why she should be embarrassed – it was only Tom – and she'd laughed with him. 'Do I look like the swamp creature in that movie we saw last week?'

'No. You're as lovely as always. And I see you definitely as a Hedy Lamarr.' It was good being always so comfortable with someone.

When the workers trudged back to the farm way after dark they found a guest seated at the supper table. Tom raised his brows. 'Louisa! Been ages since you were here last. Good to see you.' He'd meant it sincerely but felt awkward about seeing his former love. How was he to behave? He solved the problem by monopolizing Jill all the way through the meal.

'You too, Tom. And all of you. Aunt Em rang me with the news about the new baby and she suggested I come over. It's brilliant news, Lottie. I, um, don't have to get back for anyone now, so I'll share your room tonight, if that's all right?' Louisa was self-conscious about being here. She had changed her mind many times before setting off. The last time she'd been under this busy roof she'd been Tom's young lady; she had been intimate with him in his room.

'It will be really great having you here.' Lottie wagged a playful finger at her. 'You were naughty to stay away for so long. The family's not complete without you.'

When Lottie went upstairs to change out of her work clothes, Louisa carried up her overnight bag. 'Wasn't too bad, was it?' Lottie asked, standing sideways in front of her mirror in her underwear, pressing her hands over her flat tummy, imagining what she'd look like as the pregnancy bloomed.

'I'm glad I've got that out of the way. I've missed coming here so much. It was easier now that Tristan and I get along.' Louisa came over all shy. 'The reason I've stayed away for so long is I've been wondering what everyone thinks of me for sleeping with Tom.'

'That it's all pretty natural probably. One wouldn't expect Tilda to approve but she's never sanctimonious. Don't worry about it. No one else is.'

More at ease now, Louisa sat down on the bed. 'It was a good thing I didn't end up in your happy condition. I'm glad Tom seems to be getting on with his life. When we talked the day he came to the graveyard, I was shocked at how much I'd hurt him. We've forgiven each other and bear no grudges. That's the main thing. I thought Jill might have come up with us. She's your best friend. Hope she doesn't think I'm butting in.'

'Not at all. Jill wouldn't think things like that. She's very perceptive. She gave me and Nate all the space we needed. So, what have you been up to lately?'

'Oh, just the usual. Ada and I have had to come to terms at not having Bruce with us.'

'Do you think you'll look again for love?'

'Perhaps. If or when the time is right. Is… Tom seeing anyone?'

'No. We were all expecting him to take up where he left off breaking the hearts of the local girls, but he seems happy enough to stay close to home. He and Jill go out and about together sometimes.'

'I noticed he gets on very well with her.'

'They're just chums. We'd like there to be more between them. Would you mind?'

'No, not at all. I loved Tom, and I was disappointed and confused when things went wrong, but I was devastated when I lost David. I've had a lot of time to think now the house is so empty. Tom and I were carried along by passion. And let's face it, I was never cut out to be a farmer's wife. Jill is. It's easy to see she loves the life. Yes, you know, you're right, now I come to think of it, they do look meant for each other. Perhaps they know it deep down.'

'Well, if they don't soon get on with it, I'll do something to push them together. In fact, I've got an idea that might help.' Then the amusement left Lottie and she became grave. Fear drained all her colour. She plonked down beside Louisa.

'What is it, Lottie? Are you worried about the baby?'

'It's not that. Louisa, you know what it's like to have your husband killed in action. If anything happens to Nate… if I hear… can I come to you? I mean, you know exactly what it's like.'

'You don't ever have to ask for help or understanding, Lottie. I'm here for you at any time.'

'I can't stop imagining things.'

'I know. People tell you to concentrate on the good times you've had together, or to look ahead, but all sorts go through your mind.'

'Like is he in pain? Suffering? Hungry? Does he have a roof over his head every night? Is he afraid? He must be seeing terrible things at the very least. I hope, I pray, but I never know a minute's peace. At least I've got his baby. I hope my letters will reach him and he'll soon know about it.'

'It's old advice, I know, but taking one day at a time helps. If you can't cope with a whole day, break it up into little pieces, an hour or two at a time.'

'Thanks. Right now, this very moment, I'm glad to have you here.'

Chapter Twenty-Eight

He could see water all around him. That couldn't be right. There should be dull air and cloud. He should be up amid the dismal grey wreaths that had so often cancelled the number of sorties that could have been undertaken in the days and nights since he'd taken part in the D-Day assault. He was so cold and numb, he felt nothing. What had happened to the array of instruments in front of him?

He'd been up in French airspace. A daytime raid. Where the hell was he now? He'd been bombing a bridge, cutting out a critical route to disrupt the push of the slick, well-equipped Second Panzer division towards Cherbourg and Caen. The resilient German resistance to the invasion had been able to launch a series of minor counter-attacks, but despite the poor weather conditions hampering the overall effectiveness, especially from the air, the Allies had joined up and secured all of the French coastline.

When the thousand- and five-hundred-pound bombs were all dropped, Jonny had headed the Lancaster back across the Channel. Almost at once, the craft was hit by flak. He remembered now – a hard slap in the face from a spiteful choppy wave helped. He remembered his navigator saying with almost high-tea calmness, 'You've nursed a pranged crate back more than once before, Skip.'

He had. Not with this crew. Death, injury or promotion meant none of his previous crew were flying with him today. Black smoke had billowed into the cockpit and flames had suddenly burst into a flash of evil red and orange. 'Bail out! Bail out!'

He'd shouted until the smoke had threatened to burst his lungs. Hell! Bugger! And words to that effect – why he should think it funny, only God knew. Well, he'd soon be having a few words with God. Still, he couldn't grumble. He'd had a bloody good innings. Was a walking miracle to be flying and fighting at his age – well, had been… His age, the grand old age of thirty-one. Not old at all. But he'd made it a darn sight longer than those poor boys of only eighteen years. He'd waited until all the crew had thrown themselves out, praying that their parachutes would work and they wouldn't be hit by enemy fire, before jumping out himself. He didn't remember hitting the water. The chute was keeping him afloat but he reckoned not for much longer. He was so cold, hypothermia would get him if he didn't drown, and he might be horrifically injured anyway. He recalled the flames that had started to lick at his body. The searing pain.

When is my life going to flash before me?

Something grabbed him by the back of the collar. He was being dragged under. It was going to be painful. How could he be drowning if he was rising up out of the sea? Must be so starved of oxygen his mind was playing tricks. His back felt as if it was being stretched to its limits – he could hardly bear the agony.

'Here, mate, stop thrashing about! We're trying to help you.'

He tried to speak but his teeth were chattering too much. He went limp, he had no strength left. Found himself staring into shadowy faces.

'It's all right. It's Air-Sea Rescue. Your plane went down into the water as graceful as a swan. The flames coming out of her arse reminded me of myself with me heels on fire when running away from me mother-in-law,' the sailor ruined his poetry. 'We've picked up another couple of blokes. You're the big noise, eh? Lie back and let us get you comfy. Have you up in the hospital ship and in a nice warm bunk in a mo.'

Jonny hated being tugged about as he was wrapped in a blanket. He wanted to use the worst swear words of his life but no words would come out. Finally, he was frightened. The biggest terror he'd ever known. He might be dumb and paralysed for ever.

When he came to again he was in the grip of a shuddering monster. Then he saw he was in a bunk and must be in a moving ship. 'Help! Help me, someone!'

'Quiet,' a voice said, coming close. It was a medical orderly, smart and crisp, a young slim sailor, about twenty. 'I mean, quiet, sir. You'll wake everyone.'

'I can speak.' Jonny realized he was half sitting up. 'I can move.' He fell back on the pillows in relief. A wave of nausea hit him and it was several moments before everything cleared again. 'You still there?'

'Yes, sir.' The orderly came back.

'My throat hurts like hell. I hurt all over, but I was so afraid I was going to be a vegetable. Do you know if any of my crew made it? I think a sailor told me a couple of my chaps had been picked up.'

'I'm afraid you've lost two, sir. The others are more or less fine. You've come off the worst.'

'Could you get me their names? The survivors and the lost? I'm not bothered about myself.' It took a lot of nerve to ask. 'What is the damage?'

'The doctors will tell you tomorrow. It's very late. I suggest you try to sleep, sir. We'll be back in Blighty in the morning.'

'If you don't tell me,' Jonny said severely, mixing it with the foul language he'd wanted to use during his rescue, 'I swear I'll wake up the whole bloody ship.'

'I don't know all the facts, sir,' the orderly said, completely unruffled. 'Your lungs took in rather a lot of smoke. Not life- threatening but you'll be uncomfortable for some time. You've got some burns. Superficial mostly, the immersion in the salt water would have been a help to the healing. Your face is a bit scorched. The fingers of your left hand have been fused together. You'll be in for a few operations but you should be prepared to face that it's unlikely they'll ever be separated successfully. If you wanted to go out in a blaze of glory, sir, I'm afraid you'll be disappointed. If the war isn't over by the end of your recovery, you'll not be able to fight the rest of it from a cockpit. Now, try to get some sleep, sir.'

The orderly went off to a groaning patient. Jonny lifted his heavily dressed left hand. He gingerly touched his face, it was too sore to probe much. 'Oh bugger and blast!' He thought about his two dead crew members. He was alive. He had much to be grateful for. He was a career airman. The powers that be had better not try chucking him out. Life behind a desk wouldn't be too bad. Yes, it would. It wasn't worse than death, but it came a close second.

He'd wept many secret tears for dead pals, for dead crew, for the maimed. Throwing off all façade, he wept for himself. A bomb or a bullet might still claim him before this whole wretched show was over but it was a totally humbling thing never to have to face scramble ever again.

Chapter Twenty-Nine

The first thing Jill did every morning was to look out of her bedroom window and view the scene that had made her cringe before her first day's work. While the war had blasted so many places almost out of recognition – Plymouth, just across the county border, had been mercilessly bombed – the hills and valleys here had been left comfortingly the same. It brought her peace and security to watch the changing colours of the seasons, and pride to have taken part in the relentless but steady progression of the ploughing, tilling and reaping, and animal husbandry.

Today, because of something Lottie had recently been repeating to her, she lingered and took another look out from the landing window. Tiny darts of thrill touched her all over, the sensation that told her she was being watched. She knew it was Tom. She always knew when he was near. If she didn't see him for an hour or two she missed him. She turned to him, smiling. He was grinning and shaking his head. 'What?'

'You had the look of a child just then. As if it was the first time you'd seen something wonderful.'

'It is a wonderful outlook.' She drank it in again. 'I'll never tire of it.'

'Well, you won't ever have to,' he replied matter-of-factly.

'I might one day.' Lottie had been talking about her hopes of settling down with Nate on their own farm, and her hopes that she would come with them. 'I don't think I could do without you,' Lottie had stressed. 'It's like I've known you for ever.'

'What do you mean?' Tom's grin vanished. He reached her in two rapid strides. 'Mum's told you, everyone has, that you must stay on here after the war's over. We're winning, it's looking good. Uncle Tris is confident about it and he should know. There's still a lot of hard fighting to do but our chaps are gradually gaining ground. The Allies will be marching into Paris any day now.'

Jill was so used to his good humour she missed the fact he was annoyed. 'Oh, poor Lottie. There's she goes again, out into the lane waiting for the postman. I hope there's something for her and not just another lot of public information leaflets.'

'I asked you what you meant, Jill.' Tom loomed over her, breathing down her neck. 'Are you planning to leave here?'

'Not really.'

He pulled her around to get her full attention. 'What kind of answer is that?'

It was the first confrontational remark she'd ever got from Tom. The hands on her were gripping firmly. She was at a loss over his displeasure. She detailed her conversations with Lottie. 'I'd be one of the few women foremen in the whole of England. I like the idea of that.'

'Do you indeed?' he snapped sourly, letting her go. He had never thought he'd be rude to Jill or glare at her. He was hurt and offended that she could agree to such a plan. She had the right to her own life, to make her own plans. But not to up sticks and leave him.

'What's wrong with that?' Jill challenged him over his high attitude.

'There's such a thing as loyalty, you know.'

'I would be loyal, to Lottie, my best friend. She'll have a young child by then. God willing, it will actually happen, and she'll need me. I wouldn't dream of going without discussing it first with Mrs Em, of course.'

'Why bother? Seems to me you've already made up your mind. Blast Lottie! She always gets her own way.' He stormed off, leaving Jill in stunned amazement.

She rushed after him, pattering down the back stairs, trying to catch him up. At the bottom she launched herself at him and spun him round. 'Are you going to have this out with her? I don't see why. She's done nothing to upset you. Don't you dare say anything to upset her. She's in a fine state worrying about Nate. Tom, I swear, if you say one word to upset Lottie then you'll have me to answer to.'

'I'll say what I damned well like! I'm the manager of this farm.'

'Well, I'll take care never to forget it.' She would be even angrier if Tom's behaviour wasn't so at odds with his usual easy-going manner.

Their shouting had startled Paul in his pram, a few feet away on the other side of the wall. Emilia marched through from the kitchen, hands on her hips. 'What on earth's going on?'

'Nothing,' Tom barked, staring grimly above his mother's head. He couldn't look her in the eye for he knew he was the one in the wrong.

Emilia looked at Jill for an explanation. Jill shrugged. She had no idea why Tom had suddenly taken against her.

Lottie plunged through the back kitchen door, bringing a noisy wake of yapping Jack Russells with her, making such a racket herself it made her baby brother howl in fright. 'I've got one at last! A letter from Nate! Oh, I'm so happy. Sorry, Mum. Sorry, Paul. I'm going up to my room to read it.'

'Typical Lottie.' Tom stamped off outside, slamming every door after him. 'She creates bedlam even when she's happy.'

Lottie sang through every moment of the milking, oblivious to the fact that her older brother and her best friend were barely on speaking terms. Over breakfast, she repeated for the numberless time the contents of Nate's letter. 'He couldn't say where he is, of course. He says the countryside is very much like it is here, but a lot flatter, not as many hills. They're getting a mixed reaction from the French, some are very friendly and grateful, eager to share anything they have with the troops; others, understandably, are upset that the battles are costing them so much more than ever before. The blue censor pencil's done its work here and there. He got a bad nick on the cheek when he hit the shore and will have a scar, and a leg wound, but nothing serious. Tragically only he and Herv, your former supplier, Tom, survived the first day, and Herv was badly wounded. Nate hasn't seen him since and hopes he made it back and has been shipped out. We must remember them in church on Sunday. Nate might come back soon on a hospital ship himself, with casualties. Oh, I do hope so. He'll probably be stationed up-country but he might get some leave soon after that. I can't wait! I hope he's got my letter about the baby. He'll be over the moon. Of course, there's bits I can't share, personal to me.' At last she fell silent, unaware that although Tom was pleased she had received the letter, he was also quietly simmering.

'I swear the maid never breathed one single breath throughout all that,' Tilda said, dabbing her damp eyes. 'Dear Corporal Harmon. He's got through some of the worst. We must pray that he'll be spared right up till he can get back home for good. And by home I mean here. This is where his home is now.'

'How long will that be for?' Tom downed the last dregs from his tea mug, getting up tersely to start out for the fields.

'Pardon?' Lottie replied, kissing her letter again. Nothing would lessen her joy but she had now cottoned on to Tom's grumpy mood, the accusation in his question. Oh, good, it seemed the simple idea of hers was starting to work.

'How long will you and Nate be living here when he gets back?'

'What?' She made a puzzled, mocking face. 'You're thinking ahead, aren't you?'

'No. But you have, apparently.' He pointed an accusing finger.

Perry was bewildered by this turn of conversation. He had been Tom and Lottie's stepfather for thirteen years but he'd never really got used to their swiftly changing moods, although it had been with Will whom Lottie had usually sparred, not the normally peaceable Tom. He glanced, with a question in his handsome, dark eyes, at Emilia. She was playing with Paul, ignoring her older children, letting it all sweep over her. Tilda was spooning the last bit of porridge out of the cauldron for Edwin, both of them unperturbed, more used to the younger ones' stroppy ways, so Perry supposed. Jill knew something though: she was looking everywhere but at Lottie and Tom.

'Don't you two start squabbling in here,' he said sternly. 'I don't want Paul scared out of his wits again. I think I'll take him outside with me, darling. He can watch me work from his pram.'

Everyone knew Lottie wouldn't let the matter rest. One by one they drifted away until there was only she and Tom left in the kitchen. 'Right,' she went straight in on the attack, but not with antagonism. 'What's making you so crabby?'

He wanted to take her to task over insisting Jill leave the farm but saw how childish and silly he was being. It was really none of his business what Jill decided to do with her life. His explanation came out lame and to his embarrassment sounded pathetic and wet. 'I just think it's wrong to try to entice her away, that's all. She might not really want to go. She should be able to make up her own mind.'

'I'm sure she will, given the right incentive.' Lottie threw Tom into perplexity by softening and smiling mysteriously. It wasn't her plan to entice Jill away from here at all, just to make Tom realize how much he'd hate the idea if she did go. So far, so good. 'Let's get on, shall we?'

293

Shortly after Lottie had received her letter, the postman had cycled down Back Lane and popped an incongruous-looking, fat buff envelope through Tremore's letterbox. It was addressed to Tristan and he slipped off to the library to read it. There was another letter inside the envelope, addressed to Faye in Ben's handwriting. Tristan felt his insides freeze. Before he scanned the words that were exclusive to him he knew what they would say. With still no word from Ben, Tristan had been in touch with a former army colleague whom he knew to hold high office in Whitehall. He told him of his belief that Ben had accepted undercover work overseas. He knew that even if the colleague troubled to discover anything, the news couldn't be passed on to him direct, but he might be able to say that Ben definitely *had not* been involved in such an undertaking.

Now Tristan was faced with the truth of Ben's fate. *Dear Tristan… made enquiries on your behalf… your brother's whereabouts were hard to track down… chose not to be flown home… joined a shadow group… your brother was last seen alive towards the middle of May… sorry to have to inform you his body, with all the rest of his group's, was discovered some days later… easily recognized because of his scar… be assured he was given a decent funeral… whereabouts of grave on file… you'll be informed of exact location at more appropriate time. Ben operated and died courageously… strong possibility of posthumous medal… At the end of his training he requested this letter be passed on to his next of kin in the event of his death. My condolences… Yours sincerely…*

Ben. Young Ben. Dead. Poor misguided, unhappy Ben. Well, he'd always wanted to serve his country. Pray

God, he had found some contentment in laying down his life as he'd carried out his wish. Tristan stayed in solitary grief for five long minutes. Then, shrugging himself into control, he went to the door. 'Faye! Have you got a minute?'

'I was just going down to the shop to see if there's anything worth queuing for, Uncle Tris.' She appeared in a simple cotton frock, sandals and sun hat. I've got Simon and Pearl ready to come with me.'

'I'm sure Agnes won't mind watching them for a while. Come along in here, dear. I need to speak to you.'

'Sit down,' he said, trying to sound normal when she joined him.

She wasn't fooled and advanced on him instead. 'What is it? Have you heard from Father? About him?'

Tristan was fighting not to give way to emotion. The news seemed all the sadder as his brother and niece had been estranged at the time of Ben's sudden departure. He was worried about Ben's letter to her. What if he had felt he must make one last stab at sending her away? Dear God, that would be too awful. 'You were right the second time, darling. You're going to have to be very brave. I'm afraid I've received word today that Ben is dead. It happened some weeks ago. The news can't be more precise because he was away – in France, I should think – doing vital war work. I'm sure you get the picture. You can read the letter, it will explain more.' He wouldn't keep her own letter from her. Whatever it said, he had no right to do that.

On slow, slow steps she walked to the desk. Pictured her father sitting behind it, ducking his head to avoid looking at her, cutting her off, clearly wishing her far away. She cleared her throat. 'I had an idea he'd never come back. Despite everything, he was a very brave man, wasn't he?'

'Yes, he was.'

'Yet in some ways he wasn't. He couldn't come to terms with losing Aunt Em. It was she he'd always loved. He had no room in his heart for anyone but her. It's what made him so cold and pitiful.'

'I'm so sorry, Faye.'

She faced Tristan with a faint, watery smile. 'He would have liked Simon though, don't you think?'

'I'm sure he would have been very proud of Simon, and you too, darling, for being courageous enough not to lie about his parentage. Um, I hope this won't be upsetting for you. There is another letter. For you. From Ben.'

'Dad wrote to me? Let me have it?' Her hands were reaching out. She was avid to know what might have been her father's last thoughts about her.

Tristan took the letter from his jacket pocket. Faye seized it, tore it open, her hands trembling. Moments later she was flooded with tears. 'Oh, my God…'

'What?' Tristan said anxiously, not knowing how to comfort her.

'Let—let me read it to you. *M—my dear Faye, I can't go away without telling you plainly and simply that I love you. You are my dear girl, and I hope that one day I will get the chance to tell you so in person. Please forgive a lonely, bitter man for his foolish, stupid pride. I tried not to care about you, but I couldn't win against the care and concern you showered on me. If I don't make it back, darling Faye, I want you to know that I've arranged for you to be sole heir of Tremore and all my other concerns. Surely you must guess why I don't include your brother in this. Emilia can give you more of an explanation, if she cares to. Ask her, will you, to forgive me too? Please think of me kindly sometimes. I hope I haven't left it too late to make my peace with you. You are my beloved only child and my prayer for you is that you will find the sort of happiness that through my own fault, I've long denied myself. Take care of yourself, darling Faye.* It ends, *From the father who should have been devoted to you. Ben.* He's put kisses too, Uncle Tris. He loved me. At the end he really loved me. And that's all that matters, isn't it?'

She was so like a pleading child that his heart went out to her. She cried in his arms and shamelessly he wept too. 'I'm so glad Ben came round in the end. What will you say to Emilia?'

'I'll only ask about what my father's letter suggests, that Alec wasn't his son. From my brother's resemblance to the Harveys and the name he was given, there can only be one explanation, that Uncle Alec fathered him.'

'Good heavens,' Tristan whispered. 'I'd never guessed, perhaps I should have.'

'I shall ask my mother to tell Alec the truth. From my experience, and Louisa's, the cost of secrets are too high a price to pay. I think it's what the last quarrel between Father and Aunt Em was about. The past should remain in the past, and then it will mean a new beginning for all of us, Uncle Tris. I'll have what I want for Simon, he'll know where he truly belongs. As soon as he's old enough to understand, I'll tell him what a brave man his grandfather was.'

Chapter Thirty

Jill stretched her arms, rubbed her neck and circled her shoulders, all aching after the morning spent humping heavy sacks of potatoes into the storage loft with Edwin and Mrs Em. Now she was about to start sawing logs for the woodshed.

After she'd been working up a sweat for an hour, Jonny, who was on leave in between skin grafts on his hand, came to her, wearing work clothes, his bandaged hand in a sling. 'I'm here offering the service of my good hand to steady the logs for you, my sweet.' The notes of his voice were jokey but also mournful. He looked lost.

'You just take care not to get dirt in your dressings,' she cautioned kindly.

'You take care not to wear yourself out.' He swept his eyes over her, drew in on her a few more decisive steps. 'You look good, Jill, really good. Quite gorgeous. An outdoor life suits you.'

'Thank you.' She studied him. News of his injuries had made the local women fear for his looks. There had been no need. He was beautifully handsome in a different way, the slightly taut effect of his skin, the scarring on his cheeks, made him seem a battle-marred warrior. He had given up smoking, unable to bear a flame or heat near his face. Jill ignored her own need for a cigarette.

Jonny came nearer still, until she could feel his breath on her face. He was looking at her lips, then lingered over her eyes. 'Why on earth hasn't anyone snapped you up yet?'

'Not everyone needs a man in their life, you know. Shall we get on?'

They worked steadily, chatting about general things, neither mentioning their painful experiences, their need to consider a new career. 'I can see why the family value you so much. You never poke your nose in anywhere,' he said, as they perched on the woodshed steps to eat the rock buns and drink the tea Tilda brought them mid-afternoon. 'If you're wondering what I'll do next, I'm going to be a flying instructor in the Force. The surgeon is confident I'll be able to manage that. I was depressed for a while, but I'm lucky to be alive. I'm going to make my life count. I owe that to all those who died. And I've got Louisa now.'

'I'm pleased you're looking up, Jonny.'

'Can I ask you something? Is everything the same between you and Tom? Or am I imagining you don't get along as well as you used to?'

'It's something and nothing, as my grandmother used to say.' She didn't want to talk about Tom. The same day they'd exchanged cross words he'd quickly returned to his usual considerate self, but he hadn't apologized or explained his moments of pique and she was sad and bewildered that there was a barrier, something she couldn't define, between them. Gradually, they were seeking less and less of each other's company. Lottie had said sorry, that it was her fault. Jill couldn't see how. Tom alone was at fault. He had displayed superiority – she would remember her place where he was concerned.

Jonny put his face confidentially close to hers. 'I thought you and Tom…'

'What?'

He gave her one of his stunning smiles. 'You know… Louisa wasn't right for him, but you… it's a pity. Still, it gives us other chaps a chance.'

A romance with Tom? She certainly didn't want to think about that. Jonny was getting closer to her again. She didn't draw back from him. She knew he wanted to kiss her. She didn't mind if he did. 'Have you got anyone?'

'Not someone permanent.' His eyes fell on her lips.

'The way you like things.' He was the first man she had ever flirted with. It was a great experience.

He brought his face, his lips, that tiny last bit closer. His eyes were closed as he slid his good arm around her waist and sealed her against him. Jill met his kiss with gentleness, afraid she might hurt him. He was gentle too. Then he took his lips away from hers and smiled into her eyes. 'Mmm. You really are something, Jill.'

His next kiss was immediate. It was wonderful. She kissed him with eagerness, enjoying every superb sensation. He got carried away. 'Let's slip inside the woodshed.'

For a moment she considered it. It wasn't what she wanted. 'I don't think so, Jonny.'

'No? That's a pity.' He placed cajoling pecks along her lips. 'Can't I change your mind?'

'It's not the right thing. I mean you're not the right man…'

Jonny released her. 'Oh, got someone else in mind. I understand. I can't compete with that. Good luck. He's a lucky bloke. Going to tell me who he is?'

She shook her head. It rocked her to suddenly be aware who it was. She'd never tell anyone who he was. He wouldn't be interested in her anyway. She really would have to leave here when Lottie got her own place. 'We mustn't stay sitting here. Ah, here's Tilda come for the mugs.'

Tilda came hurrying, a little red-faced. 'Jill! A gentleman's turned up asking for you, my handsome. Says he come up from Falmouth.'

'A gentleman?' Aiming an uncertain glance at Jonny, Jill got to her feet. It could be Ronnie. She didn't know how she'd feel if she was faced with him now. 'Is he in uniform?'

'No,' Tilda tutted herself. ''Tisn't like me to forget to ask a caller's name. He's middle-aged. An office worker by the look of him. A quiet looking man. Come to think of it he's got the same fair looks as you about him.'

'Crumbs. Sounds like Uncle Stanley. It can't be anyone else. I wonder what he's doing here.' Jill rubbed her hands down over her dungarees. She was aware of her unkempt state in the heat.

'You'll find out if you run along inside and see him.' Tilda flapped her apron at her. She was strict on politeness and Jill was keeping her uncle, an elder, waiting. 'I've shown him into the sitting room. I'll tell him you're cleaning up. I can stretch the tea ration to a tray for you.'

Jill's only guess for her uncle's presence was that her aunt or one of her cousins, who were too young for call-up, were ill. As quickly as she could, she made herself presentable, changing her dungarees for clean breeches. She found her uncle standing about awkwardly, turning his trilby hat in his hands. 'Hello, Uncle Stanley. It's nice to see you.' She stood back from him. They had never been on cheek-kissing terms, which was more down to natural reticence on both their parts than aloofness.

'Hello, Jill. It's a very nice place here.' Stanley Laity was average of height, stocky and smart in a sports jacket and gleaming white shirt and dark tie. 'You must be wondering why I've come to see you, and not before time, I might add.' He blushed, as with shame. 'I should have made sure you'd settled in all right. I'm glad to see the housekeeper seems friendly. I must say I've never seen you looking so well. Everything is all right with you, I take it?'

'I couldn't wish to be with better people,' Jill said. It would have been an absolutely true statement until a few minutes ago. 'It's all right for us to sit down. If Mrs Bosweld, the owner, was here she'd insist on it. Is anything wrong, Uncle?'

'Not at home, m'dear. I've come about the young man next door. Ronald Trenear.'

Jill sat down woodenly in an armchair. This could only be bad news about Ronnie. 'Go on,' she whispered.

Stanley Laity stayed on his feet, treading about gawkily in his well-polished shoes. 'I can see you can guess what's coming. Mrs Trenear had already told us the tragic news about Ronald, he was killed on the eleventh of July. She came round to us last night to tell us she'd received some details from the top dogs.' Jill wrung her hands together, growing ever more misty-eyed. 'Seems he was among over three hundred and thirty men and officers, including the CO, of his battalion killed or wounded while taking a strategic place, a hill near a place called Caen, in Normandy. It's now known as Cornwall Hill, so you can tell how bravely they all fought. Ronald particularly acquitted himself, the DCLI are very proud of him. Your aunty and I always knew you and the young man had been close, Jill, and by right we should have passed on the news of his death to you before. It was very thoughtless of us and I apologize. But when Mrs Trenear went on to admit last night that you and her boy had actually been engaged, that he'd selfishly broken it off, well, I said to your aunty there and then that I must go to you in person and tell you all of it.'

'Poor Ronnie. Th–thank you, Uncle Stanley.' Her chin quivered. She so badly wanted to cry for her former friend and first love but her uncle was too much of a stranger to her to reveal her deepest feelings.

'No, you shouldn't be thanking me, Jill.' Her uncle came close with outstretched pale hands. 'I want to thank you, for seeing me, for having the grace not to send me away. Mind you, you always were a pleasant little soul. Aunty said as much before I left. We feel bad about neglecting you, for taking so little interest in you, leaving Mother to struggle to bring you up on her own. We want to put that right. We'd like you to feel welcome to come and see us, or to stay with us, for as long as you like, at any time you like. I hope you'll at least agree to us keeping in touch from now on.'

This earnest plea, so sincerely given, did make Jill cry. She sobbed softly into her clenched fist. 'Dear Ronnie. He was too gentle for war and soldiering. I'm glad he made it good at the end. It will be a comfort to his parents. Yes, Uncle Stanley, I'd really love to visit you and the family.

Of course, I get very little time off, but I'll try to come as soon as I can.'

When her uncle had gone, after giving her a shy kiss goodbye, Jill trudged up to her room. If Ronnie hadn't broken off their engagement, she would have been grieving so much more, feeling her future had been cruelly wrenched away. 'This awful, bloody, bloody war!' she screamed, needing to lash out. How many more people would have to perish before it all came to an end?

She changed back into her dungarees quickly and went back to the woodshed. There was no time to linger and brood and grieve. The only thing anyone should do is to get on with the task in hand, to fight for peace. Jonny gave her a long comforting hug and they worked on quietly until all the logs needed were cut and stored. Then he withdrew, sensing she needed to be alone.

It was strange to think that if not for the war she would never have come here. Where she enjoyed the work no matter how strenuous and tiring it was. Moulding into the village. Making so many new friends. Meeting Tom…

When Lottie had taken responsibility for the cooler way between her and Tom, she had emphasized, 'I know Tom got high-handed, but it's not what he's really like. He got all mixed up over Louisa, I'm sure he did. He didn't mean to hurt you, he cares about you, Jill. You will give him a go if he apologizes, won't you?'

'You know I don't bear grudges, Lottie.'

She missed Tom's friendship. Just as she missed Ronnie's. She had trusted them both, but both had been deceptive in their different ways. Ronnie hadn't been a bad man. Tom certainly wasn't. But it was going to be difficult to trust another man to reveal his true self. The enjoyment of working here had lost its golden edge, but she had her own family to turn to now.

–

That night Tom was in the pub, sitting alone in a dark corner, bent over a glass of whisky. It was nearly closing time – he had worked as late as possible in the fields and come straight here without telling anyone where he was going; Ruby Brokenshaw had kindly kept back some of the nightly whisky ration for him. He had no buying and selling business tonight, but was toying with calling on a girl who lived just along the road. She was guaranteed to give him a good time without hoping for anything more. No, he couldn't be bothered. He wasn't in the mood. What would Will have said about that, him losing his sex drive? Jonny would laugh at him and would try to jolly him out of his depression. He didn't want that either. He didn't want to cheer up. He wished everyone would stop trying to make him see a bright side. They all made the effort to at home. Except Lottie, who, thank goodness – because he couldn't stand it if she became all sugary sweet with him – bawled at him for being a 'miserable sod', and ordered him to apologize to Jill. As for Jill, she behaved around him as if she was walking on ice. If Jill wanted to turn unfriendly, if she wanted to mope over what was just a little row, then she could just get on with it!

'Oh hell,' he groaned to himself. 'Why am I feeling like this?' He was at the lowest ever ebb of his life. It was like a great wide pit had opened up, he had fallen into it, and he didn't have the energy or inclination to climb out.

The bar door opened and Jonny came in. Tom kept his head down. *Stay with your adoring hordes, Jonny. I'm in no mood for company.*

'Shame about Jill's former bloke, eh?' Jonny said, joining him with a pint of beer. Bright red lipstick was on his cheek from a hopeful admirer.

'What do you mean? Has he bought it?' Tom couldn't be chary about this.

'Afraid so, in Normandy. I had the pleasure of working with Jill this afternoon. Can't see why any chap would want to give her up. Even I could be tempted to make a go of things with her.'

'What does that mean? Have you propositioned her?'

'Steady on. It's not as if you're interested. Are you?' Jonny noted the fear of loss in every part of his cousin's frame. 'If you are, it's time you did something about it or you could risk losing her.'

'She doesn't care for me.'

Jonny was wondering if the man on Jill's mind was Tom. They would make a perfect couple. 'You might never know if you don't approach her. I'd make it pretty damned quick if I were you.'

Before Tom had time to digest this, Sidney Eathorne, important in his Home Guard uniform, pushed a loud entrance into the bar. 'Oh no,' Tom swore. He'd drink up and vanish.

Unfortunately Sidney was up to him and Jonny before he could put the glass to his lips. The hot tittle-tattle of Ronnie Trenear's death made him bypass ordering a drink. Then he started on something different. 'The young man had spurned her but Jill must be upset, all the same. It was good of her uncle to come personally with the news. She's going to visit him soon. He's asked her to live with his family, so I've heard.'

'What the hell are you spouting about?' Hating the notion of Jill leaving the farm for any reason, of things happening in her life without him being involved as before, was too much for Tom. He gulped down the whisky in one impatient swallow and nearly gagged on it.

'There's no need to be rude!' Sidney's chubby face turned turkey-wattle red. He was aghast, piously superior. 'It's not like you, Tom Harvey, but even so I'll be having a word with your mother if you don't watch it!' He twitched his nose. ''Tisn't like you either to enter a public place not washed up decently and changed. What's got into you these days?

Tom was experiencing the biggest panic of his life. His continuing frostiness to Jill, his omission at apologizing to her, was baffling her and making her miserable and he had chosen to ignore it. She now had the option of leaving the farm and living with her own family – she could, if she felt it necessary, ask for a transfer in the Land Army. He couldn't have that. He couldn't live without her close by, every single day. He jerked up to his feet. 'Excuse me, Mr Eathorne, I'd better be off.'

'That's better. Manners never come amiss,' Sidney aimed virtuously at his back.

Chapter Thirty-One

Tom raced along the lanes, foregoing the stone bridge beside the ford and splashing straight through the water. He had sworn he'd protect Jill, but the very moment she'd have needed him most he'd been off somewhere with his miffed nose stuck up in the air. Ronnie Trenear had cruelly rejected her but she was too good not to grieve over him. He hated the thought of her suffering. Yet he had deliberately left her feeling lost and lonely. Of all the people in the world who didn't deserve to feel that way it was Jill.

He reached the spot where he had first seen her, as a filmy shadow in the failing light. It was pitch dark now and in his troubled haste he tripped over his own feet and went crashing down. He scraped along the dusty, gritty tarmac but immediately hauled himself up and fled on as if Jill's very life depended on it. His happiness did.

He didn't stop to take off his boots or wash his hands but hurtled through the back kitchen door. A glance round the kitchen, where everyone always gathered except for on Sundays, showed that Jill wasn't there. He made for the back stairs.

His mother planted herself in his way. 'Oh, no, you don't, my son. How dare you come into the house like that? It isn't you who cleans the place, is it? Look at the state of you.'

'Mum, it's only a bit of dirt,' he said, exasperated, trying to dodge past her. 'And please don't start on about me missing supper. I need to see Jill.'

'Dirt, muddy water and blood to be precise,' Emilia said sternly. 'But if it's Jill you want to see…' She stepped aside.

Tom didn't stop to wonder why she'd suddenly broken off her lecture.

Emilia put her hands together, prayer-like, and said to her family and Tilda, 'At last, do you think?'

'I hope so,' Lottie replied, carrying on with the baby's matinee coat she was knitting. 'But I hope Jill doesn't give in too easily. He's really upset her and she should make him pay for it first.'

'Jill's not like you, darling,' Perry pointed out. He turned a page of the wafer-thin newspaper he was reading. 'And as I remember you were putty in Nate's hands.'

'Pappa!' But she happily conceded this.

The instant he was outside Jill's bedroom door, Tom stalled. He was panting. He was in a mess. He didn't smell too sweet either. He was in no fit state to present himself at a woman's bedroom door to offer humble apologies, and to say what else was on his mind. He should wash and tidy up first. Think over what to say. But he had already wasted too much time.

He knocked on the door. 'Jill, please, I need to talk to you.'

She was sitting on the bed, thinking about Ronnie, hoping he had not suffered at the end. She was thinking about Tom too, wishing with all her being that their relationship hadn't changed so much; yet even if they were still on their former matey terms, it didn't mean he'd see her as anything more than a friend. Why was life so awful for so much of the time? How was she going to cope with living here now she was in love with Tom? To her knowledge he had not seen anyone new since he and Louisa had finished, but it was going to be terrible when he did. If Tom fell in love again, gave his heart to someone else and brought a bride here, it would be unbearable. He would be just the farm manager to her, her boss's son at best, formerly a friend. His sudden presence outside her room made her plummeting heart leap straight to her throat. It took several seconds to catch her breath.

Tom thought she was ignoring him or that she didn't want to be disturbed in her grief over Ronnie. 'Jill, I'm sorry to disturb you. Can I talk to you for just a minute, please?' Afraid she might take more than a little persuading, he gazed at his skinned, work-toughened hands and rubbed the pricks of blood on them over his chin, and pleaded, 'I'm in an awful mess. In fact, I'm hurt.'

Tom hurt? She got off the bed so quickly, she dragged the counterpane with her, her feet became tangled in it and she was sent falling to the floor. Hearing the thud and her cry of alarm, Tom opened the door and rushed in to her. 'Jill, what's happened?'

She looked up at him and he looked down on her. Seeing the blood on his chin, on the palms of his hands and through the knees of his trousers, she was horrified. 'Oh, Tom! You've had an accident. Let me help you get cleaned up.'

'Let me help you up. How did you get down there?' He was with her in a moment, freeing her from the bedcover and gently lifting her up. He carried her to the chair, put her there and crouched in front of her. 'Are you badly shaken up?'

All the thoughtfulness and kindness of how Tom had been before, how he really was, was reflected in every inch of his handsome dark face. She smiled at him, a natural warm smile borne out of being back on old terms with him, and of loving him. 'I very stupidly got myself all twisted up in the cover. But what's happened to you?'

He reached for her hands, overjoyed that there was no reluctance on her part. In one mighty impact his whole being shook and was consumed even more by the force of real love. Jill had been coming out to him simply as her lovely, caring, constant self. The divine and gorgeous woman who had captured all of his heart. 'I mustn't be a fraud. I fell while hurrying back from the Ploughshare. I'd heard about Ronnie. I'm really sorry, Jill. Are you in a bad way?'

'I've had a good cry, Tom. It's Ronnie's mum and dad I feel sorry for. He was their only child. They've only got each other now.' He was gazing at her with such concern and tenderness, and she wanted to throw her arms around him and hold him close, as close as she possibly could.

'That's the saddest thing of all when there's no one left. Another young man gone, who in normal circumstances would have given so much to the world. Jill, I know about your uncle coming here today. You aren't thinking of going to live with him and his family, are you? I mean, I'd hate that. I know it's selfish of me but I want you to stay here for ever. I don't want you thinking about leaving with Lottie either. I'm sorry I was so horrid to you that day. I didn't realize then why I reacted so badly. I was a fool. I had no idea how much I cared about you.' His voice had dropped several tones and was husky and beguiling, his words emerging as if he was savouring them carefully on his tongue. He was eyeing her as if he wanted more of her. 'I do care for you, Jill. Really care for you, Jill, darling. I love you. And I mean, I really love you. I haven't left it too late, have I?'

'Not a bit.' She stroked the thick unruly hair off his forehead, then leaned forward and kissed him there. 'I love you too, Tom.'

'Oh, thank God.' He smiled, the deepest, most loving smile of all. 'While I'm down here like this, can I ask you to marry me?'

'I'd like nothing more than to be your wife.' She curled her arms around his neck. Bound herself to him by slipping off the chair and kissing his mouth. He wrapped her up in his arms. Their kisses turned rapidly from a gentle exploration to an inquisition, they would waste no more time apart. Their endless kisses were a meeting of love, of passion, of an everlasting joining of something wholly meaningful and beautiful.

'You're so very lovely, darling,' he murmured against her neck. 'I've got blood and dirt on you. I shouldn't be touching you.'

'You needn't stop.'

'Do you know, I feel a bit shy now. I've never felt shy with a woman before.' It didn't stop him taking a concentrated look over her. 'From the first time I saw you, I loved everything about you, I just didn't know it then. I'd better not stay much longer. Mum knows I've come up to talk to you. I don't think she'll let me stay in here for as long as I'd like to.'

'And for as long as I'd like you to. We'll have lots of opportunities to be alone.'

'I shall make the most of them.' Losing the unaccustomed shyness, he gently manhandled her. 'One more kiss, then let's go downstairs. I've got a feeling that Mum and Lottie will be down at the bottom hoping we'll be coming down together.'

Chapter Thirty-Two

Lottie put on her skirt and home-made smock, pinned on her corsage of a yellow rose and fern and viewed herself in the mirror. She was proud to be Jill's matron of honour today, proud that she didn't have the slim figure as on her own wedding day. She smoothed over her six months' bulge. 'This day would be perfect if only your daddy could be here.'

She'd had other letters from Nate, roughly one a fortnight. It was wonderful to hear from him, to read again and again the words that declared his love for her, and his joy at becoming a father. He'd suggested names. She was sure they were the names of the men he was serving with. Some of the girls' names were French. He had met a little orphaned girl whom he'd been particularly taken with – Madeleine – and he'd gone on to say he'd been delighted to take her on to the next village and reunite her with a grown-up cousin, who was glad to foster her. Madeleine, it was then, if the baby was a girl. *Just keep safe, darling*, was her constant prayer. As sweet as his letters were, they comforted her only for a little while, for it meant he was alive and well when he'd put pen to paper, and she dreaded all day and every day receiving a black-edged telegram.

She must hurry. There was only Jill, her Uncle Stanley and herself left in the house. The family were all at the church – Tom had been so nervous and looked so young when Jonny, his best man, had collected him yesterday to spend the night at Tremore, so as not to risk seeing the bride today until she arrived in church. Lottie had loved helping Jill put on her wedding dress, once her aunt's, a white showy affair that Tilda had altered to complement Jill's quiet character. Now, she only had to finish off herself by putting on the pearl necklace Nate had given her.

'Hey, sweetcake! Hurry up, you're keeping everyone waiting!'

Lottie was so startled she nearly dropped the precious pearls. 'Herv!' She waddled as fast as she could to the top of the stairs. 'Is that really you?'

'Sure is.' And there he was, in dress uniform, his curly black hair oiled and slick, a cigarette perched nattily on an ear; one hand missing, the sleeve pinned up. 'I was down this way and heard of the little shindig and thought I'd invite myself. Could kick myself for missing out on Jill. She's down here, looking beautiful. Well, are you coming?' Jill and her uncle came along the passage from the sitting room and waited, all smiles, at the front door.

'Yes. Yes! Just give me a moment to go back for my bouquet. Sorry to keep you waiting, Jill.'

'Wait. I've got something for you, Lottie,' Herv said.

'You've got a letter from Nate? He's written to you and enclosed a letter to me?'

'Nah.' Herv delved inside a clean white handkerchief and took out a small object set in gold. It was a pearl earring. 'He said to give you this.'

'He took it with him. I've got the twin.' Lottie was worried and disappointed. 'But he was supposed to bring it back to me himself. '

'I'd never forget a promise to you, Mrs Harmon, honey,' came a softer, quieter voice.

Lottie's heart stopped then rose up to the heavens. 'Nate?'

He appeared beside Herv, then took the stairs up to her three at a time. He swept her into his arms. 'My ship docked at Bristol last evening and I travelled through the night to get here. I thought it would be a great surprise for you and the little guy. I'm sure he'll know his daddy is here.'

Lottie kissed Nate, then put his hand on her tummy so Nate could feel the baby kicking. 'I'm sure he does.'

Together they walked down the stairs. Keeping hold of Nate, Lottie linked her other arm through Jill's. 'Right then, let's get this show on the road. Sister-in-law.'